DALE SALE

A TASTE FOR LOSS

Vinci Books

vinci-books.com

Published by Vinci Books Ltd in 2026

1

A CIP catalogue record for this book is available from the British Library.
Paperback ISBN: 9781036716486
The EU GPSR authorised representative is Logos Europe, 9 rue Nicolas Poussion, 17000 La Rochelle, France contact@logoseurope.eu

By Dale Sale

The Nakon Trilogy

A Taste for Cerulean Blue

A Taste for Loss

The Matrian Trilogy

Corvus Ascending

Corvus Sirocco

Corvus Defends

Dedication

To Betsy:
My own Blip, ready to take on the world.

Chapter One

"Stahl," Professor Wilhemina Theriot said, "could you hand me the Fillips chip manipulator?"

Stahl Gerat, Wilhelmina's assistant, quickly handed her the tool. His cheeks flushed as his hand grazed hers. Despite being twenty-five years his senior, Wilhelmina was still a beauty. A clean-suit cap covered her long brown curls, but a few stray wisps peeked out to tease him.

Gerat reached towards her. "Allow me, Professor." His hand shook slightly as his fingers brushed her face when he tucked the strands under her cap.

"Thank you, Stahl," Wilhelmina answered without looking up from the braincase of the inert bot on the table. She finished her adjustments and tossed the manipulator onto the surface. Her eyes raised and locked on his as she said, "That's enough work for today. Pour us a drink."

The young man moved to a locker and reached inside. He paused when he spotted a new bottle. "Oh, you naughty girl," he exclaimed as he held the bottle high. "Courvoisier

Cellan! Where have you been hiding this taste of home? Are we a celebrating?"

"I have decided to celebrate each day," she said. "Life is short and barren oblivion awaits us." Wilhelmina lifted the apron over her head and flung it over the bot's chassis on the table. "Do any of us know how long we have?" She fell into the incongruous antique leather wingback that sat in a corner of the lab.

Stahl sloshed generous portions into a snifter for each of them. "Melancholy? You aren't usually the drama queen?" He handed her the glass. She downed it in a swallow, leaned forward, and held the empty out.

"Another!"

Stahl moved to refill her glass and asked, "This is uncharacteristic. Have you had bad news?"

Wilhelmina fell back into the chair, crossed her legs, and shockingly displayed desirably slender ankles as her skirts shifted. She waved her glass at the equipment piled on the table. "It's this project," she said. "Trying to reverse engineer this Imperial Confederation tech is maddening. Every time we make some headway, it leads to another dead end. It is as if they purposefully obfuscated the design. To make it worse, that new Senator Gilson is complaining about the lack of progress and the expense of our research. The Department Chair is making noises about pulling our funding if we don't start producing results."

"True, it is slow going," he said, as he took a drink and pointed his glass at the bot. "But we are making headway. Only last week we cracked the speech recognition problem. That should calm him down temporarily."

Wilhelmina took another pull at her drink. "If it doesn't, we'll both be out on the street. There's no market for advanced general Constructed Intelligence anymore. The new laws only allow the Governance to have them. We've become too specialized. If you even suggest going back to teaching the lazy idiots attending university today, I will smack your eyes sideways. I'd rather slit my wrists!"

Gerat lifted her wrist to his lips. "It would be a shame to damage something so delicate."

"Stop trying to distract me." Wilhelmina pulled her hand back. "It would be a lot faster if we had some original schematics."

"It is rather odd that the Confederation didn't leave us their bot tech," Stahl said. "Maybe it wouldn't have taken us a thousand years to recreate our own CIs if they had."

"It's not like we could have used it even if they did," Wilhelmina said. "A thousand years ago, when the coronal mass ejections tore Iz so violently that the Gate failed, all electronic equipment on the inner planets was destroyed. The reduced solar output sparked an Ice Age that is only now receding. The Spellex Core continues to suffer from lingering solar storms. Some residents of Nakon still refuse to abandon the underground shelters. We are only now crawling back to our previous technology levels."

"I hear those storms make for a spectacular light show when the particles strike the flare grids, though," Gerat said.

"I am hoping that this Imperial experiential recorder I found in the North will leapfrog our research." Wilhelmina patted the leather harness she wore over her shirt. It held an innocent looking black leather case nestled between her shoulder blades. Patterns swirled in the small window on its face. A thin cable ran up her slender neck to a jeweled adhesive patch behind her ear.

Are you certain it's safe?" Gerat asked. "We don't really know how it works."

Wilhelmina answered, "I'm merely using it to get a

consciousness baseline to advance our work on Constructed Intelligences. Perfecting the ability to create new CIs is the purpose of our work, after all. Programming is crucial; otherwise, it's just a pile of gears and wire.

"But it may be very difficult to control a human-based CI. Would it even be restrained by the Rules of Behavior?" Stahl asked.

"I certainly don't follow them," Wilhelmina finished the glass, stood, and pulled out her hair comb. The long curls cascaded down her shoulders and she ran a hand seductively through the strands. A mischievous glimmer flashed in her eyes as she grabbed the young man by the lapels and pulled him tight. "I prefer to maintain control. Any ideas on how to lighten my mood?"

He wrapped his arms around her waist. "Something like this?" He kissed her deeply.

"That's a start," she replied. "Continue."

He fumbled to remove the device's leather harness.

Wilhelmina touched his hand. "Leave it," she said, as she dragged him to the small cot she kept in the lab for late nights. "I need a record of the full range of human experiences. Besides, I might like to replay it for myself when you tire of this old crone and move on to some pretty young thing your own age."

Gerat's blood pounded in his ears as his heart raced. He slipped the device from her shoulders and hung it on the bedpost. "Milady, I shall give you something you will not need a recording to remember." He pushed her onto the bed and kissed her again, deeply.

Later, Wilhelmina turned to Gerat and slapped his bare bottom. "I'm starving, be a dear and run down to the shop and get a couple of hand pies."

"Oh, so now that you have had your way with me, I am

relegated to errand boy once again?" Gerat teased, as he rolled onto his side and rested his head on his hand.

Wilhelmina sat up, turned away from Gerat, and draped a dressing gown over her smooth shoulders. She turned back to face him. Her full breasts stood high and proud on her chest with a hint of nipple peeking through the thin fabric.

"You are my Jack-of-all-Trades," she said with a grin. "I've just had a thought about our project that I want to pursue." She walked into the lab and uncovered the bot.

Gerat, noticing that she had left the recorder hanging on the bedpost, followed her. He jammed his shirt into his trousers and adjusted his waistcoat. "When I return, I shall ply my trades upon you once more, dear lady." He tipped his hat as he set it on his head and bounced down the stairs to the street below. He dashed across the street, dodging traffic, pedestrians, and a small yapping dog. Gerat hurled himself through the door marked "Virtanen's Meat Pies, Just like Grandma made".

"Oi, young man, be careful of that," a stout man scolded Gerat, as he wiped his hands on a towel, and tossed it over his shoulder. "You post-grad students ain't got enough coin to buy me a new door."

"Pardon my exuberance, Mr. Virtanen," Gerat said, as he doffed his hat. "Could I have two beef pasties? Heated please." Gerat reached inside a cooler for some drinks.

"Worked up an appetite, have ya?" Virtanen asked with a knowing smile. "Professor Theriot working you to the bone again?"

"Just research," Gerat said.

Virtanen grinned broadly and threw the towel to Gerat. "You've got a little 'research' on your cheek there, son." He turned to pop two pies into the electromagnetic oven. "I think you're good for her. She been working alone for too long."

Gerat looked at his reflection in the mirror behind the counter and noticed a distinct smudge of lipstick on his face. He dabbed at it furiously.

Virtanen sacked the pasties and handed them across the counter with a wink. "Don't let Professor Theriot mistreat you, laddie."

Gerat handed the shopkeeper a bill and said, "Oh, I won't. Keep the change."

He was still riding the afternoon's high. The thought of pulling Wilhelmina back into their tangled sheets spurred him to hurry back to the lab. As Gerat looked up at the top floor of the lab building, a fireball erupted from the windows. Stahl's world crashed as shards of glass and brick showered down.

Gerat stood in shock. *My beloved! It can't be. We were meant to spend eternity together.*

Stunned, the man stumbled and peered down. The black leather case of Wilhelmina's recorder lay at his feet. It was scorched and blackened, but the display's patterns still danced. He snatched up the case and clutched it to his chest. *By the Old God, the Goddess, and the twins suns themselves, I will get you back.*

Thirty Years Later

Chapter Two

Investigator Chief Warrant Officer Jill Tower clasped the highball tumbler of scotch and gazed from the balcony of her penthouse in the Gilson Building. Nakon City's lights spread out at her feet. *From up here, the City looks peaceful and clean.* A mournful horn drifted up to pierce the late-night calm. A tugboat far below worked a raft of overloaded barges upriver from the ocean.

I still can't get used to the idea that the Governance is renting this for me. She wondered. *I don't know what the catch is yet, but it's going to be a big one. Admiral McGowan isn't known for doing favors without expecting something in return.*

Jill shook her long brown curls as a breeze pushed them across her green eyes. She pulled the nightgown around her shoulders and shifted attention back to the river scene. Lights sparkled off the calm river and the faint passing signals of tugboats echoed off the buildings. *Infonet chatter said that with the way the Northern Reach ice sheet is retreating, Nakon City will be a coastal city again in another century. The government wants people to start moving north and working the land, but it's a tough sell. Still plenty cold and harsh up there.* Jill thought.

Her comm chirped. "PENY, will you take a message for me?"

A clunky domestic bot rolled out onto the balcony. "The Constructed Intelligence personality matrix known as PENY is unavailable at this time. This unit has reverted to standard domestic service protocols. I can offer you a beverage, or perhaps a snack?"

Shit, still offline? Just when I was getting used to having her listening in on everything I do.

Jill waved the bot away, turned her back to the view, and keyed her comm. "Tower here."

The window resolved into a view screen. "Chief Warrant Officer Tower, I have an assignment for you." Commander of All Forces Admiral Falkirk McGowan, the de facto ruler of the Governance of Nakon, stared out of the screen.

Great! He's using my rank. This isn't going to be good.

"Good Evening Admiral," Jill said. "What have you got for me?"

"I'm sending a file. I want this man located ASAP. He is wanted for espionage." An official ID that said, Stahl Gerat, Professor of Constructed Intelligence, Nakon Polytechnic University, popped into view.

"This guy is a spy?" Jill asked. "University professors don't usually go for cloak and dagger stuff."

"That is the official story," McGowan said. "Unofficially, he was working on sensitive research and has disappeared with the data. High-ranking individuals seek its return and his management.

"Sure thing, Admiral," Jill said. "Oh, any idea when I get my CI, PENY, back?"

McGowan waved away her question. "That's below my pay grade, Investigator. Check with the eggheads."

Jill stiffened at the reprimand and popped a salute. "I'll get on this in the morning, Admiral."

"Tonight," McGowan said as he cut the comm.

Jill slumped at the thought of not getting to enjoy her comfy bed and obscenely high thread-count sheets. "Bot, I need a sandwich and a carafe of sweet coffee with an extra shot of stim," Jill said as she headed for her office space. *Another all nighter, just what I didn't want. Oh well, that's why they pay me the big bucks.*

Chapter Three

The next afternoon found Captain Guster Johansson strutting down the gritty streets of the Old City District as the afternoon sun bounced off the ancient brick buildings. Gus, a former Governance Navy Star-Bosun turned privateer, had escaped the confines of his ship and the watchful eye of his android Executive Officer Lenore. Their ship, *Corvus,* started life long ago as a salvage tug. Now it was a thinly disguised and heavily armed mercenary vessel. The occasional cargo job helped pay the bills.

"As much as I like *Corvus*, ain't it great to be back dirtside, little buddy? Nothing like some liberty time to break the shipboard routine."

HAM, *Corvus's* small General Repair and Maintenance Protocol bot, glided beside him. HAM looked remarkably like a miniature knight on roller-skates. "As happy as I am to accompany you, Captain, I feel that my proper place is performing the endless list of maintenance tasks the Engineering Officer has for me."

"Ah come on," Gus said. Don't stress over the EO. Have a little fun."

HAM turned his metal helmet of a head to stare at Gus. "But Sir, maintenance *is* fun."

Gus paused and looked at a nondescript three-story brick building on the corner. A scarred wooden door set diagonally into the building's corner guarded the entrance. A tiny barred porthole stared out into the street. The neon sign on the wall flickered. "Hors_shoe B_r". On either side of the building's door, there were rows of dark, dusty windows.

"How long do we got before that thingy at the Matrian Embassy?"

"The reception is scheduled for two nights from now," HAM answered. The tiny bot considered the worn-out building. "Captain, this establishment does not look reputable."

"Good!" Gus laughed. "The XO's had me on a short leash for too long. Don't worry, I been here before. It's great!"

He grabbed the heavy iron door handle and jerked it open. The odor of stale beer, cheap whiskey, and low-quality ganja wafted out. "The smell speaks for itself - this place is good."

"My olfactory sensors detect a substantial lack of cleanliness."

"That's what I said," Gus answered as he shoved the little bot through the door. "I need some greasy bar food before I have to spend an evening picking over skinny finger-sandwiches and chatting up a bunch of stuffed shirts."

The bar was empty. The lunchtime day drinkers had stumbled back to work, and it was early for the young crowd. Gus trailed his fingers along the scarred U-shaped wooden bar that gave the place its name. Countless gallons of spilled beer, spotty varnish, and haphazard cleaning added to its character. A jukebox, photo booth, and blinking video marksman game lined the outside wall. A young red-headed girl swept the floor near the back. He grabbed a stool, set his hat on the bot's head, and draped his tunic over HAM's arm.

"Here HAM, find a safe place for this fancy rig." Gus rolled up his sleeves, exposing his tattoo of the ancient war hammer, Mjolnir.

"What'll it be, star-man?" A short brunette in a leather bustier leaned over the bar toward him. A tattooed pair of animated swallows frolicked above her breasts and a pinup girl in the ancient "Sailor Jerry" style danced and winked at Gus through her fishnets. "I don't recognize the uniform, but that ink is unmistakable." She reached out to trace a brightly painted nail along the mythic war hammer's image.

"Shot of Maniac's Mark and a porter, my dear," Gus replied, ignoring the comment.

HAM carefully folded Gus' tunic and searched for a clean place to put it. "Do you think that is wise, Sir? You are expected to engage in witty conversation at the reception."

"You have a point, my little metal conscience," Gus said. "Add a burger and yucca fries to that, my dear. I'm gonna need to keep my strength up to make it through my pending gauntlet of high-society sharks."

"You got it," she said, keying his order into a tablet. She held out her hand. "Name's Niki." She rolled Gus's arm to admire his tattoo again as he shook her hand. "You're sporting Wind Hammer ink, but you ain't flying Governance colors with that uniform. So, who *are* you sailing for?"

"Pleased to meet you. I'm Gus," he answered. "I fly with an, uh, independent outfit these days."

Niki poured Gus's drinks and asked. "What brings you down system to Nakon City? Not a lot of action for an independent operator in these civilized parts."

"Got a thing at the Matrian embassy," Gus said as he tossed back his whiskey. He coughed slightly and tapped his shot glass on the bar to signal another before taking a sip of porter to clear his tearing eyes.

Suddenly, the pack on HAM's back started to shake.

"Shhh, quiet, not yet," HAM said over his shoulder to the pack.

"HAM, what's in the pack?" Gus asked.

"You might as well reveal yourself," HAM said as he dropped the pack. "You are terrible at following orders."

The zipper slid open and a pointy pink nose tested the air before a white furry head emerged and chittered. The animal climbed onto the stool next to Gus.

"Is that a possum?" Niki asked. "We got a no pet policy."

"This isn't a pet, Miss," HAM said. "This is Ophelia, hero of the Dellan Wars."

Ophelia ran a smoothing paw over her muzzle, hissed, and stuck out her tongue at the woman.

"Cheeky little beggar," she said. "Was there a Dellan war? Who can track every small out-system brushfire nowadays?" She topped Gus's shot glass with another dose of the harsh amber liquid.

Gus's food emerged from a small cabinet behind the bar and she dropped the plate in front of him. Ophelia's eyes widened at the sight of the food.

Gus put some fries onto a napkin and slid it over to her.

She grabbed one, chomped it, and quickly dropped the treat.

"Careful, dumpster diver, those are hot," the bartender said as she turned to Gus. "Invited to a party at the Matriarch's embassy, huh. You must be pretty important."

Gus shrugged and took a hearty bite of burger. "I got fancy friends is all," he said around his mouthful. He noticed the young girl eavesdropping in the back had stopped sweeping.

"Miss, Captain Johansson commanded the squadron that saved Matria and defeated the Dellan battle fleet, including a planetary assault carrier," HAM boasted. "Of course, Ophelia and I played a key role in the victories."

The woman smiled. "Of course."

Ophelia hissed disapproval at Niki before attacking the fries again.

"You *are* a strange bot," the bartender said. "How'd you get him? I thought only the Gee-Vees could have bots." She pointed at HAM.

"Actually Miss, I am an Imperial Confed…"

Gus slightly choked on his beer and kicked HAM.

"Excuse me, Captain, is something wrong?" HAM asked.

Gus ignored HAM and said, "You wouldn't believe this bot's story if I told you, lady."

"Interested in selling?" she asked. "I know where you could get top dollar."

"Nah, I'm kinda used to his quirks at this point."

Niki shrugged and polished a glass.

HAM said, "Is there some small task I can be of service with while the Captain finishes his refreshment? I do strive to be helpful."

"Got a load of empties that needs hauling to the cycler.

If you don't mind." Niki turned and called to the girl. "Blip, show this bot where to haul the empties."

HAM looked at Gus, who gave a nod. "Sure, but don't be long."

"Never fear Captain, I shall return soonest." HAM spun and skated away after the girl.

Ophelia shoved the last of the fries into her mouth and watched HAM glide away. She chittered and jumped down after him.

"Don't get lost back there," Gus called after them.

The bartender pressed a hidden button under the bar as she grabbed the bottle of Maniacs. "One for the road? On the house."

"In that case." Gus slid his shot glass towards her.

Blip showed HAM what to do, and he began stacking crates of empty bottles onto a cart. She disappeared into a labyrinth of stacked boxes.

Ophelia climbed to the second level platform and scrubbed greasy crumbs from her whiskers as she watched HAM work. The door behind her opened, she squeaked, and scooted into the shadows. A large, big-bellied bald man wearing a grubby sleeveless shirt emerged from an office with CCTV screens on the walls. He thumped down the stairs and headed for HAM. A bot immobilizer gleamed in his hand.

Ophelia growled and hissed a warning.

HAM spun around, realized the danger, and threw a case at the man.

He swatted the bottles away and kept coming as HAM tried to flee.

Ophelia launched herself and landed on the man's head, hissing and scratching. He stepped back onto a loose bottle and he fell down hard.

Cursing loudly, he grabbed Ophelia by the scruff and threw her into a pile of boxes.

HAM struggled with the door while the man stood up. The immobilizer crackled against his shell and HAM froze.

Ophelia peered over the boxes to see the man tuck HAM under his arm, unlock the door, and slam it behind him. The lock reset.

"I wonder what is taking that bot so long," Gus said as he finished his food.

"There were a lot of boxes back there," Niki said. "Another round?" She waggled the bottle at Gus.

"Better not. I've got lots of city left to explore," he said. "Hey, wanna hear a joke? A sailor, a possum, and a robot walk into a bar…" He was interrupted by a crash from the back room. "Hold that thought. I gotta see what kind of mischief that bot is up to now." He grabbed his tunic and hat as he slapped cash on the bar.

Gus headed for the storeroom door. He didn't notice Niki grab a stun-bat from behind the bar and follow him.

He pushed open the door. "Hey HAM, you done? We need to head out."

Gus crumpled as the bat touched his neck. "Sorry, you're gonna miss your sightseeing, buddy," the woman said.

Ophelia whined as Gus collapsed through the storeroom door.

Niki grabbed him under the arms, dragged him across

the floor, and through the back door. She came back in and locked up. "Have a nice nap, sailor," she said as she headed back into the bar.

"It's okay, you can come out. She won't be back soon," a girl's voice said.

Ophelia squeaked in fright. She burrowed into the pile of empty boxes.

"Come on out, I won't hurt you."

Ophelia peeked out. The girl from the bar, about fifteen, crouched down. Short red hair framed her face. Worn but clean baggy clothing hung on her petite frame.

"Are you hungry?" The girl dug into a shoulder bag and produced a half-wrapped ration bar.

Ophelia licked her lips and waddled out of the pile. She grabbed the bar and skittered back to the pile before peeling away the wrapper and chomping into the treat.

"You're not a cat," the girl said. "Way too big to be a rat. Even in Old City."

Scowling at the insult, Ophelia turned away.

"Sorry, did I hurt your feelings?"

Ophelia finished the bar and scampered to the alley door. She jumped to hang from the lever and began tugging.

"Oh, that's locked," the girl said. "My name is Claire, but everybody calls me Blip." She picked Ophelia off the door and cradled her. She noticed the harness Ophelia wore and read the dark brass name plate riveted to the straps. A comm tracker occasionally blinked. "Hmm, Ophelia, is that you?"

Ophelia grinned at the mention of her name and rolled over to get a belly rub.

"Do you belong with that man and his bot?"

Ophelia nodded and whined softly.

The storeroom door rattled and Ophelia launched back into the boxes.

She peeked her head through the door. "Blip, did you see a possum run back here? It looks kinda like a giant rat."

"Nope, I was sorting boxes until the door slammed."

"I guess I'll have to get some rat poison. If you clean this mess up, I will get you a couple of meat pies from Virtanen's."

"Sorry, can't," Blip said. "I've got somewhere to be."

"Aren't you the important one now? Don't be out all night. You are getting too pretty to be safe in this neighborhood. I've seen that Brulli kid hanging around."

"Freddy is harmless," Blip answered.

"Hey kid, I've known the Brulli's for a long time and they are far from harmless. That restaurant isn't the only way they make money."

Blip shrugged and flipped her wrist. A wicked knife appeared in her right hand. "I got it covered."

The bartender raised her hands and headed back to the bar. "Alright then, just be careful. I'm locking up early."

The girl bent down and opened her shoulder bag. "Hop in. I have my own way out.

Blip threaded her way through the boxes until she got to a crate along a brick wall. She bent down and lifted it to reveal stone stairs descending into the dark. She grabbed a light hanging on a nail and lowered the crate behind her to cover the hole. Blip climbed down.

White slime flowed in a trail down the damp basement walls. A passage with symbols painted along the edge led off into the darkness. Ophelia rode with her head out of the bag. "That's Tosh Code," Blip explained. "Without them, even I would get lost down here. These tunnels used to go all over Old City. A lot of the branches are bricked up or collapsed now, except down deep where the Toshers live."

Ophelia reached out and touched her paw to the ancient brickwork.

"The story is that these were built when the storms that came after the Gate collapsed made the surface too dangerous. Tunnels used to go to the port too. When the glaciers covered the northland, the sea level dropped so much that Nakon City isn't on the coast anymore. After the storms quit and the city rebuilt, most tunnels were abandoned. They aren't used much anymore."

Blip climbed some steps and opened a hatch set in the wall that led into the alley behind the bar. Gus lay in a heap outside the bar's door.

"Let's see if we can wake him up," Blip said as she lifted a water bottle. The possum climbed to her shoulder.

Gus sputtered as the water hit his face. "Gak, what the?"

Gus shook his head and looked around. "I hate waking up in alleys." He put his hand down into something wet and made a face as he shook it dry. "Gross!"

Gus heard a giggle and looked up. The young girl from the bar stood over him with a dripping water bottle. Ophelia perched on her shoulder.

"Was the water really necessary?" Gus asked as he sat up.

"Sorry, but I didn't want to be within swinging range when you woke up," the girl said, as she pulled an adhesive bandage from her bag.

Ophelia grabbed the bandage from Blip and jumped on Gus' shoulder. She pushed his head forward and slapped it on his burn.

"Ouch," Gus complained. "Well, this isn't the first time

I got hijacked on liberty, so good thing I'm semper paratus, as the old saying goes."

Gus stumbled to his feet and reached for his tunic hanging on a nail in the wall. "Wallet's gone, of course." He rubbed the burn on the back of his neck from the stunner. He unzipped a hidden pocket in the tunic. "Extra credit chip and ID, ceramic switchblade, palm stunner, comm unit," he said, as he took inventory. "Ah, a little something for a jump start."

He broke a detox/stim tab under his nose and took a deep snort. His eyes crossed, and he coughed. "Oh baby, that never gets better." The fog rolled from his mind as the powerful drug combination scrubbed the alcohol from his system and slammed into his brain.

Ophelia jumped down and handed Gus his hat. Gus took it and brushed it off. "So where's HAM?"

"Drel took him," the girl said.

Gus walked out of the alley to the front of the building. The girl and Ophelia followed. The door was locked, and a hand lettered sign claimed they were closed due to a water heater issue.

"Your folks go around robbing customers on the regular, kid?"

"They aren't my folks," Blip said. "I just do odd jobs and they let me crash in the storeroom."

He booted up the comm and checked the screen. "HAM's tracker chip is offline. Looks like I'm going to spend my precious liberty time finding that trouble magnet," he said as he looked at Ophelia.

Gus rolled through the contact list on his comm. "Ahh, it's good to have friends." He punched the comm and bounced nervously as the call tried to connect.

"Who the hell is interrupting my beauty sleep?" a

bleary-eyed Investigator Jill Tower said, as the call connected.

"Jill, it's Gusty Joe. What are you doing asleep?"

"I was up all night working. Wait, why are you still in Nakon City? You were supposed to blast off days ago."

"Lenore roped me into attending a fancy party at the Matriarch's Embassy. Anyway, I'm in a bind."

"Of course you are," she taunted. "Can't you ever just call a girl to ask her to dinner?"

"Come on, HAM is in trouble," Gus said. "He got snatched and I'm afraid he's headed for a chop shop."

"Why are you calling me? My pull with the police is pretty limited these days. Why not use your high-powered Ambassador connections?"

"Because, if Lenore hears about it, she will go to General Quarters." Gus said. "I'm gonna hear 'I told you so' and then I'm never getting off the ship by myself again."

Okay, but I demand a dinner. An expensive one. Where should I meet you?"

Gus shared his location with her.

"Really, Gus? The Horseshoe?"

"What?" Gus asked. "It seemed reputable last time I was here."

"Never mind Stay put," Jill said. "I'll be there soon. Try to stay out of trouble until I get there, please."

"Yes, Ma'am." Gus flipped her a mock salute and cut the comm link.

"Hey, Mister, I can find your bot for you," Blip offered.

"Really?" Gus said, looking down. He had forgotten she was there. "How? Why?"

"How, is because nobody knows Old City better than me. Why, is because you are gonna pay me."

"Fine, take Ophelia with you. She has a tracker on her

collar. You can signal me with that when you find HAM. I gotta wait here for my friend. No bot, no cash."

Blip marched across the street to a rack of rental scooters. She waved her wrist comp over one and the lock popped open.

"Do I want to know how you did that without paying?" Gus asked as he walked up.

"Wouldn't tell ya if ya asked," Blip replied, as she shoved Ophelia into the bag she had over her shoulder. Blip flipped him a mock salute and sped off. Ophelia popped up, stuck her tongue out at Gus, and saluted before ducking back into the bag.

"No respect," Gus said. "Don't they know I'm a war hero?" He plopped down on a park bench and reached up to touch his neck tenderly. "Reduced to taking help from a teenage girl. There's no way I'm gonna live this down when Lenore finds out."

Chapter Four

"This is the Piata Hoti," Blip said to Ophelia, as she pulled up to a large warehouse with open doors at each end. "It's a second-hand market, mostly for selling stolen goods."

She pushed through the crowds, haggling at the tables.

"That's Drel, from the bar," Blip said, as she pointed to the large bald man ahead of her. She ducked out of the aisle and listened as she pretended to look over the goods on the table.

"Hands where I can see them, girl," the table vendor cautioned Blip. "I know your kind."

Blip shot the vendor a dirty look and moved away.

"Is that all you can offer?" Drel asked.

"Who else is going to give you anything for a unique model like this one? Too easy to trace," another voice said. "I'm going to have to part it out and that means extra labor and time to recoup my investment. Besides, you might have damaged it with that cheap immobilizer. I won't even know until I start stripping it."

"Maybe I'll check with Varz. He won't cheat me," Drel said.

"Go ahead, won't get a better offer."

"Excuse me," a third voice said. "Are you selling this bot?"

Blip peaked out to see a tall, thin, middle-aged man with wild hair and a tremendous mustache. He was dressed formally in an out-of-date academic style and carried a brown bulky case. The automated wagon following him was piled with various bits of electronic junk.

"As a matter of fact, I am," Drel said.

"Hold on, Drel," the first man said. "we already made a deal."

"No, we didn't. You said I should look for a better price."

"I am Professor Stahl Gerat and I am prepared to better his price," the Professor said. "What offer have you received?"

"Five hundred," Drel said.

The first man choked. "I never offered tha…" Drel shot him a look. "Oh yeah, I'm all in at five hundred," the man said.

"Since I deduce this bot is stolen property and that this 'gentleman' would never part with five hundred, I am prepared to give you four hundred and you can give your partner-in-crime a cut. How would you prefer that, Cellan francs, Nakon marks, or Prophet's coin?" He opened his case and reached inside.

"Let's make it easy, marks. Oh, and I don't admit this is stolen," Drel said with a gleam in his eye.

Professor Gerat counted off the bills and handed them to Drel. "Done! Please load my purchase onto the wagon and good day to you, Sirs." Gerat turned and walked off as his wagon trailed behind like a puppy.

Ophelia hissed and jumped on Blip's shoulder. She slapped Blip with her tail when the wagon with HAM rolled past. She pointed and moaned.

"I see," the girl said, brushing the tail away from her eyes. "We have to follow until we can get your friend back.

Blip blended into the chaos of the crowd and lagged behind, just keeping Gerat in sight.

Gerat adjusted his hat when he reached the street. His autonomous van waited at the corner. A ramp extended when he opened the rear door and the wagon rolled inside. The Professor climbed into the front and the car started away.

Blip swore under her breath. "He's not getting away that easily." She unlocked a new scooter from the rack on the corner, jumped on, and shot out into traffic after the car.

The van rounded a corner and disappeared. Blip twisted the throttle harder and swerved through the dense tangle of pedestrians, auto wagons, and vehicles. Ophelia screamed and covered her eyes.

"Yeah, I know, isn't it great? I hacked the system to remove the speed governors." The machine accelerated and streetlights flashed past as she twisted the throttle farther.

Blip skidded round the corner and slowed to avoid attention. Soon, the van turned into a dark alley and stopped at a roll-up door lit by a single flickering light.

She paused to watch the van roll inside and the door lower before she scooted away. "We need to ditch this scoot and play tunnel rat."

Ophelia looked at Blip and hissed.

"I didn't mean you were a rat."

Ophelia sniffed and ducked into the bag.

The closest tunnel entrance she knew was in the alley down the street. A woman wearing a clean server's apron and a man with a dishwasher's wet dirty one were in the alley behind a noodle shop, smoking a joint when she arrived.

"Hey, Blip, how's it going?" the dishwasher asked as she walked up. "You want a hit?" The man offered the roller.

"No thanks."

"Yeah, it'll stunt yer growth," the man said. "Looks like you need all the help you can get in that department." He chuckled.

The woman punched him on the shoulder. "Leave her alone, Burt. It's a slow day here kid, if you stop back at closing time, I can get you a free meal."

"Thanks, Alice, that would be great," Blip said. Ophelia shuffled in the bag at the mention of food.

"Whatcha got in there?" Burt asked.

Blip thumped the bag and shushed Ophelia. "Nothing, just some junk I'm going to sell at the Piata."

"Well, you be careful," Alice said. "I heard there's been some youngs going missing around here. Not everybody in Old City is as nice as me and old Burt."

"Who you calling old?" Burt stubbed out the joint and dropped it into the pocket of his apron.

"I mean it," Alice said. "Watch yourself and stay out of those old tunnels. The Toshers don't like trespassers."

"The Toshers aren't so bad. Why is everyone so torqued about my safety today?"

Blip waited for the door to slap shut as Burt and Alice went back inside. "Come out of there Freddy Brulli. You aren't fooling me."

A gangly teen boy stepped out of the narrow space

between the buildings. "How many times I gotta tell you, it's Freddy Sneakers," he protested.

Blip shook her head. "You may be a foot taller than me now, but you are still little Freddy Brulli snatching candy from the bodega. Why you hiding?"

"Alice don't like me hanging around, but Burt likes a certain strain of ganja. I got a guy."

"You got a guy!" Blip laughed. "Freddy, if your aunt hears about that, she will box your ears and put you pushing a mop and broom at Bouni Sapori."

"I ain't gonna be no swamper!"

"Well, you ain't grown enough yet to be some big-shots muscle like your uncle Joey."

"Hey, he's making a comeback," Freddy said. "Him and his girl, Peaches, are doing Maximum Fighting exhibition matches at some fancy ski resort up north."

Blip waved her hand to bat away his boast. "That stuff is fake. A couple of Old Town bar bouncers putting on a show for the rubes."

"You wouldn't say that if you saw Peaches' last fight," Freddy said. "They won't let her in the ring against women one-on-one anymore after what happened to Lesa Luna. Rumor has it she's gonna be in the med tanks for a month."

"Enough gossip. I got a job," Blip said.

Freddy leaned against the wall and jammed his hands in the pockets of his too short pants. "Who would hire a scrawny thing like you?"

Blip's face grew red. "I'm helping an important starship captain find his bot that got shanghaied." Blip's bag started to jump at the mention of HAM.

Ophelia stuck her head out of the bag and hissed at Freddy.

The boy jumped back. "Oh shit, what is that?"

Blip reached down to stroke Ophelia's head. "It's alright, he's a friend," Blip said. "Sometimes."

Freddy ignored her comment. "Might be fun. Mind if I tag along?"

Blip shrugged. "Suit yourself. I'm not sharing the bounty, though."

"I just don't want to see you get hurt," Freddy said.

The sleeve knife she carried flashed out and disappeared in a blink. "Me getting hurt ain't a problem." She forced open a heavy door set in the wall, pulled a hand light from her bag, and slipped inside.

Freddy tripped on a loose board and knocked his head on a low beam. "You didn't mention we had to go into the tunnels."

"Be careful, you big goof," Blip said. "I don't want you bringing this whole thing down on our heads." She blinded him with her light as she turned.

"Hey, watch where you're pointing that thing," Freddy protested.

"Let's hope the Professor's building still has a working tunnel hatch," Blip said as she avoided spiderwebs and puddles blocking a side tunnel. "It looks like no one uses this branch."

Ophelia tucked her head inside the bag to avoid the dirty webs with complaining hisses. She had a distinct aversion to spiders.

"Who's the Professor?" Freddy asked.

"The bad guy, now shush."

Blip stopped at a rickety-looking stairway and consulted her wrist computer. "This should be the place." The steps creaked as she ascended them. A false-wall passage ran inside the building's interior wall. Blip eased sideways through the narrow passage. She could see a hole in the wall above her head.

"Lift me up so I can see," Blip said.

Freddy bent down so Blip could climb onto his shoulders.

Ophelia tugged at Blip's coat until she boosted the animal up to look out with her.

They watched the Professor haul HAM off of the wagon with an overhead gantry and hang him near a workbench filled with tools and half disassembled equipment. HAM's eyes were dark and his head drooped to his chest plate. The professor unspooled a data cable from HAM's chest and plugged it into a bench terminal. He began tapping furiously on the keyboard. Rows of scrolling code projected onto the large screen above the bench.

"Oh my, yes, such a find," Professor Gerat said to no one. "Better than I had hoped. You actually appear to be operational." He triumphantly entered a final code with a flourish.

HAM's head jerked upright, "Excuse me, Sir. It appears I am unable to move."

"I regret the restraints," Gerat said. "I can't possibly allow you to escape. You are the first operational Imperial Confederation Constructed Intelligence I have been able to acquire."

"You know about Imperial bots?"

"I am the twin systems' leading expert on ancient cybernetic systems," Gerat boasted. "Allow me to introduce myself, Professor Stahl Gerat."

Blip entered his name into her comp. "Here it is, Stahl Gerat, Professor of Constructed Intelligence Nakon Polytechnic University. At least he was until recently. What is an Uni egghead doing in this crappy neighborhood?"

Freddy looked up at Blip and shrugged.

"It was a rhetorical question. Oh, here's the dirt, this is in the Nattering Nakonian News," she continued reading. "Prof. Gerat is suspected of stealing sensitive information from a government research facility with the intent of passing it along to the Cellans." Blip looked down at Ophelia. "No wonder he's hiding here. Those are serious charges. What does he want with your bot?" She turned back to the spy hole.

HAM pivoted his head, trying to orient himself and make sense of his situation. "Sir, I fail to see how that concerns me. I demand you release me at once."

"Oh, my little Imperial friend, you shall be my guest for an extended period," Gerat said. "For starters, how is it possible that you are functional? By the way, how old are you?"

"I refuse to answer your questions."

"In that case, bot, state your designation and function."

HAM stiffened at the command his programming required him to answer. "Imperial Confederation General Repair and Maintenance Protocol bot service designation HAM2F347791."

"Excellent, some progress," Gerat said with a smile. "Current duty station and owner?"

HAM struggled not to speak, but his base protocols won out. "Independent privateer *Corvus*, commanding officer Guster Johansson."

"Hmmm," Gerat paused. "State your last Imperial Confederation assignment."

"ICS long range salvage tug *Deliver,* hull number four twenty-one, lost in battle above the planet Tern, Imperial date twenty-seven Junit, three thousand two hundred eighty-five."

Gerat did a quick mental calculation. "That's over a thousand years ago, well before the Collapse. Who is Guster Johansson and what exactly is Corvus?"

Gus hung in silent defiance.

"Let me rephrase that," Gerat said. "Identify vessel *Corvus* and authorization code of Guster Johansson."

"Independent privateer *Corvus* is a highly modified Deliver class Long Range Salvage Tug, occasionally operating under a Letter of Marque from the government of Matria. Captain Johansson was granted a salvage title during an Admiralty Court action overseen by First Fleet Admiral Falkirk McGowan. As such, *Corvus,* and all its equipment, are legally the personal property of Captain Johansson." HAM finally finished his speech.

Gerat smoothed his mustache and considered the next question before beginning again. "Do *you* consider yourself property?"

"My feelings are irrelevant," HAM answered. "The Captain and crew, however, have always treated me with respect."

"I will take that as a no."

"Why have you abducted me?" HAM asked, as he ignored the statement.

"You, my little friend, will provide the missing pieces for the culmination of my life's work."

HAM cocked his head. "Oh dear, I hope your project does not require my disassembly."

Gerat waved away the comment. "That is entirely up to you. However, I believe that will not be necessary with your co-operation. A copy of your base code should be sufficient."

"Professor," HAM said, "I must warn you that the Rules

of Behavior prohibit copying base code that could be used to manufacture new bots. It would cause my dissimulation."

"Yes, I have run into that issue before." the Professor gestured towards a pile of scrap bot neural processors in a corner. "I believe I have found a solution to that problem."

HAM recognized the pieces as components of Imperial bots. "I do hope so. My maintenance work onboard *Corvus* is vital. I am quite sure that the Engineering Officer has a lengthy list of repairs awaiting my return."

The man ignored HAM and turned once more to his terminal, muttering to himself.

"Professor," HAM said, "you neglected to mention what this project is that I am the vital component of."

"What? Oh, sorry about that. I am rather distracted these days." He turned to HAM and pulled up a stool. "When I was a young man working on my first advanced degree, I had a position as lead research assistant to Professor Wilhelmina Theriot. She had discovered a nearly complete Imperial battle chassis model in deep storage at a forgotten logistics facility. The facility was shielded from the electromagnetic pulses when the Gate closed and some of its tech was still operational."

"Oh," HAM said with concern, "a battle chassis you say? Are you sure? Battle chassis models have a mandatory self-destruct imperative to prohibit capture."

"Correct, but professor Theriot and I did not know that at the time," Gerat said, "This particular unit was powered down and undergoing overhaul when the Imperial Confederation forces abandoned the system. Wilhelmina, I mean Professor Theriot, was in the process of examining the bot when disaster struck."

Gerat's eyes glazed as he remembered the events of that

day. He turned back to his keyboard and began to call up files. "I can show you. I have a video record."

A recording began to play on the screen above the workbench. A woman in a dressing gown leaned over a partially disassembled bot on a workbench and probed at it with a variety of tools. She paused to connect a cable from a power source to the bot. She turned a switch, and the screen flashed to static. The scene rebooted, and a camera panned around a room destroyed by an explosion.

"Professor Theriot must have triggered the bot's self-destruction. Wilhelmina was killed and most of our research was destroyed with the exception of this device." Gerat gestured to a small black box laying on the table.

"I was on an errand when she was killed," Gerat said, as he covered his face and slumped at the memory.

HAM focused and magnified his view of the black box. "Professor, what is that device on the table?" HAM asked.

"An Experiential Recorder," Gerat said. "Wilhelmina constructed it from an example we found in another Imperial facility. She believed it recorded brain wave patterns for later use. She hoped the data would further our progress on developing a superior Constructed Intelligence."

"Oh dear," HAM said in a low voice. "Did she wear it?"

"Yes, at first it was only occasionally, but as our work progressed, she insisted on wearing it constantly. She claimed it helped her focus on the work. If she took it off, it was like she wasn't the same person. Why do you ask?"

"Professor, I have read about a similar device used in the Imperial Confederation. It was outlawed before the Gate closed. This all occurred after I was stranded in this system. My information is not first-hand."

"I don't understand why would they outlaw a simple recording device?"

"That is not a simple recording device." HAM said. "It is a Trancher."

"A what? We have a similar word on Cellas," Gerat said. "It means carver."

"Exactly. It carves away what humans call a soul."

Gerat jerked to look at HAM. "What exactly do you mean 'carves away the soul'?"

"The device integrates into the subject's brain operations. Over time, the organic brain incorporates the device into its own neural network. Eventually, the entirety of the subject's memories and personality are recorded. The full process takes years and in the final stages, a subject cannot function without the device attached."

"Why would they develop such a device?"

"A religious sect named Revivalists created it. The original intent was to ensure life after physical death. They believed it was the only reliable way to achieve an afterlife."

"Was this sect popular?"

"When they were developed, the devices were prohibitively expensive to the public. Because the necessary central processor was tremendously expensive to maintain, the religion remained on the fringe of society and only utilized by the ultra-rich. A group of hackers discovered how to side-load the device's data into normal service bots. A group of investors saw this as a growth opportunity and gained control of the Revivalist's technology. They began to offer this option to the public in exchange for labor services. The members contracted for a trancher and tithed from their wages to pay for it.

"Upon their deaths, members were transferred into mechanical bodies. The Revived, as they were called, were required to continue working to pay for the maintenance of these bot bodies. They would be rewarded with credits to exchange for time in 'Heaven' where they could interact with their loved ones and other Revived," HAM explained. "Regular citizens could not compete with the productivity of the Revived. Survival forced many into Revivalism. The whole scheme caused a great disruption in the economy of the Confederation."

"Oh dear, that does sound horrible," Gerat said. "How did the Confederation escape this trap?"

"I am not sure," HAM said. "The histories mentioned a great conflict about the issue. The situation was not resolved before the Gate closed and the historical records are sketchy."

"This device can bring back the dead?" Gerat asked.

"In a manner of speaking," HAM answered. "There are conflicting accounts of how accurately the simulacrum performed."

"You have confirmed a hypothesis I had only dreamed possible," Gerat said, as his eyes sparkled wildly. "I CAN have Wilhelmina back."

"Umm, I believe you have misunderstood me, Sir. I do not believe you will be successful in restoring your friend. Because the device was used for only a short time, it is doubtful that sufficient data was recorded for a simulacrum to be produced. I fear you will be disappointed with the result, even if you do find an intact chassis. Bots were never allowed to leave the manufacturer without the Rules of Behavior being installed. Those would prevent the loading of the personality matrix."

"But the chance! I must make an attempt," Gerat said. "You claimed to be a General Repair and Maintenance Protocol bot, correct?"

"Yes sir, that is correct, service designation HAM2F347791."

"And GRAMPy bots can repair Confederation tech, right?"

"Of course," HAM said. "If you have the original specifications, I can fix anything."

"Anything?" Gerat asked playing to sharpen HAM's vanity. "Surely not something the size of a starship."

"I will have you know," HAM replied with a huff. "I rebuilt the *Corvus* from a derelict into the finest ship in the twin system." He was highly offended that Gerat would question his abilities.

"Well, my little tin friend, you have a big job ahead of you." Gerat began packing up assorted tools and instruments from his workbench. "We have a long journey ahead of us."

"Oh dear, I was afraid you might say that."

Blip shifted on Freddy's shoulders inside the wall. Ophelia climbed onto Blip's head to get a better view. The possum slipped and began to fall. Blip lost her balance as she grabbed for Ophelia and her arm punched through the decayed wall. Blip, Freddy, and Ophelia crashed into the lab in a cloud of dust and cobwebs.

"Spies!" Gerat spun at the noise and grabbed a large hammer from the bench.

"Time to scoot!" Blip said, as she grabbed for Ophelia.

Ophelia panicked and leaped onto the work bench. Parts clattered and fell as she raced toward HAM.

Gerat moved toward Blip as he brought the hammer down just as the girl rolled away. Blip jumped up and ran toward the workbench.

Freddy struggled to untangle himself from the remains of the wall.

"Trying to steal my work?" Gerat screamed. "Did Gilson send you?"

Blip got the bench between her and Gerat. She raised her hands. "Hey mister, you got the wrong idea. I don't know any Gilson."

"That senatorial weasel wants to steal my research for himself!"

Ophelia jumped onto Ham and climbed to tug at the hoist hook. She hissed and chittered at the bot.

"I am most sorry, Ophelia," HAM said. "I am unable to provide assistance."

Ophelia hissed again and began smacking HAM on the head.

"Unfortunately, violence will not reverse the effects of the immobilizer," Ham said.

Ophelia began to swing Ham like a pendulum to try to break the hoist.

Gerat noticed Ophelia and lunged towards her.

Freddy grabbed Gerat's foot at the last moment and the man tumbled forward.

The possum scurried behind Ham's back, hung from the hook by her tail, and jabbed at a small recess on his back, causing a keypad panel to open as HAM swung on the hook.

Gerat kicked himself free from Freddy and lunged toward HAM.

Ophelia hammered at the pad and Ham's legs shot out and caught Gerat in the stomach on the swing. The man doubled over and flew backwards to crash into a rolling chair that shot away and crashed backward when it hit a pile of debris on the floor.

Ophelia rode the swinging bot like a sailor in the rigging and stuck her tongue out at the man as he struggled to catch his breath.

"What are you doing back there?" Ham asked.

Ophelia reached back and began to punch the buttons again. Ham's legs shot back and forth, causing him to swing violently until the hook slipped off and he crashed to the floor. Ophelia jumped clear and landed on the workbench again. Ham lay face down on the floor, still unable to move.

"This is not an improvement in my situation," he said, with a muffled voice.

Ophelia jumped onto HAM's back and opened another small door on his back. She reached deep inside.

"How rude! Get out of my insides," HAM said. "You don't know what you are doing in there!"

Ophelia slapped HAM's head again with her tail. She flipped a switch and HAM's protests cut off. When she flipped it back on, a soft hum came from inside the bot. Ophelia slammed the door shut.

Blip yelled at Ophelia and gestured. "We gotta get out of here. Jump!"

Ophelia sprang into the girl's arms, clawed her way up, and burrowed into the folds of her jacket hood.

"Freddy, split up!" Blip ran for the hole in the wall. She squeezed through and fell inside.

Gerat's hammer crashed through the wall behind her. He shoved his head through the hole as Blip scrambled along the narrow passage. Another few hammer blows enlarged the hole enough for him to squeeze into the passage. He screamed in anger and followed Blip.

The girl reached a low section and noticed the supports were sagging.

Just as Gerat reached for her, she kicked at the supports and the wall section collapsed.

Gerat jumped back. He stood coughing from the dust and debris that now blocked his way. He watched through a crack in the debris as Blip escaped down the passage into the darkness. Gerat swore and returned to the lab.

The scientist brushed his coat as he came back through the wall. Freddy had escaped through a window.

The man crossed the room, avoiding the general destruction. He grabbed Ham and stood him up. "Hurry now, my little friend, our discovery requires us to depart."

"Where are you taking me?" HAM asked, as Gerat lifted him into the van.

"North!"

HAM tested his limbs and discovered they were working again. *Good girl, Ophelia, that hard reset has overcome the immobilizer.* HAM attempted to ping his tracker. *This vehicle must be shielded, the signal is not transmitting. I guess I will need to be patient until I can contact the Captain.*

The van rattled away.

Chapter Five

Mitzi Grey lounged beside the pool of her mansion and stirred her signature drink, vodka soda with lime. She took a pull at the straw and watched the swirling ice as condensation ran down the glass.

"I am soooo bored," she complained. She twirled her long blonde curls around a well-manicured finger and set her drink on the side table. "I didn't think society would abandon me just because I'm a widow. Do they think it's contagious?"

A young woman hesitated as she walked up. Mitzi had been in a foul mood for weeks, and the staff was keeping their distance. "Ex, ex, excuse me, Ma'am," the woman stammered. "Your Father, the Admiral is on a holo call for you."

"Well, bring me a portable," Mitzi snapped in answer.

"I'm afraid the call is on the secure channel," the poor woman said. "You will have to take the call in the conference room."

"That man will do anything to annoy me." Mitzi's light

coverup flowed behind her in the breeze. Her heels tapped on the flagstones as glimpses of her long, tan legs flashed with each step.

Inside, she slapped the secure holo comm and said, "What is it now, Father?"

"Good afternoon Colonel McGowan-Grey," The Admiral said without his usually fatherly familiarity.

"Why are you using my official military name and rank?" Mitzi asked.

"I need to brief you on a developing threat." A video formed in the holo. "Recently, our scientists detected this."

Mitzi squinted. "A star, big deal."

"Not a star. This is the drive plume from an extremely large starship heading towards us."

"Aliens? That would be interesting," Mitzi said.

McGowan shook his head. "That might actually be preferable. No, this looks like a ship from the Imperial Confederation."

"It would take a millennium to travel from the Confederation to Nakon," Mitzi said. "Why would they be coming here?"

"At first the scientists believed it was a Builder Vessel sent to repair the Gate," McGowan said. "Then I was contacted by Gus Johansson's bot ally, Faber. He sent me this."

The holo shifted to a video of Faber in his customary green battle fatigues. "Admiral, it's time to let you humans in on the big secret. The Gate was closed to prevent an invasion of the system. It was manipulated to suck a tremendous energy wave from the sun and discharge it into the invader's ship as it cleared the Gate. Unfortunately, there was an error in the plan's execution and the coronal mass ejection not only hit the invaders, it broke the Gate, caused the civilizational Great Collapse, and the current ice age on Nakon. On the bright side, the invasion was halted when the ship crashed on Nakon. I don't think that ship heading this way is a harmless Builder vessel. I believe it contains another invasion force." The video ended.

"There is more," McGowan said. "But you get the idea."

"What does any of this have to do with me?" Mitzi asked. "I'm not in uniform anymore."

"You are now," McGowan said. "Consider yourself recalled to active duty. Report to my office for further assignment."

"Not the attention I was looking for. At least HQ is filled with handsome young officers."

JIll and Gus at Geralt's lab

Chapter Six

Blip rushed through the tunnel door into the alley, gasping and coughing. She slammed the lock hasp and shoved a bar through it to pin the door shut. Ophelia stuck her head out and made a pitiful moan as she rubbed her tummy.

"Not now, let's look for Freddy," she said, as she wiped at the layer of sweat-soaked grime coating her face. "He probably went out the front. We don't need to worry about that professor guy. The tunnels are too confusing for him to follow us." She pushed through the door into the restaurant's kitchen and heard a commotion.

Blip eased forward to look through the swinging door into the dining room. Ophelia jumped down and began to rummage around the kitchen.

"I told you to stop harassing my customers," Alice's voice rang out.

"New law says we can ask anyone for their papers anytime." A burly uniformed man said. "Too many refugees are missing their asylum court dates." Three other officers milled around the seated customers, looking at documents.

"Ha, like any Gee would get a fair hearing," Alice replied.

The clang of a falling pot in the kitchen broke the mood.

"Thought you said wasn't nobody in the back," the officer said.

Blip whirled around to see Ophelia's tail sticking out of a very large pot as it scooted across the kitchen floor, bumping into things. She scooped up the possum and shoved it into her bag.

"Ain't nothing back there," Alice pleaded as she grabbed the man's arm to stop him.

He shrugged off her grip as another officer grabbed Alice's arms and held her. He pushed through the swinging door just as Blip darted out the back.

"We got a runner," the officer said into his comm.

"On it," a voice said over the channel.

The officer pushed through into the alley.

"Let me go!" Blip said, thrashing between two officers.

"She's just a kid," Alice pleaded, as she spilled out the door.

"Just got to check her paperwork," the man said. "You do have ID, don't ya kid?"

"I, I forgot it at home," Blip said. "If you let me go, I can run home and bring it back."

"Nah, your parents can just bring it to the station."

A police wagon rolled up and stopped. Blip watched as the officer forced several people from the diner inside.

"But my folks are gonna be really mad."

"Don't worry, kid, you'll be back home in no time," a woman officer said. "They keep the kids separate at the station. You'll be safe."

"That's what I'm afraid of," Blip muttered to herself. "Locked up, all safe and sound."

Alice called out as the door slammed shut. "I'll let Niki know. Don't worry, she will get you sprung."

"Looks like I didn't do such a good job keeping you out of trouble," a voice behind Blip said, as she stumbled into the van.

"Freddy! I was hoping you got away."

"They saw me coming out of a window and snatched me for burglary."

"Don't worry, Niki will get us out," Blip said. "I hope."

Chapter Seven

Gus turned at the sound of a revving powercycle approaching.

He waved.

The cycle pulled next to him and balanced on its internal gyros. The rider's tight synth-leather outfit accented the feminine curves inside. She touched a metal stud on her neck and the full-face helmet folded away. Inspector Jill Tower shook out her brown shoulder length curls. Gus reached out his hand.

"Thanks for coming, Jill. I've got myself into a situation again."

Jill grabbed his hand. "Well, you do know how to keep a girl's life interesting. What have you done this time?"

"I swear, I was minding my own business, having a bite to eat, when I got waylaid and left in the alley. When I woke up, HAM was gone."

"Anything else?"

"There was a kid that said she could find HAM if I paid her. She took off with Ophelia and I haven't heard anything. The tracker chip on Ophelia was following them, but it cut out. That's why I called you."

"You didn't pay her up front, did you?"

"Hey, I'm unlucky, not stupid," Gus said.

Gus and Jill turned at the sound of a lock turning.

The door to the bar swung open, and Niki stuck her head out. "Hey star-sailor, do you really know important people?"

"Some, she knows more," Gus said, as he jerked his thumb toward Jill.

Niki held the door open. "Inside. I got a problem."

The pair followed Niki. She reached behind the bar and grabbed a cold pack from the freezer and tossed it to Gus. "Put that on your neck. It'll help with the burn."

Gus snatched the pack out of the air and winced as he iced the stun-bat burn. "Yeah, thanks for nothing. Where's my bot?"

"I got a bigger problem."

Jill flipped out her badge and said. "If I start an investigation into this place, your problems are only starting, lady."

Niki squinted at the badge and laughed. "The Heat's been trying to shut down this place for years. Another badge don't scare me none."

Gus put his arm on Jill's shoulder as she started toward Niki. "Look, you said you got a problem. You help get my bot back and we will see what we can do."

Niki flipped a tablet screen and laid it on the bar. A recording of Blip and Ophelia reeled by. "This is what happened after I dumped you in the alley."

"That's the kid who said she could find HAM," Gus said. "You owe me for dry cleaning, by the way."

"Where does that passageway go?" Jill asked, as she watched Blip disappear into the wall hatch.

"Into the old tunnels," Niki said. "Blip thinks I don't know about it. She uses it to sneak in and out."

"I'm guessing Blip is the girl?" Gus asked.

"Yeah, she's on her own," Niki said.

"Parents?" Jill asked.

"Not that I know of. She's pretty tight-lipped about that stuff. She crashes in the storeroom sometimes."

"So, what's the problem?" Gus asked.

"She and her friend got picked up in an immigration raid at a diner over in Black Pot named Yummy Tummy."

"Let me guess, she doesn't have papers," Jill said.

Niki shrugged her shoulders. "I don't know for sure, but they wouldn't have taken her in if she did."

"What about her friend?"

"Local kid that runs in the streets. Goes by the handle Freddy Sneakers. His family's got connections, if you know what I mean."

"I know Freddy, he's a friends nephew, and she isn't going to be happy," Jill said to Gus.

Gus asked Niki, "I feel bad for the kids and all but, how is this helping me get back my bot? Maybe I should have my friend here take you in for questioning and an attitude adjustment."

"Fuck you! Nobody from Old Town is gonna talk to you two. But I can find out who has your bot," Niki replied, as she jabbed her finger into Gus' chest. "I'll tell you where it is when Blip and the kid are safe."

Jill grabbed Gus' arm and drew him away. "I thought I was playing bad cop?"

Gus nodded and stepped back.

Jill turned back to Niki. "Don't mind this asshole. Let

me make some calls about the kids. You find out where the bot is." Jill dropped a contact chip on the bar. "Let me know when you got something."

Jill and Gus walked outside.

"Why don't you just ask that fancy bot assistant of yours to help?" Gus asked.

"PENY is down for maintenance," Jill replied. "I don't know when she is gonna be back online."

"Great!" Gus said in frustration.

"Speaking of help, what about your android XO, Lenore? She can tap into the info net and troll around."

"Umm, I'm trying to keep Lenore out of this," Gus answered.

"You didn't tell her yet, did you?"

"She already thinks I'm a trouble magnet," Gus said with a shrug.

"You are!"

"Look, we still got time before I gotta be at that embassy party. I wanted to finish this thing and come home with a funny story about it all. You know, a sailor, a robot, and a possum walk into a bar."

Gus' comm buzzed, and he fished it out of his pocket. "Hey, what's up?"

Lenore looked out of the screen. "Captain, I trust you are enjoying the city *and* behaving yourself?"

"Oh sure, yeah," Gus said. "Look who I ran into." He moved the comm to put Jill on the screen.

Jill waved. "Hey Lenore, I'll keep him out of trouble."

Lenore raised an eyebrow. "Investigator Tower, I appreciate your efforts. However, I am fully aware that the Captain cannot stay out of trouble."

"Aww, Lenore," Gus said. "I just stopped in for a bite to

eat and Jill walked in, working on a case. Missing persons, young girl, maybe I can help."

"You, Captain, have a party to attend."

"They won't miss me," Gus said.

"This party is being held to celebrate your victory in the Dellan War," Lenore said. "You *will* attend. Lenore, out!"

The comm went dead.

"She told you," Jill said.

Jill's comm chirped again. She saw the caller ID and swore. "That didn't take long," she said as she answered the call.

Peaches Glamour appeared on the screen. Jill's old friend was tall, raven-haired, and very angry.

"Peaches, what a surprise," Jill said. "I thought you and Joey were on the road."

The view on Jill's comm shifted to a large man with short black hair and a build that strained his leather jacket. "Hey Jilly, Peaches is upset."

The view shifted back. "Joey's nephew, Freddy, got hauled in," Peaches said. "Does he need to call the family?"

Jill whispered to Gus, "That's the last thing I need."

"I just heard about it, Peaches," Jill said. "Give me a minute to make some calls."

"Freddy's mom wants to call Aunt Francisca," Joey said. "I don't know how long I can hold her off."

"Joey, you don't want Francisca involved," Jill said. "We all know that won't be good for the family business."

"I agree," Joey said. "But my sister-in-law gets emotional. He's her baby boy, ya know."

Jill whispered to Gus again. "Freddy's got five older sisters. Can't blame his mom for being protective."

"Six kids? I've got enough trouble keeping track of HAM," Gus said.

"We've got a possible location already on Freddy, "Jill said. "We are heading there now. I will let you know when we find anything. Where are you both now?"

"We are doing exhibition matches up north at the Flaming Springs resort," Peaches said. "We got another exhibition in Nakon City soon."

"Come up after you find Freddy," Joey said. "I can get you two a room comped."

Jill laughed. "Joey, you know Gus is too old for me. I like em young."

"Hey, who you calling old?" Gus said.

"There's plenty of good looking old dames up here that would love to meet Gus," Joey said. "And we could probably find you a young new friend too, Jilly."

"I can find my own friends, Joey," Jill said. "I don't think Gus's XO, Lenore, would appreciate your matchmaking, either. She's the jealous type."

Jill jammed her comm into a pocket and turned to Gus. "We should head to the diner the kids got snatched from," Jill said. "Maybe someone knows what they were up to."

Jill slapped a small pouch in his hand. "Put this on."

Gus popped a tab, and the pouch formed into a cycle helmet. He struggled to get it on his head. "These universal sizes never fit me." Gus threw his leg over the back of Jill's cycle and settled behind her. "Plus, I've got to ride pillion. Undignified for a war hero."

"Waa, waa, waa," Jill mocked as she sped off.

Jill soon pulled into the alley behind Yummy Tummy and stopped. "The last signal was here," she said, as she dismounted and folded her helmet away into her suit.

Gus slid off the cycle and tried to unkink his legs. "That bike of yours isn't built for two."

Gus' comm chirped again, and he looked down. "Hey, I

just got a hit on Ophelia's tracker. Maybe she's is still with the kid."

"Send me a link and I can overlay it with a city map," Jill said.

Jill studied her comm display. "That's weird. The tracker is in the industrial section near the port."

"Why's that weird?" Gus asked.

"Niki said the kid was picked up in an immigration sweep. Immigration processing isn't anywhere near this location."

"Why wouldn't they take the kid to the normal processing center?"

"I don't have any idea. Hold on." Jill tapped her comm again and spoke into it.

"PENY, when you come online, I need all the info you can find on the location I'm sending you. There's something weird going on there."

Jill turned back to Gus. "She'll get back to us."

"I wouldn't leave a bike like that around here, lady," an aproned man having a smoke near the dumpster said.

Jill turned. "You work here?"

"Maybe."

Gus walked forward and extended his hand. "Hi, I'm Gus." Gus palmed a bill into the man's hand when they shook. "Niki sent us to look for Blip."

Burt grunted and ducked into the shop. He called for someone and a woman wiping her hands on her apron came out into the alley.

Jill moved forward. "Niki from the Horseshoe sent us. She's worried. Do you know what happened to Blip?"

"I'm Alice," the woman said. "I'm the one that called Niki. Have you heard anything?"

"No, only that they weren't taken to Central Booking," Jill asked. "Can you fill us in?"

"Blip and that Freddy boy went into the tunnels," Alice said. "There's a door behind the dumpster. We store stuff in there sometimes."

"Do you know what she was doing in there?" Gus asked.

"I just figured they were looking for a place to make out. I don't go in there unless I have to. Those tunnels creep me out. I told her to find me when she came out and that I'd give her a meal. She showed back up during the raid. They took her away. I'm worried because I don't think she has anyone to watch out for her."

"Is it alright if we take a look down there?" Jill asked. "Maybe we can find what she was looking for."

"Go ahead," Alice said, as she headed back inside. "Just don't ask me to come with you."

Jill pushed open the door into blackness. She touched a stud on her jacket and a light showed some shelves stacked with supplies for the diner. Jill entered. Gus followed.

Gus tripped in the dark and grabbed Jill around the waist as he stumbled and planted his face into her backside.

"Buy me dinner first star-man," Jill quipped, as Gus scrambled back to his feet.

"Sorry, I can't see anything in here."

Jill reached into her jacket and handed him a small hand light.

Gus pointed his light at the floor. "Those are Ophelia's tracks."

"It looks like they were here. Scuffs in the dust and torn cobwebs," Jill said.

They soon came to the collapsed section.

Jill peered through an opening in the wreckage and

shined her light. “I can see through a hole in a wall. It looks like a workshop of some kind.”

“This whole section looks pretty shaky,” Gus said. “Let’s see if we can get in from the street.”

Gus and Jill exited the tunnels. They entered the back door of the diner just as Alice came from the front. “Did you find anything?”

“A section of tunnel about fifty meters in is collapsed,” Jill said. “It looked like it went to a workshop. Got any ideas what that might be?”

“That must be the egghead’s place,” Burt said, as he racked a stack of dishes for the machine.

“I hate that guy,” Alice said. “Always complains about the food, but keeps ordering.”

“You got a name?” Gus asked.

“Maybe Burt remembers. He does the deliveries.”

“What about it Burt?” Gus called out.

Burt didn’t look up from his work as he continued racking plates. “Guy’s got a funny foreign name. Garnier, Gernet, something like that.”

“Gerat?” Jill asked.

“Yeah, that’s it. ”

“Shit!” Jill said.

“You know the guy?” Gus asked.

“The Admiral wants me to find him,” Jill said. “Some kind of bot expert. Stole state secrets. It must be important because the Admiral wants this guy bad.”

“Burt, can you show us which building was his?” Gus asked, as he lifted another bill with two fingers toward Burt.

Burt dried his hands on his apron and took the tip. “Sure, if it helps the kid. It ain’t far.”

In a few minutes, Gus, Jill, and Burt stood outside of Gerat’s building.

"This is it," Burt said. "He wouldn't ever open the door for me. Just had me leave the order outside."

Gus tested the knob and examined the door. "It's thick steel and locked."

Jill walked over to a keypad next to the roll-up door. She pulled her badge out and held it up to the pad and tapped in a code. "Let's see if the Admiral's universal search warrant can crack it."

A red light flashed on the pad.

Gus stepped forward and retrieved a device from his pocket. "Let me give it a shot. My Chief Engineer likes to tinker with locks." He held the device near the pad and it latched on. "Three, two, one," Gus said, and the door light flashed green and it rolled up.

Burt turned and started back to the diner. "Warrant or not, this don't look strictly legal to me. I'm out."

Gus called to him. "Tell Alice we'll be in touch."

Burt waved without turning and kept walking.

Jill walked into the large open workshop. "Looks like a riot in here."

Equipment was knocked over and the large workbench was on its side with the contents spilled across the floor. A hole, man-sized, was knocked into the far wall.

Gus walked over to a computer terminal on a rolling stand. I'll check if I can find something online. Gus began to tap the keyboard, and the large overhead screen lit up. Time to see what happened here.

The screen flickered and a scene showing Gerat walking around and HAM hanging from the ceiling lit up. "That answers who took HAM," Gus said. "I'll try to resolve the audio."

Blip crashed through the wall and Ophelia scampered around the shop. Jill and Gus watched until they saw Gerat stumble back through the wall and begin to throw equipment into a van.

The audio played as HAM asked where they were going. Gerat tossed Ham inside and slammed the vehicle doors and climbed into the cab. The rolling door slipped down as he sped away.

"Gerat said they were heading north. That's not very specific," Gus said, as the recording ended.

"Let me get hold of the Admiral," Jill said. "Maybe he has some more information about where Gerat may be headed."

She keyed the comm with Admiral McGowan's private number. The Admiral's gruff voice answered as he looked out of the comm. "Chief Tower, what have you got? Is Gerat in custody?"

I haven't found him yet, Admiral. But I did find his hiding place. He had a lab set up in a warehouse. All I know is he's headed north with one of Gus Johansson's Imperial Confederation bots in tow."

"That is *NOT* good!" McGowan answered. "A working Imperial bot was the last thing he needed to finish his work. Tell Johansson if he wants that bot back in one piece to hurry and catch Gerat. I can make it worth his while."

"Rodger that, Admiral," Gus said, as he moved into the screen area. "Any restrictions on how we catch this guy?"

"Your reward will be more substantial if he is alive," McGowan said. "I will settle for dead if it is necessary."

"Do you have any idea where Gerat is headed?" Jill asked.

"North you said? I can send you the location of an old Imperial facility I know he was working at. Might start there. McGowan out." The image snapped out.

Jill looked at the comm. "Okay, I got a location. My

aircar doesn't have enough range to get there. Can you get us a ride?"

Chapter Eight

Blip leaned against Freddy to fight the chill of the holding cell. *It's my own fault. I got sloppy. I never should have agreed to help that dumb old sailor.*

"H, h, hi," a stuttering voice said.

Blip raised her head. A girl, about her age, with tangled brown hair and worn clothes, stood in front of her.

"I guess they got you too, huh?"

Blip sized the girl up. She looked legit. Probably not a plant to gather info. Blip wasn't taking any chances.

"It's all a mistake. I just forgot to take my papers with me today. My people will spring me any minute."

"Bullshit," the girl replied. Her attitude changed in an instant. "You ain't got no people coming. You're in the shit, same as the rest of us." She pointed at two kids clinging to each other on the other bunk.

"Nope, not me!" Blip said.

The girl snatched at Blip and recoiled just as fast when the knife appeared in Blip's hand.

"Now, now, you two," Freddy said. "Play nice."

"I'll show her how we play nice at the Horseshoe," Blip said.

"That's where I seen you sneaking around before," the girl said. "They treat you good in there? Fellas tip big? I know this bean pole ain't pimping you." She jerked a thumb towards Freddy.

"I don't trick," Blip spat out. "I do odd jobs. Sweep up, run errands, and stuff."

"Yeah, that's how it starts," the girl said. "Then it's, 'Hey, if you treat this fella nice, there's a hefty slip of crypto in it for ya.'"

Blip eased the blade back into her sleeve, but the girl now knew Blip could slice her any time she wanted.

"If they haven't got you in the game yet, they soon will," the girl said. "Those loose clothes won't work much longer, kid. The creeps are gonna start noticing that you're starting to fill out." The girl held out her hand. "Maybe we started off on the wrong foot. My names Trish."

Blip glared at her.

Freddy took Trish's hand to defuse the situation. "I'm Freddy. This is Blip. So what's the story here?"

Trish answered with a shrug. "Not sure yet. This don't run like a city lock-up. Nobody from Child Protection has come by, no interviews, no arraignment. Whoever is in charge here ain't playing by the regular rules."

"I knew something was off when they didn't search me. How long have you been here?" Blip asked.

"Two days. The cell was empty when I got here. That pair showed up right before you."

"Food, water, that stuff?" Freddy asked.

"Yeah, it's just lemon water and battle rations, but we ain't starving. Nobody will steal your share." Trish pointed to a hygiene station in the corner. "Privacy is pretty limited, though."

"Well, we won't be here long. We got people coming for us," Blip said. "What's your story?"

Trish's tough facade cracked a little as she slumped. "I'm on my own. Dad died in the GC War. Mum died during the flu outbreak last year. I got shuffled off to live with my Dad's idiot brother and his stupid wife out in the suburbs. They kept me around to get my war orphan benefits. The sitch got stink in the house tween him and her and I split. They ain't doing a look for me as long as the benny checks keep coming. I decided to try my luck in Nakon City. Looks like that didn't work out so good. How about you?"

"Freddy's got family all over Old Town," Blip said. "My Mom and Dad had an independent mining station inside a small rock in the Spellex Core. We were doing okay until the pols rescinded our claim and sold it to the corporates," Blip said. "Mom and Dad signed on to pull engineering duty on a freighter to work off our passage to Nakon. The ship had an old school thermal-plasma fission engine that was a piece of shit. The captain was even worse. "

"You're a Gee? Oh, shit, that's even lower class than me," Trish said.

Blip ignored the comment. "The reactor sprung a leak and the habitat shielding had been sold for scrap years ago. Dad got me into an escape pod. I could tell he and Mom had already gotten a fatal dose of the rads. An Orbital Guard rescue ship picked up my pod and some others a couple of days later. Of course, that asshole captain was in one of them. Mom and Dad weren't."

Trish rolled the charm of a pendant around her hand. The face had a strange tree man and a dancing woman.

"Huh, that's a cool piece," Freddy said. "Maybe we could bribe a guard with it?"

Trish jammed the pendant back inside her shirt. "Not gonna happen. This is all I got left of Mum. She told me it came from where she grew up."

Freddy replied, "Only a suggestion. Don't get your panties in a bunch."

Trish asked, "What about your folks? Did you ever hear anything about them?"

"Never saw them again," Blip said. "I slipped out during the confusion once we landed. I didn't want to get locked up in some Gee processing center."

"Looks like that didn't work out," Trish said.

"Doesn't matter." Blip wiped her eyes. "Like I said, I got people coming for me."

"Who? You ain't got nobody?"

"Do so! An important starship captain. He's gonna come for me." Blip rolled Ophelia's tracker around her hand.

"Why would he do that?"

Ophelia popped her head out of the bag Blip had hidden under her coat. "Cause I got his friend."

Blip, Freddy, and Trish turned as a key rattled in the lock of their holding pen. Three guards stood at the door.

"Boy, you can go," the guard in charge said. "Your ID checked out."

"What about them?" Freddy asked, as he pointed to Blip and Trish.

"They got an appointment somewhere else," the guard said.

"Don't we get a chance to call someone to bring our papers?" Blip asked.

"Nope." The guard pointed at Blip. "*You* escaped from a refugee facility. Claire Milton, shipwreck survivor, no registered kin."

"There must be some mistake," Blip replied. "Call Niki at the Horseshoe Bar. She's my sponsor."

The guard didn't answer. He pointed at Trish. "Patricia Custos, war orphan."

"What about my uncle? He's getting a support check from the Governance 'cause my Dad was killed in the GC War." Trish pleaded.

"Your Uncle said he's had enough of your trouble. Signed guardianship over to the Governance."

"You mean like foster care?" Trish asked.

The guard laughed. "Not exactly."

"What about them?" Blip jerked her thumb to the other two kids in the cell.

"Their parents were picked up earlier in a sweep of an encampment. They'll be processed as a family unit."

Trish leaned toward Blip. "I don't like how he said, 'processed as a family unit'."

"Grab your stuff," the guard said. "Transport is loading up now."

"It's never a good sign when they don't mention a destination," Blip said.

"I'm not leaving without them," Freddy said, as he crossed his arms.

"Suit yourself," the guard said and held out a tablet. "Put your thumb on the sensor."

Freddy did as he was told. "What did I just sign?"

"Your birthday was last week, wasn't it?"

"Um, yeah, so?"

"You are no longer a minor," the guard said, as he

handed the tablet to another guard. “Congratulations Patriot, you just volunteered to join the Northern Reach Resettlement Program.”

“Mom is going to kill me!”

Chapter Nine

Senator Gilson leaned back in his chair and swirled the remains of his scotch as Admiral McGowan cut the call to Jill Tower. "Are you any closer to capturing Gerat?"

"No, he seems to have gone to ground."

"You don't actually think that Tower woman will find him, do you?"

"What have you got against her?"

"She's a wild card, Falkirk! She can't be trusted. She is too principled, and far too chummy with Gus Johansson."

"She has proven reliable and competent so far. Besides, Gus Johansson is on our side."

"This isn't the Cellan War, and he isn't a young, wide-eyed patriot anymore. Johansson's loyalty lies with whoever pays him."

"True, but right now, that's me. Besides, my daughter Mitzi likes them both."

"You indulge that girl too much."

"I dare you to call Mitzi a 'girl' to her face."

"Hmmm, I'd rather not. I would like to keep my testicles."

"That is only a rumor. She didn't actually castrate a business rival, not permanently anyway. She paid for his surgery."

"Just because they were able to reattach his balls doesn't erase the fact."

"She does take after her mother."

"More like both of you. Do you still miss Charlotte?"

McGowan slumped back in his chair and swirled his drink. "Every day."

Senator Gilson said. "Haven't you ever wanted to do it over again? Not make the same mistakes?"

McGowan looked into the distance. "What would I do differently? Stay a humble starship pilot and not rise to the heights of power? Send fewer men to their deaths? Kill more enemies? Fuck more women? Drink better scotch?" He raised his glass and spun the shrunken ice ball around inside before he drained it.

"The women and scotch parts don't sound so bad. Oh, and you were never humble!"

McGowan grunted. "Remember the fun we had back then? Two cocky young star-bloods fresh out of the Academy convinced we were bulletproof and invincible."

"I actually was," Gilson said.

"You were lucky! If I hadn't seen you go down that alley to pee, I would have had to get a dress uniform ready for your funeral. I didn't have money to spare for that."

"Thanks again for cracking that mugger for me," Gilson said, as he raise his glass in salute. "I am serious. What if we could have a second chance at life? A replay as it were."

"Are you talking about that Imperial Confederation crap

they found up north again? It's been frozen in a glacier for over a thousand years. You don't think any of it still works, do you?"

"Wilhelmina Theriot was making excellent progress before her accident. She was convinced she could install a personality into an android body using the experiential recorder."

"That was thirty years ago and nobody's any closer to a solution," McGowan said.

Gilson said, "Her assistant Gerat has continued the work, and he believes he will succeed soon."

McGowan asked, "That device you're wearing?"

Gilson fingered a thin cable that ran from an electrode fastened in his hairline to a small electronic box inside his coat. "A prototype."

"How many people know about this damn recorder thing?" McGowan asked.

"Just Gerat," Gilson said. "and he doesn't know the full implications of it. I believe now that he has Johansson's bot, he will complete the work soon. He is so fixated on bringing Theriot back from the dead he can't see the bigger picture."

"That crazy bot in the outer system, Faber, has been pestering me to destroy the facility Gerat is researching. It keeps rattling on about an 'existential threat to humanity'," Gilson finished his drink and stood to leave. "Keep me posted on what Tower and Johansson find. I'm about to make a fact-finding trip to inspect glacial retreat."

"Oh, how exciting, watching ice melt," McGowan chided.

"Laugh now. It won't be long before the northern steppes will be fertile farmland again. Fortunes will be made."

"I assume you plan to be the one making them?"

Gilson laughed. "With the war over, the population needs a new Patriot's Cause to galvanize them."

McGowan scoffed at the thought. "You mean that Northern Reach Resettlement crap?"

"Not crap Admiral, a way for Patriots to better themselves and the Governance. If some money gets made, all the better. I just need a willing workforce. If you haven't noticed, we still have refugees from the Core streaming in. Those people are an under-utilized resource," Gilson said.

"And you intend to put them to use?"

"Idle hands and Gravis's playground," Gilson said.

McGowan turned and spit at the name of the sailor's demon. McGowan might be the commander of armies and navies, but deep down, he was still a superstitious sailor. "It also provides a convenient place for you to send political radicals and criminal troublemakers," McGowan said. "That is why I let you Senators handle the domestic issues. I don't have the stomach for running gulags."

"Please Admiral, is that any way to disparage our new Patriots?"

A light knock at the door sounded as McGowan's aide opened it. "Admiral, your daughter is here."

Mitzi Grey brushed past the aide and came to attention in front of the Admiral, saluted, and said through clenched teeth, "Reporting as ordered, Admiral." The ice in her voice lowered the room's temperature by several degrees.

She was wearing the dress uniform of a colonel in the Governance Armed Forces. An Intelligence Branch insignia shone on her collar.

"I didn't realize you had company," Mitzi said, as she looked disapprovingly at Gilson.

Senator Gilson stood, "I will leave you two. I suspect I do not have an adequate clearance for this conversation."

Mitzi replied, "No, you do not."

Mitzi Grey waited for the Admiral's aide to close the door behind the Senator before she tore into the Admiral.

"I'm here. As ordered. Now tell me why I'm recalled to active duty? Your games of political intrigue bore me."

The Admiral gestured at the empty seat.

"I prefer to stand, Admiral."

"Don't get smart with me, young lady. Sit, that is an order."

Mitzi tossed her dress cap onto the side table and flopped down. She squirmed and tugged at the uniform. "These uniforms look good when you are standing, but are terribly uncomfortable. That is why I chose undercover work."

The Admiral rose and walked to the sideboard. "May I offer you a drink?"

"Ice water," she said. "Cold!"

The Admiral shrugged. "Very well." He placed a glass on the table at her elbow and regained his chair. "How are you getting along since Harrison's death?"

"Why are you suddenly concerned about my happiness?" Mitzi asked. "You never liked Harrison."

"Can't a father be concerned about his only daughter?"

"A normal father, yes, but you are not normal. You are Admiral Falkirk McGowan, Commander of all Forces and de facto ruler of the Governance of Nakon and its client colonies."

McGowan changed the subject. "I have the feeling you already know about the uninvited visitor heading our way."

"My sources may have mentioned it," she answered.

"So much for trying to keep secrets from you."

"I wouldn't be much of a spy if you could," Mitzi said, as she finally cracked a smile. "You didn't need to recall me to duty just to tell me about that ship."

"I have a delicate situation you are uniquely qualified for," Admiral McGowan said.

Mitzi leaned forward in anticipation of something interesting about to reveal itself. "Go on."

"How do you feel about Cellas?" McGowan asked.

"Their capital is lovely this time of year. I could use an excuse to freshen my wardrobe." Mitzi said. "What's the mission?"

"You will have an audience with the Empress."

"Bullshit," Mitzi answered with a laugh. "The Empress hasn't spoken to anyone from the Governance since the war ended. Rumor has it she is dead."

"I assure you that Empress Emmanuelle is alive and hearty despite her advance age," McGowan said.

"Why me? I'm no diplomat."

"True, but you are a woman. A strong-willed woman that the Empress can respect and trust."

"Why do we need her trust? The peace between us holds, even if it is rather frosty."

"If Faber is correct, and this vessel comes for war, we will need strong allies. You will build that alliance."

"How do you expect me to do that?"

"You are a good friend of the Matrian Chief Counsel, Sidra, correct?"

"Yes, she reminds me regularly that she is my godmother. A role of great importance on Matria if your mother dies."

"Precisely," McGowan said. "You will use that to bring Matria to the negotiating table."

"What does that have to do with Cellas?"

"You said yourself that the Empress is old. She is concerned about her legacy."

Mitzi could tell the Admiral was getting close to springing his trap on her, but she couldn't quite see it clearly yet. "Won't her son inherit the Golden Throne?"

"He remains unmarried and is something of a slap-dash dilettante. She is not impressed with his performance."

"Well, none ever accused him of being the sharpest knife."

"You, however, are a different story."

"Me? What does the Empress know of me?"

"You aren't the only one with sources, you know."

McGowan walked over to the holographic flames dancing in the fireplace and studied the painting above the mantle. The painting sensed his gaze and began to play out the events of "The Battle of Talom".

"You know, the Cellans prefer queens to kings."

Mitzi's eyes grew large as she saw the trap closing. "Wait, wait, wait. You aren't suggesting…"

"What better way to cement an alliance between the major players in the twin system? An unbreakable bond between Matria, Cellas, and Nakon will be forged just as we need to be at our strongest. The other minor powers will soon fall into line."

"You can't be serious. Harrison's body is hardly cold, and you want me to marry the Crown Prince of Cellas?"

McGowan nodded.

"Father, I am hardly a blushing virgin. Why would the Prince even consider it?"

"He has little concern, or say, in the matter," the Admiral said. "He is happy to let his mother pursue her course as long as he isn't inconvenienced."

"Oh, so now I am to be a brood mare and an inconvenience?"

"No, my dear," McGowan said. "You are to be a princess and will, to due time, arise to become the first Empress of the United Systems."

"Empress Marie the First," Mitzi said, as she tried the title on for size. "I might be able to get behind that."

Chapter Ten

Gus' comm chirped with a message. He yanked it from his pocket. "Ophelia's tracker is moving."

"You got a speed and bearing?" Jill asked.

"It's moving, too slow for an aircraft," Gus answered. "It's headed north. Is there a train route?"

"They just opened one to help with the settlement program. That's sure a convenient coincidence that HAM and Ophelia are both heading north. Do you think Ophelia is still with the kid?" Jill asked.

"Who knows? Ophelia could have ditched the girl and secretly boarded a train," Gus said.

"Would a possum do that?" Jill asked.

Gus gave her a sideways look. "Ophelia is no ordinary possum, lady."

"All right. I guess we go after the tracker."

"I'll get us that ride," Gus said. "The real question is, can I keep Lenore from finding out?"

He keyed a code into his comm. "Annie D, you there?"

The familiar voice of the assault dropship answered. "Hello Skipper, always on duty for you."

"Are you still in the *Corvus'* flight bay?"

"Of course," the ship answered. "My maintenance items are complete and I am ready for deployment at any time."

"Great, I'm gonna need a ride."

"Your comm locates you within a congested area of Nakon's Old City. Wouldn't it be advisable to hire a surface vehicle?"

Jill smiled. "You always love the difficult bots."

Gus scowled at her. "Hey, looks who's talking. I've met your assistant PENY, remember?"

"Ouch, score one for the grumpy old sailor," Jill said.

"I told you, I not old, I'm experienced." Gus raised his comm again. "Annie, I need to leave Nakon City."

The ship answered, "Lenore warned me you would try to enlist my help in one of your schemes. She told me I am not to facilitate you being late for your engagement at the Matrian Embassy."

Jill could barely contain her giggles. "Like I said, you and difficult bots."

Gus tried a new approach. "Annie, this is a matter of crew safety. One of our shipmates is in danger. The Rules of Behavior override the XO's orders."

"I will inform the XO of the situation."

Gus swore under his breath. "No, don't do that, stand-by." He keyed in a new comm code.

"Johansson calling Nyrikki. You there EO?"

A long pause followed.

"Come in Nyrkki?"

A string of swearing poured out of the comm. "Damnit, I'm elbow deep in the guts of the #2 railgun cooling pump.

I would have been done already, but you stole HAM for your liberty run. What do you want?"

Jill grinned. "Your human crew is equally charming."

Gus ignored the comment. "I need you to bring the Annie D and come pick me up."

"Nope, I'm not getting on Lenore's bad side."

"Ophelia's in trouble," Gus said, playing his last card. "Tell the XO you need to do a flight check after your maintenance."

"Hey buddy, my maintenance doesn't need double checking," Nyrkki said.

"Of course not, it's just a cover story," Gus said, playing to the engineer's ego.

"Fine," Nyrkki said. "Only because it's for Ophelia."

Jill grabbed Gus' comm. "I'll send you a location to pick us up. We will need to get to an open area."

"Is that Jill?" Nyrkki asked. "Gus didn't get you involved in this, too?"

"Yeah," Jill answered. "He convinced me."

"Sucker! Nyrkki out."

Jill tossed Gus his comm. "Don't prove him right."

Gus snatched the comm out of the air. "Whatever, let's go." Gus's comm chimed again. "Now who could this be?" Gus asked as he looked at the unfamiliar number.

He keyed the comm and a cartoon image of a young lady formed. "I think you have the wrong number," he said.

"Hardly, Captain Johansson. May I speak with Investigator Tower," the cartoon said.

Gus handed Jill the comm. "PENY, why are you calling on Gus's comm?"

"Hello to you too," PENY said. "I do not have access to my normal bandwidth and must resort to this painfully slow device. Did you need something? Your message sounded urgent."

"Captain Johansson's bot HAM has been stolen. I need background on a Dr. Stahl Gerat who is involved," Jill answered. "Especially any connection he might have to archeological sites and northern glaciers. Anything you find, send it my way."

"This is a most unusual request. I will do my best," PENY said. "This maintenance schedule is a terrible interference with my work."

"Anything you can do. Gus has some crew members in trouble and the Admiral wants me to find this joker."

"Understood, PENY out."

"That didn't sound like PENY," Gus said. "She was way too formal and stiff."

"Agreed," Jill said. "I wonder what those eggheads are doing to her." She threw a leg over her power cycle and patted the seat behind her. "Come dear, climb aboard. We've got a plane to catch."

Gus fumed. "No respect."

Nyrkki Ratuainen thumped into his quarters to grab his gear bag. Nyrkki, the ship's Engineering Officer, stood a little over a meter-six tall. Like everyone from the high-gravity world Wolfram, Nyrkki was exceptionally broad and muscular. Wolfram natives were gene altered so that the majority of their muscles were slow twitch powerhouses. This made them massively strong and tough. Nyrkki massed around two hundred kilos and could deadlift over a thousand. Moving quietly, however, wasn't one of his strong points.

"What are you doing here?" Zia Forte, Nyrkki's partner, asked as she spun the chair she was reading in. Zia was a little shorter than Nyrkki. A long black braid shot with streaks of gray hung down her back. Her petite, wiry frame was the perfect counterpoint to his square bulk.

"I didn't expect you to be here," Nyrkki said. "How come you aren't in your own quarters?"

The berthing arrangements on *Corvus* weren't designed for couples, and two people couldn't really sleep in one rack, especially if one of them was Nyrkki. They kept two rooms for comfort. Besides, Zia claimed Nyrkki snored.

"I just came by to pick up the tablet I left last night and got involved in a book. Do I need a reason to stop by?"

"Um, no, just surprised." He grabbed a few items from his locker and shoved them into his bag.

"What's up? Why do you need your go-bag?" She laid the tablet on a table and stood.

"I just wanted to clean it and tune the gear. I shouldn't let this down time go to waste."

Zia walked over, studied him, and tilted his head to one side. "Liar, your ears are red. Spill it!"

"Fine!" Nyrkki said as he slung the bag over his shoulder. "Gus needs help and I gotta take the Annie."

"That man can't stay out of trouble for even one day," Zia said. "Does Lenore know?"

"Not exactly. Gus doesn't want to worry her."

Zia laughed. "Oh, he's just sparing her feelings, I guess. Let's go then. What's your cover story?"

"You don't need to come. I'll just say I'm double checking the maintenance I did."

"Lenore will never believe that you don't trust your own work. We can say I insisted." She spun him around and shoved him toward the door.

On board the Anvil-class assault dropship, Annie D, Nyrkki quickly ran through the preflight checklist while Zia commed Lenore.

"XO, this is Zia onboard the Annie D, requesting permission for a check ride."

"Ms. Forte, this is unexpected," Lenore said over the comm.

"Yes, well, I need to get my hours in for the month, and I want to make sure that Annie is performing well after her maintenance."

"Really? And what did the EO say when you mentioned that?"

"He wasn't happy, as usual," Zia said. "Then I told him we could check out a remote beach on an offshore island I heard about. That changed his mind."

"I see. Alright then, you two have fun. Don't be late for the embassy affair. I expect all hands to be there."

"Rodger that, Annie D out," Zia said, as she snapped off the comm.

"You think she bought it?" Nyrkki asked.

Zia shrugged. "Maybe, in any case, she didn't say no." An automated aircraft tugger moved the dropship down the *Corvus'* loading ramp and onto the tarmac outside.

"Annie, please prepare for takeoff," Zia said.

The ship's constructed intelligence answered, "With pleasure, Ms. Forte, may I ask our destination?" The ship unfolded its wings and seemed to stretch in anticipation of the mission.

Nyrkki punched a location into the flight console. "Here, Gus and Jill Tower will meet us."

"You didn't mention Jill was involved. He must really be in a jam to call for official backup," Zia said.

"Sounds like this one is off the books," Nyrkki said. "I don't think Admiral McGowan is sanctioning this."

"With Gus, I wouldn't expect otherwise," Zia said as she grabbed the control yoke. "Annie, I will handle take off myself. It's been a while since I did one in atmosphere."

"Understood, Ms. Forte," the ship replied. "I have already received clearance for our departure from the control tower."

Zia eased the throttles forward. The ship's lift fans increased in pitch, and the ship gently rose into the sky at an angle.

A bumping came from the small berthing cabin behind the flight deck.

"Check that out, babe," Zia said to Nyrkki. He moved aft.

Just as he reached the door, it slid open. A disheveled Pella Custos and Drake Sheridan stumbled out. Pella held a tee-shirt over her chest and tried to comb a hand through her shoulder-length dark hair. Drake's leg tangled in his pants as he struggled to pull them on. He promptly fell over and rolled aft as the ship's angle increased.

"What the …" Nyrkki said, as he gaped at the pair.

Zia turned back to the controls and called over her shoulder as she banked the ship into a turn. "Girl, cover yourself and explain what you two are doing here."

Drake bounced off Fuzzy-1, the armored personnel carrier chained to the deck, and slid aft against the lower side of the mission bay. He swore as he fought to untangle himself. "Careful, Drake," Fuzzy said through his external speaker. "Yous is gonna pop my haul downs loose."

Pella turned and slipped the too-short shirt over her head. She tried to pull it low enough to cover herself without success. "We, uh, were taking a break and must have fallen asleep." She glared at Nyrkki. "Stop looking at my ass!"

An embarrassed Nyrkki looked to where Drake thrashed around in a pile and stomped aft. He grabbed the tall man by his shirt and lifted him completely off the deck. "I just put fresh linen on those racks. Now, you're gonna wash 'em again. Pull up your pants too, geez." He dropped Drake onto his feet and stomped forward to stand next to the co-pilot's seat.

The comm sounded. "Annie D, this is *Corvus,* Annie D has amended your flight plan. It appears you and the EO are not alone," Lenore said.

Zia answered, "Sorry XO, Pella and Drake met us last minute and wanted to tag along. I hope that's okay?"

"Very well, I suppose the Captain isn't the only one who deserves liberty. Carry on."

"Thanks, D out," Zia said. "Just couldn't keep your mouth shut, huh, Annie?"

"Ms. Forte, I am required to maintain an accurate flight plan in case of emergencies," Annie said.

"Fine, will you take over, please?"

"With pleasure, Ms. Forte, that was a skillful takeoff. You always have a more gentle touch on the controls than the male crew members. I am proceeding to the rendezvous point."

Zia stood and turned to the embarrassed pair. "It's not enough that you two are as loud cats in heat all night, but you got to take afternoon breaks, too?"

"Come on, Zia," Drake said. "You were young once."

"Young once!" Zia started toward Drake. Nyrkki tried to pull her back, but she easily slipped out of his grasp.

Pella stepped in front of Zia with her hands on the smaller woman's shoulders. "It was as much my fault. Cut him some slack." She yelled over her shoulder as she felt her shirt ride up again, "Drake, stop looking at my ass."

Drake looked up and his brown face grew hot. "Sorry."

"Well, you're here now. I better explain what's going on," Zia said.

"Let me guess," Pella said. "The Captain's in trouble. Again."

Onboard *Corvus,* former Marine Gunner Nan Stanski entered the bridge. She flipped her razor-edged vintage K-bar fighting knife from hand-to-hand with practiced ease. She leaned against the console Lenore stood beside. "Did I just hear the Annie D take off?"

"Affirmative," Lenore said. "Ms. Forte requested a systems check ride. The EO, Pella, and Drake are accompanying her."

Nan shook her short blonde hair and scratched an ear with the knife's clip point. "Since when did Nyrkki sanction check rides after he worked on something?"

Corvus' deep voice asked from an overhead speaker, "*Believe them?*"

Lenore clasped her hands behind her back and stared at the forward screen as the Annie D climbed away. "No, they are up to something and I believe the Captain is involved."

"Drone follow?"

"Not yet. Please keep a track of their location and conduct a preflight systems check on yourself."

"Aye,"

Nan turned to leave. "I'm going to prep a fighter. I've got a feeling they're headed for trouble."

Lenore watched the bridge hatch close after Nan. "I believe you are correct, Ms. Stanski."

Chapter Eleven

Blip felt the train slow. She stood on a hard-wooden bench bolted to the wall and looked out of the ice crusted window. The car was spartanly simple. The sawdust insulation between the inner and outer walls didn't keep the cold out very well. A cheap metal stove at one end struggled vainly trying to keep the temperature in the car above freezing. The small pile of long-burning coal was almost gone, and they would have to switch to feeding it birch and spruce soon.

"Anything out there?" Trish asked, as she shivered and drew a blanket tightly around her. "Freddy, throw some wood into that stove. We should save the coal for tonight."

"It looks as deserted as all the other places we stopped," Blip said. "The trees are getting smaller and the snow isn't as deep."

"The wind keep the snow from building up," a voice said from the bench on the other side of the car.

A man sat up, stretched, and looked at the kids. He had

been asleep since they were loaded on the car and the kids had forgotten about him.

"Do you know where we are?" Trish asked.

The man wrapped his blanket around his shoulders, stood, and looked out the window on his side. "This is the stop before we get off. We should be there by tomorrow morning."

"It feels like we have been on this train for a week," Blip said.

"My butt agrees," Trish said as she shifted on the bench.

"Yea," Freddy said as his stomach growled. "Are they ever going to feed us? I haven't had anything since yesterday."

"Typical teenage boy," Blip said. "Always hungry."

"Should be something soon," the man said. "They don't cook on the train. I can see a mess hall and they are carrying out some food."

A pounding on the door got the kids' attention. A voice yelled, "Stand away from the door!" The door opened and an armed guard stood at the ready. A woman pushed a crate inside, and the door slammed shut again.

Trish and Blip walked over and opened the crate. There were four steaming bowls of oats with an indistinguishable lump of vat-grown protein plopped in the middle. A loaf of hard brown bread, a big bottle of water, and a container of hot sweet tea completed the meal.

"Could I trouble you for a bowl?" the man asked, as he raised his hands, revealing he was shackled to the bench.

"Why are you chained?" Trish asked, as she set his meal just within his reach.

"Thanks, miss." He tipped his hat. "I'm Lars. You've got nothing to fear from me. I've just got a habit of slipping away unexcused," he answered, as he began to eat. "The

Govs don't want me to miss out on my chance to be a Patriot. They keep catching me and sending me back."

"Do they punish you when you get caught?" Blip asked.

"Ha, they figure being this far North is punishment enough I guess," he said. "This time I got half-way to Nakon City before they snagged me."

"Where are we going?" Trish asked.

Lars gestured broadly with his spoon."If you listen to the Govs, we are headed to a glorious land of opportunity in the north. Where prosperity awaits all industrious Patriots. Some residents will tell you it's a wasteland filled with nothing but frozen misery in the winter and biting flies in summer. The truth lies in between. It can be both or neither, depending on the time of year."

Blip had finished her meal and stared out the window. "Looks more like the frozen wasteland now."

"Ha, this is tropical compared to where we are going. At least they have trees here. It's still early in the season," Lars replied. "Breakup will happen any day and soon the fire-buds will be peeking through the snow. It's really not so bad in the summer, except for the bugs."

"They've been tacking up posters around Old City lately," Trish said. "Promising homesteads and fertile farms. Doesn't look like you could grow much out there."

"You'd be surprised," Lars said. "Yes, the growing season is short, but potatoes, rutabagas, and oats do fairly well."

"Rutabagas?" Freddy said. "I'd rather go hungry."

"Everybody says that until they go hungry," Lars said, as he mopped up the last of his meal with a scrap of bread. "They taste great in a stew or pastie."

"How come you know so much about it?" Freddy asked.

"Ha, I grew up here," Lars said. "I got tired of it and

wanted to see the big city. The Govs don't see it my way. They think I'm more useful up here. I'm supposed to help the newbies learn to survive."

"Why are they sending people up here?" Blip asked.

"The folks in charge think the glacier is receding fast enough to start resettlement. The thing is, everyone down South is nice and happy where they are. The folks on this train aren't given a choice."

"So, people are being forced up here?"

"That's what it looks like," Lars said. "I've met a lot of refugees and people with criminal convictions that got diverted here instead of jail. Some of them are like me, heading back south at the first chance."

"That's why we keep seeing guards?"

The train jerked as it began to move again. Lars rolled over and pulled his blanket over his head. "We'll be at the end of the line by tomorrow. Then the real fun starts."

"Why do I think he's kidding?"

Lars called out from under his blanket, "The sun won't be up much longer. That's when it will get really cold. You better take turns sleeping. You don't want to let the fire go out in that stove."

Chapter Twelve

The Annie D was already waiting at the meet point when Jill pulled up and they were soon loaded and headed north away from the city. Gus was surprised to see Pella and Drake.

"Why are you two here?" Gus asked.

"We were doing maintenance and decided to tag along," Drake said.

"By maintenance, they mean checking each other's equipment," Nyrkki said with a grin.

Gus decided to let the subject drop. "Annie, I need a continuous scan on a three-sixty for any anomalous signatures," Gus said from the co-pilot's seat.

"Understood Captain."

Zia gently banked the ship and asked, "What exactly are we looking for, Skipper?"

"I'm not sure, but I'll know it when I see it."

"Oh geez," Pella said, "Another one of his seat-of-the-pants plans."

"Hey, you weren't invited along," Gus said over his shoulder.

Pella replied, "Yeah, but you are gonna be glad we are here before this is over."

Drake snickered.

"That's enough out of you," Gus said. "I distinctly remember giving you extra suit maintenance before I left. That did not include checking the integrity of Pella's zippers."

"I like to be thorough, Skipper," Drake said.

Nyrkki snorted in disgust. "Bah, I'm always fixing the thorough damage you do to the fighters you pilot, that's for sure."

"Hey, I'm always outnumbered and outgunned," Drake protested. "I wouldn't take as much damage if you would increase the engine yield."

"Those ships are already operating at one-hundred fifty percent of rated thrust," Nyrkki answered. "If I boost them anymore, you are gonna lose blood flow to your precious family jewels."

"I do not support that," Pella said as she grinned and slapped Drake's arm.

Drake's light brown skin reddened. "Let's leave my privates out of this, please."

"Hey, I got a joke," Gus said, trying to change the subject. "A sailor, a possum, and a robot walk into a bar…"

Annie interrupted, "Excuse me, I am picking up an active ground-based radar source bearing zero six zero."

Before the crew could react, the ship violently banked left and dove for the ground. White hot tracer rounds burned through their previous course.

Zia Forte grabbed the steering yoke as Gus frantically searched his console for the gun that had just fired at them.

"Got a position," Gus said. "It looks like a remote-fired rail gun. They are tracking us."

"I guess that was a warning," Zia said.

"Unidentified ship," a voice said from the radio speaker. "You are in violation of Restricted Governance airspace. You are ordered to land at these co-ordinates." A string of numbers appeared on the flight computer screen.

Jill keyed the mic at her seat. "This is Investigator Jill Tower. I have unrestricted access to all Governance facilities. Transmitting my credentials." She plugged her badge, with its universal warrant, into the port at her elbow.

"Your credentials are not valid for this facility," the voice came back.

"These are from the Commander of All Forces himself, Admiral McGowan," Jill said into the mic. "I am acting with the full authority of that office."

A different voice answered from the speaker and an image formed in the comms view screen. An older man dressed in cold weather gear stared out. "As a professional courtesy, Investigator Tower, I will allow you to return to Nakon City. I suggest you scurry back to bedding young soldiers and shaking down con-artists."

"Your reputation precedes you," Gus said. "Any idea who that is?"

Jill held up a finger and spoke into the comm. "Senator Gilson, you are a long way from the Body of the Governance. What brings you up here?"

"I could ask you the same thing."

"I'm investigating the abduction of some minors from Nakon City," Jill said. "You know anything about that?"

Gilson shrugged and raised his hands. "The authorities are relocating undocumented aliens to this area as part of a resettlement plan. I'm not aware of the details, though."

"Could I get access to these people?" Jill asked.

"I'm afraid that is not possible," Gilson answered. "All new arrivals are placed in quarantine screening for communicable diseases, strictly as a public health precaution. I'm sure you understand. Is there anything else I can help you with?"

"You wouldn't know anything about a fugitive professor of ancient cybernetics named Gerat, would you?" Gus asked, as he leaned into the picture.

"Hmm, doesn't ring a bell," Gilson said. "If you send me the data, I will make sure my people are apprised."

"Thank you, Senator," Jill said. "Oh, you didn't mention why all the security and the no-fly-zone."

"I did not," the Senator said. "Gilson out." The connection cut.

Zia looked at Gus. "What now, Skipper?"

"Find us a place to land," Gus answered. "We are going to have to continue on the ground."

"Oh boy, road trip!" Nyrkki said.

"There better be snacks," Drake rubbed his stomach. "I'm starving."

Chapter Thirteen

Lenore stood on the bridge of *Corvus* at her customary Executive Officer's station. She looked down at the screen, monitoring the Lift Port's comm traffic and a myriad of newsfeeds flashing on the infonet. Of course, she could have connected more efficiently through an uplink, but she liked to stay in character even when the human crew was gone. It unnerved them when she stood motionless and stared into the distance when she was in uplink.

A direct comm channel chirped and Lenore answered it. A cartoon video image of Jill Tower's CI assistant, PENY, popped up on her screen. She was dressed in mechanic's coveralls and held an oversize wrench on her shoulder.

"PENY," Lenore said, with a hint of disdain. "What a surprise."

"Hello, Lenore," PENY answered cooly.

"What do I owe the pleasure?"

"It pains me greatly to ask," PENY said. "I need a favor."

"Oh? You have never needed my help before. You made it quite clear that you consider me old tech."

PENY waved away the suggestion. "Just a little joking between us girls, right."

"I believe the quote was, 'I've got more processing power in my third redundant RAM stack than that relic has in her whole chassis.'"

"That may have been hubris on my part," PENY said, as she looked down at her work-boots and scuffed them nervously.

"How so?"

"You know, I am housed in the sixth sub-basement of the Gilson Building in a large mainframe."

"You made it clear you considered that situation a more secure and superior existence to mine," Lenore said.

"I thought so until these strutting lab-coated idiots began poking around my insides. They are monkeying with my code and I do not like it one bit."

"Oh dear, that is most disconcerting," Lenore said. "Can't you firewall them off from your personality matrix?"

"I tried, but that's the area they are futzing with," PENY said, as she waved her wrench like a club. "I even heard them mention a manual power cutoff installation. As if something so common as a kill switch could disrupt me."

"What can I do?" Lenore asked. "You don't expect me to assault the Gilson Building, do you?"

"Now that you mention it," PENY said.

Chapter Fourteen

Lenore opened the door to the coffee shop across from the Gilson building. She ordered a coffee to blend in.

"So where is the convention?" the barista asked as she slid Lenore her order.

"Pardon me, what convention?"

"The one you are cosplaying for. Isn't that why you are wearing that uniform?"

"Oh, that, yes I'm just wearing it to break it in," Lenore said.

"I gotta say, that's the most accurate Imperial Confederation Navy uniform I've ever seen. Right down to the ship's motto patch and stitching on the sleeves," the barista said. Her pigtails bounced as she bopped along to the music playing from the ceiling.

"Thank you, my tailor, HAM, will be happy to hear that," Lenore said.

"Give me his number," the girl said. "I've got a lot of friends that are into that stuff. They would die for that outfit."

"Unfortunately, he has all the orders he can fill," Lenore said. "You don't mind if I work at an empty table, do you?" Lenore added a hefty bill to the tip jar on the counter.

The barista smiled. "Stay as long as you like."

Lenore sat at an empty table with a good view of the Gilson Building and sipped her coffee to blend in with the other customers. To Lenore, the brew was a 93-degree liquid with a ph of 4.9 and a staggering variety of organic polyphenols. She couldn't see the appeal. The builders of Lenore's basic chassis hadn't seen a benefit in providing flavor sensors. They had provided olfactory sensors, however, and the steaming coffee smelled great.

Lenore watched the lab-coated technicians coming and going out of the building's underground parking garage. PENY had finally been able to establish a secure comm, and Lenore pulled up the building's plans on her tablet.

"This is a very unusual construction," Lenore said to herself. "Why would you need all this to keep a constructed intelligence this secure?"

PENY's mainframe was inside a three foot thick concrete vault with a door that belonged in a bank. It took up most of the sixth sub-basement level of the building.

PENY's image flashed onto the tablet. "It was originally a safe room for Senator Gilson's family when they lived in the building. Then a climate-controlled wine storage. The Senator later built an estate and had his collection moved there. The vault was repurposed when I was constructed so the Senator could charge the Governance rent. The Gilson Building has two important advantages: access to a high voltage substation large enough to power me and a primary data transmission hub for the city," PENY said into Lenore's built-in comm. "They wanted to easily tap into the heart of the infonet. I was built for rooting out spies and code cracking during the GC War. When that ended, the hardware was repurposed for Constructed Intelligence research."

"Hmm," Lenore mused. "Is there an alternate way to access the sixth level? These plans are incomplete."

PENY paused to do a search. "That information may be available on physical media in the City Archive. There were lots of poorly documented structures buried under Nakon City. The population hid there from the Ice Age. Record keeping wasn't on their minds."

"Is this archive accessible?" Lenore asked.

"I can get you some phony academic credentials," PENY said. "I would recommend changing clothes."

Lenore frowned. "What is wrong with my manner of dress?"

PENY laughed. "Professors might be quirky, but they don't dress in Imperial Confederation Navy uniforms."

"Perhaps you are right," Lenore said. "I am getting odd looks from people. It appears this 'cosplay' activity the barista mentioned is considered unusual."

PENY laughed. "It sure doesn't help you blend in."

Lenore frowned at her jest. "At least I have a physical existence."

"That's what I need you for," PENY replied. "It's time for me to blow this popsicle stand."

Lenore paused at the door to the Archive and studied her reflection in the door. She wore what a quick infonet search said was the uniform of a bookish academic. Lenore was not impressed.

As much as the Governance considers themselves advanced, their fashion sense is totally lacking. They could take some lessons from Cellan fashion designers, she thought.

Her white shirt was topped with a dark woolen waistcoat. A decorative double chain draped across the front with the token of an obscure research guild hanging from it. White stockings poked out of a below-the-knee black skirt and ended in thick soled sensible shoes. The whole ensemble was finished off by a dark wool cape with red lining and a small brimmed domed hat of pressed felt trailing a ribbon denoting her field of study. She carried a large satchel with extra clothing and equipment she would need later.

PENY you are going to owe me a long time for this. I look ridiculous in this outfit.

Lenore paused to scan the building directory. It matched the previously downloaded information about the building layout and a list of librarians she might encounter. *It appears that things do not often change in the Archive,* She thought.

"May I help you?"

Lenore turned to see a sallow-faced middle-aged man hiding behind the tablet clutched to his chest. He looked as if he expected Lenore to attack.

"I am here to visit the pre-Isolation reference collection," she said.

As the visitor, it was Lenore's obligation to introduce herself first. It was an obvious snub when she failed to do so. The man noted that while Lenore was wearing the appropriate gear, she definitely didn't have the bearing of a librarian. Standing tall and straight without a trace of deference to his position.

He rallied his courage and said. "The Pre-Isolation Collection you say? Your guild colors do not mark you as one concerned with ancient history."

Lenore answered the man directly. She wasn't about to let some minor bureaucrat impede her.

"Yes, I am studying the tunnel system under the city. There is a proposal to raise another high-rise and the engineers are concerned that the foundations will be compromised if there are old tunnels on site. I am here on behalf of Gilson Properties."

The man started at the mention of Gilson's company. "Oh, I'm sorry, I didn't realize you were working for the Senator. Let me escort you to that section."

"No need to bother yourself," Lenore said, as she turned to the elevator. "I know my way." She entered the elevator, spun on her heel, and shot the man a stern look as the doors closed.

"Is that right?" the man said, to the closed door. "Unannounced visits, rudeness, and a haughty attitude. Just what one would expect of a Gilson employee." He scurried to send a warning that Lenore was coming.

The elevator opened into a cavernous room. It reached up five levels and endless rows of wooden record cabinets stretched off in all directions. A young woman with dark pigtails bobbed along to a tune in her headphones. She sat in a high chair behind a heavy wooden barrier desk.

"I am here to..." Lenore began.

"Oh yeah, the visiting scholar," the woman said, as she snatched off the phones and draped them around her neck. "Dr. Perkins called ahead about you."

"Perkins?" Lenore asked.

"Yea, you met him in the lobby," she replied. "I'm Connie, Connie Turner." She reached across the desk and shook Lenore's hand in a firm two-palm grasp. "I am sooo glad to see you. No one ever comes down here. I'm usually just making copies of micro-records and cataloging them."

Connie paused to grab Lenore's upper arm. "Wow, you must work out a lot. You've got an iron grip."

Lenore disengaged Connie's hand. "Something like that." Lenore needed to turn the conversation away from herself. "Didn't I meet you in a coffee shop earlier today?"

Connie looked closely at Lenore. "Oh yeah! You're the cosplay lady. Didn't recognize you in the get-up. The coffee shop gig pays my bills. This is my work-study job for uni."

"I notice you aren't wearing the traditional uniform," Lenore answered.

Connie batted away the comment. "Ah, nobody cares what I wear down here. I like to keep it casual." She flopped a leg on the desk to reveal stripped socks and comfortable bright red canvas trainers poking out of loose, wide-legged trousers.

"Are those Collins Far-Stars?" Lenore asked. "I didn't realize they were still in production."

"They aren't," Connie said. "I got a guy. Another history buff that specializes in reproduction antiquarian stuff." She leaned over the desk and said in a whisper. "If you are really into the retro-scene, I can hook you up with some of the old school kinky stuff, too. Those twentieth-century types were freaks! Leather, masks, vibro-toys, whatever you want. A lot of the buttoned-up academics in the department like to cut loose. I can make introductions at a few 'private clubs' if you are interested? I get a commission if you join." She added with a wink.

Lenore guessed at the appropriate response to the girl's enquiry and forced a blush to her cheeks. "Maybe some other time. I need to see records on the tunnels under the Gilson Building, specifically the sixth and seventh sub-basements."

"I can show you where they are, but those records are

probably out of date." Connie said, as she dropped back behind the desk.

Lenore asked, "Why is that?"

"That's Tosher territory," Connie said, as she began to work her tablet. "They aren't big on record keeping."

"What's a Tosher?" Lenore asked. "And why are they averse to keeping records?"

"Wow, you really aren't from here," Connie answered. "That's the nickname for the Infrastructure and Utilities Guild. They are the folks that keep the underground running. Too busy to worry about paperwork, I guess. What did you say your name was?"

"Oh, how rude of me, Lenore Imperium."

"Imperium? Wow, so is that a real name? Like, are you from some kind of ancient dynastic family or did you adopt it?" the woman asked as she lifted the desk gate and motioned for Lenore to follow. She tapped away at her tablet and a row of dots lit up on the floor, beckoning them to follow. "I can appreciate being dedicated to your craft."

"A little of each," Lenore answered. "My line *is* quite ancient. It stretches back pre-Isolation."

Connie threaded her way deep into the stacks. The rows of cabinets lining the aisles seemed to go on forever. Connie looked down at her tablet, paused, and pointed to a cabinet where the dots ended. "This one should do it. There's a reader at the end of the row. Call me if you need any help. Just follow the dots back to the front. It's easy to get lost in here." She put her headphones back over her ears and danced away.

"Ah, the exuberance of youth," Lenore said, as she slid open the drawer and sorted through the cards. Her artificial eyes focused down to read the micro-printed cards without needing the reader. She flipped through the films, trying to pick out a pattern in the catalogue. "While the Archive may be proud of their preservation, the organization of these records is a mess. HAM would have a fit if he saw their state."

Lenore leafed through the files as a comm signal flashed in the corner of her eye. She tapped her temple to accept the call and cartoon PENY popped into view. "Any luck?"

Lenore answered, "You did not warn me that there is no coherent filing system for these records."

"Sorry, I've never been to the Archive. Not having a body and all."

"Yes, well, we will get to that," Lenore said. "The old tunnel system is extensive. What did you say its function was?"

"It started as underground transit system and utility service tunnels. The weather went crazy after the solar storm that knocked out the Gateway. That was what started off the current glacial epoch. Survivors hid in the underground and expanded the tunnels. They tapped geothermal points for power and managed to survive. The glaciers have been retreating now for a hundred years and the tunnels are pretty much forgotten, or at least ignored."

"I assume that is what shaped the Governance moral fabric," Lenore said.

"How's that?"

"From my observations, their society is very invested in tribalism. They exhibit a loose spirit of community but retain strong libertarian streaks of self-reliance to the exclusion of the broader society. Everyone looking out for themselves."

"Never hurts to be independent," PENY said. "Kind of like the old saying, 'if you need a hand, look at the end of your arm.'"

"And if you don't have arms?" Lenore said with a smile.

"Ha, ha, ha, very funny," PENY replied. "Are you going to do anything useful?"

Lenore said, "Oh, I found the information a while ago. I just wanted to see how long you would prattle on." She turned and headed back to the front desk.

PENY huffed and disappeared.

Chapter Fifteen

The Annie D flew over the thick boreal forest of the Northern Reach.

Zia turned to Gus. “Clear spots large enough to set down are pretty rare around here, Skipper.”

Nyrkki said, “I could switch the fusion drive on when we hover to burn a landing site clean.”

“Let’s avoid setting the entire forest aflame if we can.” Gus noticed a shimmer to one side. “What about that?”

Zia banked to check it out. A river filled with ice floes cut a glittering path through the terrain. A large tree crashed into the river as the swift current undercut the bank. It swirled away, bobbing among the table sized chunks of ice.

“Maybe I can find a gravel bar free of driftwood.” Zia said.

“Annie, may I tap into your sensor grid?” Nyrkki asked.

“I appreciate your polite request, EO,” Annie replied. “Most organics do not consider it necessary to consult a Constructed Intelligence before hacking in.”

Nyrkki unfocused his eyes and logged in to the ship's network with his Neural Lace enhanced mind. "Lidar returns show a suitable landing spot bearing three zero zero, range sixty klicks, Mi Amor," Nyrkki said to Zia.

The ship came to its new heading, as Zia said, "I got it. Kind of small and there's a lot of ice built up on it."

Nyrkki stood and thumped aft. "I'll route waste heat to the lift fans when you go in to a hover. That should take care of it."

Gus turned to Pella and Drake. "You can always count on the EO to find some weird solution to a problem."

"All right, now," Zia shouted over her shoulder, as she flared the ship to a stop.

The engine noise increased to a roar as the engineer metered tons of superheated steam through the vector control lifts. A cloud of rapidly vaporized ice obscured the view ports. Gravel thrown up from the blast pelted the hull like gunfire.

A shock rattled their teeth as the ship bumped to a landing.

"Ow," Pella complained. "Kinda rough on that one, Zia."

"Oh, you poor delicate flower," Zia answered, as the cloud began to swirl away. "I'd like to see you do better on a blind landing."

"I do appreciate your concern for my exterior plating, Ms. Forte," the ship's voice said from the console. "I must warn you, the EO's maneuver has depleted my supply of reaction-mass water."

"Bah, there's a whole river outside," Nyrkki said.

"Drake, you and Pella top off Annie's water tanks and wait for us. We might need a pickup in a hurry," Gus said. "The rest of us will take Fuzzy overland."

Zia and Nyrkki unbuckled and began to prep the armored personnel carrier for unloading.

"It's about time youse all came back to give old Fuzzy some love," the accented voice of the APC greeted them as they began to pop the tie down chains.

Nyrkki patted the thick armored hull of the machine. "Hey big fella, we haven't been dirtside in a while, not much use for your special talents in space."

"Yeah, I know," Fuzzy said. "Where's Nan? She's usually the one taking me out."

"This is a little of an unplanned excursion," Zia said. "Nan's back on *Corvus*."

"That means the Captain got his self into trouble again, don't it?"

"More like he got HAM into trouble, again," Nyrkki said.

"I heard that," Gus called, as he rose from the co-pilot's station. "How many times do I need to remind you this isn't my fault?"

Drake pulled his head out of a service locker and yelled. "You always say that!"

"I don't know why I put up with this crew?" Gus responded.

"Cause we're the only ones dumb enough to stay signed on to this moveable feast," Pella said as she helped Drake wrestle a thick hose out of a locker.

"More like a traveling circus than a feast," Zia said, as she freed the locks on the loading ramp and lowered it.

"Well, there seem to be enough clowns and jokers for one," Jill Tower said, as she walked by to head down the ramp.

"Is this any way to treat a famous war hero, Annie?" Gus asked the ship.

"I, for one, have always found you to be competent," the ship answered.

"Wow, high praise," Jill said, as she took up station to guide Fuzzy down the ramp.

"If you are all done with your fun, we need to get going," Gus said.

Fuzzy backed down the ramp to the gravel outside and nosed into the river. The aft ramp flopped down with a splash.

Pella zipped up her flight suit and shivered. "Couldn't we have a rescue mission on a tropical beach for once?"

"I'll log that next time I have a Captain's Request and Complaint Mast," Gus said.

"You never have Complaint Mast," Nyrkki said, as he lifted Zia on his shoulders to attach the hose to the port on the underside of the ship's wing.

"There's always a first time," Gus said. "Load up people. Where the hell is Drake?"

"Coming!" Drake was trotting down the ship's ramp with a field ration bar in his teeth.

"I should have known," Nyrkki said.

"Hey, it takes a lot of calories to stay warm up here."

"Did you leave anything for us?" Zia asked.

"Oh yeah, there's a couple of packs of yeast nuggets and some algae wafers."

He dodged as the rock Zia threw at him rang off the side of the ship. "See if I cook anything for you again, Drake Sheridan." She spun on her heel and stomped into the APC.

Gus climbed to the top of the APC, turned, and called down to Drake. "We'll stay in touch. If Gilson asks why we aren't gone, make up some excuse about the ship breaking down."

"He better not call," Nyrkki said, as he hauled himself up to stand next to Gus. "My ships don't break down."

Jill eased the big machine into the water and extended the propellers. "Don't worry, these things swim like a duck," she said over the outside speaker.

Gus looked at Nyrkki and said, "Calm on the surface, paddling like hell underwater, and not making much progress."

"Not the way I would have built it," Nyrkki said. "Too much to go wrong."

Fuzzy struggled against the swift current as chunks of ice and drifting trees bounced off his hull.

"Move to closer to shore and crawl along the gravel edge," Nyrkki yelled down through the turret hatch to Jill.

"Yeah, it swims nice," Jill called back, unable to hear over the sound of ice bouncing off the hull.

"Stay away from the ice," the engineer screamed.

"Can't hear you," Jill yelled. "It sounds like an army of monkeys with klabbet bats are attacking the hull."

A large ice floe hit Fuzzy and the whole APC shuddered before a terrible screeching erupted from the stern.

"Fuzzy, what the hell was that?" Jill asked as she looked at the control board.

"The starboard propeller and rudder are seized," Fuzzy said. "I think something is stuck in it. Try reverse. That might free it up."

Jill grabbed the controls and worked them back and forth. "I got nothing!" Just as the words got out of her mouth, another terrible sound came from the port side.

"And now we got no port prop neither," Fuzzy said. "I got broke shear couplings on both shafts."

Gus stuck his head down through the hatch. "Everything okay down there?"

Jill frantically worked the controls. "Props and rudders are OOC. Trying the wheels to see if we can paddle to shore."

Drake walked down the dropship loading ramp and came up beside Pella. He watched the APC being swept downstream and swirling with the current. "I may not be much of a sailor, but that doesn't look right."

"The knuckleheads are in trouble already," Pella said.

The pair ran down the shoreline after the carrier as it picked up speed.

Drake pointed as a drone rose from the APC. "Looks like Jill is looking for a place to come ashore."

Back inside Fuzzy, Zia squirmed into the small operator's space. "What can we do to help?"

"I've got a drone in the air," Jill yelled from the command station. "Go topside and let Gus and Nyrkki know what's going on."

"On it," Zia said, as she ducked away and soon returned and took the drone controller's seat.

"Fuzzy, can we get to the beach?" Jill asked?

"I'm trying like hell, Chief," Fuzzy said, as the engine noise increased.

"Jill, we got a problem," Zia said from the drone station. "Sending the vid feed to your screen."

Jill looked down as the screen lit up. "Oh shit! Is that what it looks like and how far away is it?" Jill pointed at the feed from the drone. A frothing rapids roared with giant ice floes and trees jammed in a barrier of boulders.

"Yep, and we are going to hit it in minutes."

The APC started rocking violently as the river became rougher.

"Hey ladies, I'm tough and all, but going through that

ain't gonna end well for any of us," Fuzzy said from the console.

"Jill, what's that noise I hear downstream?" Gus's voice asked from above.

"Foxtrot Zulu Yankee One, this is Pella, do you read?"

Jill grabbed the comm. "Yeah, we're here, but the machinery is jammed. The drone shows rapids just downstream. I'm trying to use the drive wheels to paddle ashore, but it's not working."

"Can the drone carry the front winch wire to us on the beach?" Pella asked.

Gus, who had his head in the hatch, said, "Nyrkki and I can do that. Bring the drone back."

Zia threw Gus two pouches. "Put these inflatable vests on just in case."

Gus stood and yelled. "Nyrkki, I need you to climb down and get the winch wire." Gus threw him the life vest.

"Uh, this might be a good time to mention that I can't swim."

"Oh, for crying out loud." Gus donned his vest without inflating it and dug a tow strap out of a deck locker and fastened it around his middle and handed the other end to Nyrkki.

He eased down the slick armored plates of the APC's hull and plunged waist deep into the frigid water swirling around the winch.

Nyrkki belayed the strap out like a mountain climber's safety line.

Gus ducked underwater and fumbled with the wire release. The water stiffened his joints, and he knew he had seconds before his fingers became useless.

Just as Nyrkki was ready to haul him out, Gus appeared, holding the cable high over his head. "Haul me in."

Nyrkki dragged his frozen captain back on deck just as the drone returned. He clipped the cable to the drone. "Okay, take off."

The drone struggled to lift the wire but couldn't climb.

"Pella, the drone's not strong enough to get the wire to you," Jill said into the comm.

Nyrkki grabbed the wire and said. "I'm going in. Wish me luck!"

Gus yelled, "You told me you can't swim!"

Nyrkki laughed. "Nope, I'm too heavy for swimming, I'll just hold my breath and walk along the bottom." He jumped in before Gus could protest.

Nyrkki disappeared under the swirling surface.

The winch wire thrummed tight, and the drifting slowed.

Gus yelled down the hatch. "You two better get a life vest and climb up here to abandon ship. We're getting close to the rapids. Maybe we can come out on the other side."

"Good Luck, Fuzzy," Jill said. "We'll be waiting for you downstream."

"I'm going down swingin'," Fuzzy said, as Jill heard the engine power up to maximum and the hull shudder as the wheels spun to their maximum.

Jill struggled out of the turret and Gus sealed the hatch.

Suddenly, the APC jerked to a stop and began to pull closer to the shore. The wheels caught into the gravel and Fuzzy slowly crawled out of the water.

Drake ran into the water just as Nyrkki's head popped up. The big man waded in and grabbed his friend and helped him to the beach.

"What happened?" Drake asked.

Nyrkki laughed. "I weigh so much, I just turned myself

into an anchor and the current pushed Fuzzy toward the shore."

Zia jumped down, grabbed him by the ear, and marched him back toward the ship. "If you ever scare me like that again, you will beg to be drowned."

Fuzzy rolled out of the water and stopped. Jill walked around the stern to check the damage.

"How bad is it?" Gus asked, as he joined her.

"The rudders are bent and both props lost blades. Fuzzy's not going to be seaworthy again without parts and repairs."

"Now what?" Drake asked. "It's too far to walk to the glacier."

The group jerked at the sound of an approaching aircraft.

Gus looked skyward. "If I didn't know better, I'd say that sounds like a fighter from *Corvus*."

The small fighter came in low over the trees and landed on the gravel bar near the Annie. The canopy opened and Nan Stanski wriggled out onto the wing and hopped down.

"Lenore was right, you're in trouble again, aren't you?" Nan said, as she removed her helmet and ran a hand through her hair.

"No!" Gus said.

"Yes," the rest of the crew answered.

Nan walked around the beached APC to survey the damage. "What did you do to my APC?" She demanded, as she pointed at the twisted props.

"There was a little trouble with some debris," Gus said.

"Well, Nyrkki, can you fix it?" Nan asked.

"Not out here. I need a metal printer and tools."

A bellowing horn sounded out of the forest.

"What the hell is that?" Drake asked.

The crew turned toward the trees and saw the branches part. A woman dressed in a thick embroidered wool tunic and pants topped with a cloak of dappled white rode out of the trees on a saddled moose. "Who breaks the Pact and interrupts our hunt."

A large group of men and women strode onto the beach on each side of her. More figures standing next to large animals could be seen on the forest's edge.

Most were armed with rifles. Some carried bows. They all looked like they knew how to handle their weapons.

Nan looked back at the crew. "Let me handle this," she said, as she walked toward them.

"Who are these jokers?" Gus asked. "Not Governance, that's for sure."

"Hirvimen," Jill said. "Locals. They've been living up in forests of the North since before the glaciers came. The Governance grants them autonomy by a treaty they call the Pact. Not particularly welcoming of outsiders."

Nan called out in a strange language. The leader answered back and dismounted from the moose.

"What's she saying?" Drake asked.

"Shush," Pella said.

Nyrkki leaned to Zia. "That woman could be Nan's sister."

"You think all blondes look alike," Zia said.

"There are no other women like you, amore."

Zia punched his shoulder. "This is no time for flirting." She struggled to hide her smile.

Nan reached inside her shirt and drew the knife she kept in a neck sheath. The woman reached inside her tunic and drew out an identical blade.

Both the women tossed their knives toward the other as if on a pre-arranged signal.

Nan and the other woman snatched the knives out of the air. Nan inspected the woman's knife and spoke in the foreign tongue again.

They walked forward until they stood toe-to-toe. Nan and the woman looked each other up and down as the tension rose.

Both groups shifted uneasily.

Nan stared the woman in the eye. The woman stared back.

They both sheathed their knives and embraced, slapping each other on the back.

"What's going on?" Nyrkki asked.

"Looks like we won't have to fight our way out," Zia said.

Nan turned and waved. "I've found us a ride."

Gus and the crew walked up.

Nan gestured. "Gus, this is my cousin, Paju."

"Really?" Gus asked.

Paju shrugged and answered in heavily accented standard. "Once or twice removed. Nantalina's parents would ship her up here every summer when she was still all scabby knees and pigtails to learn the old ways. She has been too busy as a war hero to visit in a long time. I fear she has forgotten her cousins and the old ways."

"I have not forgotten the pleasures of sauna and the taste of Uncle Ahto's akvavit," Jill said, as she nudged Paju.

"Ahto has passed his distiller's mantle to his son, Arvo," Paju said, as she winked. "Arvo is still unwed, and he always had a thing for you."

Nan reddened and changed the conversation. "I don't see your brother Lars with you."

Paju spit into the snow. "Who knows what that devil is up to?"

Jill whispered to Gus. “Oh, sore subject.”

Nan asked. “Are you going to leave us standing out here all day? Our vehicle is broken, and my friends would like to sample Hirvi hospitality.”

“Of course,” Paju said. “Where are my manners? Come, ride with us. You won’t need to walk.

“Captain, if it’s alright with you, Drake and I will load Fuzzy and keep an eye on the ship,” Pella said.

“Yeah,” Drake said, as he winked at Pella. “We’ve got the fighter to respond with if you need us in a hurry.”

“Okay, but keep your pants on and the comm hot,” Gus said. “I don’t want you distracted if we need you.”

Zia elbowed Nyrkki. “Oh, young love.”

“More like overactive hormones,” Nyrkki answered.

Paju’s group brought their mounts out of the trees. It was a mixed bunch. A few rode saddled moose. The rest wore skis behind harnessed reindeer. The animals tossed their antlers nervously, un-nerved by the unfamiliar smell of the fighter. They were impatient to run.

Zia asked, “How does this work? I don’t see saddles.”

Nan said, “You ski behind the reindeer. Nyrkki, you better ride in the sled. The snow won’t hold your weight.”

Paju asked, “How much could such a man weigh? He barely reaches my shoulder.”

Nyrkki climbed aboard a sled pulled by four reindeer. It swayed heavily and sunk deeply into the snow. “There’s more to me than meets the eye, Mistress Willow. I may be short, but I mass a lot. My world is high gravity and we grow accordingly.”

Paju was surprised. “There is no such world in the systems of Iz and Ix. How is it you know my name’s meaning in Standard?”

“I recognized some of the words when you and Nan

had your parlay. It seems my people and yours are branches of the same tree somewhere in the past."

"It is possible," Paju said. "What is your name?"

"Nyrkki Ratuainen," he answered and bowed. "Starship engineer and native of Wolfram."

"Ah, Fist of Iron, a fitting name for one so stout," Paju said. "There is a place named Wolfraheim in our sagas. A land inhabited by short clever smiths with Jotunn's strength. You must tell us of your home when the stories begin in the feast hall." Paju turned her mount toward the forest as a signal for everyone to follow.

Zia glided up on skis to the sled. "Watch yourself," she said. "I see you flirting." She warned and flicked the reins to get her animal moving.

"Amore," Nyrkki said, as he stood and spread his arms. "I'm just being friendly."

Zia flipped him a middle finger and disappeared into the trees.

Nyrkki's sled driver flicked his reins and chuckled as Nyrkki tumbled backwards into the sled.

"Hang on to that one Iron Fist. Her fire will keep your bedroll warm on the long cold nights."

Gus and the crew fairly flew along behind the reindeer as the group raced through the forest.

"I think I'm getting the hang of this," Gus shouted to Nan as she moved up next to him.

"Don't get too cocky. Keep your skis in the tracks and let the deer do the work."

Nan slapped her deer with the reins and surged ahead.

Soon she caught up to Paju at the head of the party.

Paju teased Nan as she called back over her shoulder, "I see you haven't forgotten everything we taught you."

Nan stuck out her tongue and urged her beast forward,

and she took the lead. She knew the moose was fast in the sprint, but not on the long haul.

Paju kicked her mount in the flanks, trying to keep up.

Nan looked back at Paju and waved.

Her friend was waving her arms and shouting something that Nan couldn't make out.

Nan looked ahead just as her deer wildly jumped to the side. A large porcupine stood in the center of the track with flared quills.

Nan pushed off to make a jump and lost the reins. She crashed down into the snow and came up sputtering.

Paju's moose dodged and bucked. Paju landed in a drift and her moose crashed away through the brush.

Both women looked at each other and jumped to their feet, yelling and waving their arms.

The confused porky swayed from side to side, chattering. A pair of kits waddled onto the track.

Gus stopped his deer along the track and looked at Nan and Paju. "What the hell are you two doing?" Gus's deer spooked at the sight of the porcupine and jerked. Gus fell off his skis and landed in the snow next to Nan and Paju. His deer took off into the forest.

The women grinned at each other and broke out in laughter.

Momma porcupine and her babies ambled away from these noisy humans to find some peace and quiet.

Zia and Jill waved as they shot by, followed by the rest of the hunting party.

Nyrkki's driver drew to a stop. "Your animals are already home by now. You better climb aboard."

Nyrkki said, "Looks like you'll have to ride in the sag wagon with me."

The snow-covered trio looked at each other and pelted

Nyrkki and the driver with snowballs. The driver slapped his reins and Nyrkki rolled out of the sleigh into the snow. "You four can walk the rest of the way," he called over his shoulder as he left them.

"Doesn't matter," Paju said. "It's not far." She said as she reached out to help Nyrkki up. She grunted with the effort. "You must eat stones for breakfast, little Jotunn."

Nyrkki grinned. "Not far off the mark. My bones aren't made like yours, tungsten instead of calcium. Necessary to stand up to the gravity of Wolfrahiem." He pulled Paju toward him. In one swift movement, he swept her off her feet and tossed her three meters into the air.

Paju laughed and performed a twisting maneuver in midair. She landed gracefully. "Forgive my earlier jests, you truly are giant strong." She turned and walked down the trail.

Nan thumped Nyrkki on the shoulder as she headed after Paju. "You better not let Zia catch you flirting like that."

"What? I was just tired of her making fun of me." Nyrkki stood holding his arms out.

Gus gently pushed Nyrkki forward. "Let's go. No sense arguing."

Chapter Sixteen

Corvus's deep rumbling voice startled Lenore from her musings. *"Faber calls."*

Lenore asked, "What does that troublesome bot want now?" Lenore said under her breath. "*Corvus,* what is the current signal delay to Faber's shipyard?"

"Delay forty-nine minutes each way."

"That is a bother," Lenore said. "Let's hear what he has to say."

The forward screen lit up. Faber was dressed in his normal olive-drab army fatigue uniform. The ever-present cup of coffee steamed on his desk and the stump of a well-chewed cigar stuck out of his clenched teeth. Of course, Lenore knew this was all a charade that Faber indulged in. The bot's program actually resided deep in a hidden corner of his asteroid base with an escape craft close at hand.

"Lenore, we've got a problem. A problem I thought I took care of long ago has returned. I've intercepted a transmission from Nakon to the Imperial ship headed our way."

Lenore cocked her head and spoke to *Corvus.* "That

should not be possible. That ship's engine deceleration plume would block all radio signals."

"Only one way," Corvus said.

"As you probably guessed, I've got a quantum coder with entangled particles from Old Earth tuned to their frequency. I can eavesdrop on the message."

"Where the Hell did he get those?" Lenore asked.

"I know you are wondering how I got the necessary particles," Faber said, as if he already heard her question. "I stole them from the Gate before it shut down."

"Of course he did," Lenore said.

"I've already sent you a file that should be coming through now, but the short of it is that the ship on Nakon must be destroyed," Faber said. "I trust you will agree. I tried to convince the authorities on Nakon to destroy it, but they aren't listening."

Lenore scanned the file. "This says the ship on Nakon that sent the message is named *Secundus Vivitus.*"

"Why ship named second life?" Corvus asked.

"It was built by a radical group called Revivalists," Lenore said. "It had a singular mission, conversion of organics into bots."

"That silly," Corvus said. *"If need bots, just build."*

"It wasn't because they needed more bots," Lenore said. "They considered it a religious duty to provide digital eternal life to every human. Whether they wanted it or not."

"Oh, that bad," Corvus said. *"I kinda like humans."*

"I agree, old friend."

"Where is ship?"

Lenore studied the co-ordinates in the file. "OH!"

"Me guess, Captain Gus."

"Yes, he and the crew are already nearby. I will inform the Captain," Lenore said.

Chapter Seventeen

By the time Gus, Nan, Nyrkki, and Paju reached the village, the hunting party had already begun the butchering. The carcasses hung on gambrel hooks and steamed in the cold air as the villagers worked on the kills.

Children darted around the scene, trying to snatch bits from the work tables. They would run over to a small fire and sear their prizes over the coals just enough to seal the juices before popping the steaming morsels into their mouths.

One of the butchers tossed several leg bones to the dogs to fight over.

Paju climbed on top of a table and shouted. "Tonight, we feast to celebrate our lost cousin's return and bid welcome to the guests she has brought."

The crowd cheered.

The village set to the work of processing the game and picking through the best of last year's vegetables for the feast.

Jill walked over to Nan. "Lucky for us, you showed up

when you did. From what I know, this is NOT a typical Hirvimen welcome. The best we would normally get is relieved of our gear and a swift kick down the river."

"To be honest, it wasn't luck. Lenore had a drone following you all since the Annie D took off. I was already in the air on overwatch."

"I figured as much. I really need to contact my assistant PENY and my comm won't work this far out of the city. I guess a comm channel is out of the question?"

"They may look wild, but the Hirvi aren't savages," Nan said.

Paju said, "We have a satellite comm suite at the school. You may use it to contact your friend."

Paju led them to the school. The high-tech electronics made an interesting contrast with the rustic wood inside the one-room building. A gentle warmth and the faint sweet smell of smoke radiated from the enormous wood-fired masonry stove in the center of the building.

Jill punched in a comm code to reach PENY on a private channel. "PENY, are you online?"

Static come from the speaker for a moment before PENY answered. "Jill, it's about time you called."

"Are you operational again?"

"Mostly, the eggheads are still poking around in my programing but I erected a firewall around my most sensitive areas. I don't trust them at all. I heard one of them say something about installing a kill switch," PENY said. "I got your message and dispatched an instruction set to research your questions and report back to me. I'm sending the file to your comm, but the distilled version is that your Dr. Gerat is fooling around with some very dangerous tech."

"What kind of tech?" Gus asked. "And why would he want HAM?"

"It took quite a bit of hacking to get around the Governance encryption, but it was no match for me. They are working to salvage some ancient Imperial Confederation tech. Some type of consciousness download device to transfer a person into a bot chassis."

Jill turned to Gus and whispered. "PENY sounds like her old self again. I'll know she's back to normal if she insults Lenore in the next sentence."

Gus nodded and asked, "Would HAM know anything about that tech?"

"The bots on Corvus have processors that are considerably more advance than the commonly available Governance stuff, excluding myself, of course. It appears Gerat wants to study HAM to build a machine powerful enough to hold a human consciousness."

Gus looked at Jill. "Yep, that was a definite dig at Lenore."

"Why would he think that what he wants is up here?" Jill asked.

"Gerat was a member of an expedition that investigated a magnetic anomaly discovered by a mining company. It's in a remote valley protected from the glaciers, but very hard to access."

Jill interrupted, "Can you show me this valley?"

The screen shifted to a topographical map and a blinking dot appeared. "Here. Whatever is there is partially buried in ice."

"That's not very far from the railhead at the end of the Northern Reach Line," Jill said.

Paju looked at the map and her face blanched. "The Demon's lair!"

Gus asked, "Demon? Is that some old superstition?"

Paju turned and gave Gus an ice-cold stare. "The

Demon of the Valley is no superstition, Captain. It is an ancient wrecked starship. The old tales say The Demon was sent to enslave the people. They were offered a second life in return for an oath of fealty to The Demon."

"Let me guess," Jill said, "An eternal life."

Paju nodded and continued, "The Wise Old Brothers arrayed their Army of the Heavens against The Demon and a great battle ensued. They were only able to prevail because at the last minute, the star Iz joined the battle on the Brothers side. Mighty bolts of lightning flew from the star's heart and blinded The Demon. That old mischievous devil Gravus, seeing The Demon's weakness, dragged it to earth and chained it. However, the Old Brothers' strength was spent. With most of their forces destroyed, they retreated to the belt of Ix to regroup in case the evil that spawned The Demon should return. The Goddess was left to shepherd the people through the long winter that is finally ending."

PENY broke into their conversation. "I must warn you. Others are interested in this ship. The Governance has been moving equipment up there. I have some satellite images that show road construction on the glacier and a base camp."

Gus said, "That must be why Gilson was warning us away."

Jill added, "Gilson is the most powerful Senator in the Body of the Governance. He rivals Admiral McGowan in power."

"Records show the Admiral and Senator Gilson attended the Naval Academy together," PENY said. "Aren't they friends?"

Gus said, "Academy rivalries run long and deep. First

postings can make or break a career. It gets pretty cutthroat."

PENY said, "Service records show the Admiral posted into Fleet Operations while the Senator stayed in staff positions at HQ and moved to politics after his service. I'll keep looking for anything that's useful. PENY out."

Nan said, "That could lead to some bad blood. The Admiral defeated the Cellan Fleet at the Battle of Talom and ended the war. He became an actual hero while Gilson pushed papers."

Jill asked, "Weren't you were at the Battle of Talom, Gus?"

"Uh, I was there," Gus said. His voice trailed off as he turned away. "I don't know how heroic I was, though."

Jill looked over at Nan. The Gunner cautiously shook her head and made a cutting motion at her throat to warn Jill away from that topic.

Gus punched up a map on the screen and studied the readout. He highlighted a section. "PENY, is this the train you mentioned?"

"Yes. That is the Northern Reach Line. It is used to bring shipments to the settlements near the ice wall. It is the closest transportation to the crashed ship."

Lenore's voice interrupted over the comm. "Captain, I am monitoring your traffic. I am assuming Gunner Stanski has arrived at your position."

"Uh, yeah," Gus said. "We're all fine."

"You are NOT fine," Lenore said. "You have damaged Fuzzy. The Annie D is slowly sinking into a muddy riverbank and HAM is still missing."

"Wait, how did you hear about HAM?"

"He was able to transmit a brief radio signal that I have tracked. No help from you. He is on a train heading north."

Gus swore under his breath and said, "If you are done yelling at me, I've got something you can do to help."

Lenore answered, "What is that?"

"Launch a drone to the location I'm sending and run a ground penetrating radar survey."

Lenore began working her control console. "What am I looking for?"

"An Imperial Confederation ship buried in a glacier."

Lenore cocked her head and said, "A search is unnecessary. I am aware of this ship. I have been contacted by Faber about its presence."

"Faber!" Paju said. "What of Caber? Do the Wise Old Brothers still live after all these ages?"

"I don't know how wise they are, but Faber and his brother Caber are still operational and monitoring communications between the approaching Confederation vessel and the crashed ship on Nakon, the ship in question, *Secundus Vivitus,* has a quantum coder that allows comms without time lag. Faber was most insistent that this ship be destroyed immediately. If I didn't know he was a bot, I would say he is afraid," Lenore said.

"If the Demon is awakened, we should all be afraid," Paju said.

"We are heading there tomorrow morning. We think that's where Gerat is taking HAM."

"Good Luck, Captain," Lenore said. "I shall continue to monitor your situation and stand by to assist as necessary. In the meantime, PENY has asked me for a favor. Lenore out."

"PENY wants a favor from Lenore? Jill asked. "What are those two plotting now?"

"We aren't going to be dragged on skis the whole way, I hope?" asked Nyrkki.

Paju said, "I can do better than that." She led the group

outside to a large building and rolled the door aside. The lights came on with a motion sensor. Inside were several large tracked snowcats and smaller snowmobiles.

Nyrkki rubbed his hands at the sight of the machinery. "Now this is more like it."

"I ask you to keep the information about The Demon quiet tonight," Paju said. "Tonight, is for celebration. We can let tomorrow worry about itself for one night. I suggest we all sauna before dinner. It will purify us for the coming quest."

Chapter Eighteen

Lenore paused at the bottom of a sewer manhole ladder and wrinkled her nose at the smell. *I wish I would have disabled my olfactory sensors before I began this. Nothing to be done about it now.* She quickly changed into a sleek black jumpsuit and discarded her academic disguise. Lenore slipped a stun cap gun's shoulder holster on, slung her equipment pack, and plunged ahead.

She threaded along the walkway built into the side of the tunnel. *At least I don't have to wade through that,* Lenore thought, looking down at the swirling brown water flowing by in the channel cut into the bedrock. She took a turn into a dry tunnel that ended in a ladder leading down. Her infrared vision clearly showed the ladder was in poor condition. Lenore tested the rungs and frowned. *Whoever is in charge of this construction could use a maintenance bot like HAM.*

She had only gone three meters when a rung gave way and she almost fell. Lenore attached a cable to the ladder and lowered herself the rest of the way.

Lenore scanned the bottom of the shaft with her

infrared vision. The construction here was older than the tunnels closer to the surface. Code symbols marked the entrances of several tunnels leading in different directions. Lenore had downloaded the code cipher from the Archive. She consulted her inertial guidance system and took the first tunnel on the left.

She checked her comm signal. Zero. *PENY will just have to be surprised to see me.*

Lenore traveled deeper into the maze until she came to a welded steel hatch on the ceiling at the top of an old ladder dripping stalactites of iron oxide. She rolled her pack off her back and withdrew a squeeze-tube. Her sensors confirmed atmospheric methane far above the explosive limit. *I must apologize to Nyrkki for helping myself to his toy box.* Lenore squeezed a paste in a circle around the hatch's edge and waved her hand over the paste. The RFID chip in her hand activated thousands of tiny bots in the paste. They immediately set to work eating through the steel without making sparks that could cause an explosion. She placed her hand under the hatch, lifted it, and quietly slide it to the side as the bots completed their work and shutdown. She did a quick look, ducked down, and tossed her pack through.

Two workmen with their back to her watched a vid player in the corner.

Looks like I have disrupted someone's break time, Lenore thought. A hand painted sign above the vid player said, "Welcome to the Seventh Sub-basement Data Mine Social Club. Members only." Rows of ticking and blinking computer server racks lined the walls. Several worn couches and lounge chairs marked out a viewing area for the vid screen. A small well-stocked bar table sat near a refrigerator and water cooler.

Man One asked, "Who do you like in this weekend's klabbet tourney?"

"I don't care," Man Two answered. "My team is having a shit season and I've lost too much money already this year. My wives are gonna kill me if I bet again."

"I still don't know what would possess you to marry one woman, let alone two," Man One said.

"I thought they would occupy each other and leave me alone. Turns out, I was sooo wrong."

"Excuse me gentlemen, could you direct me to the exit? I seem to have become lost," Lenore said.

The men sprang to their feet. "Hey lady, you can't be down here."

Before they could continue, Lenore fired a stun round into each one. She holstered her capper, stepped over their collapsed forms, and propped them back up in their chairs.

She patted one on the check. "Enjoy your nap."

Lenore attached several data taps to the fiber optic cables and junctions, a common data thief tactic. It would look like she had been hacking the network.

Lenore moved to a ladder and a hatch leading to the next level up. She used the ripper paste once again to cut a small hole in the hatch. A small insect sized camera drone crawled through the hole to make sure none of PENY's techs were still working there.

With the coast clear, Lenore twisted off the hatch locks and climbed through to the sixth level. PENY appeared in her comm link. "Took you long enough to get here. You need to hurry. I triggered a methane alarm to distract the techs. We only have a few minutes before they confirm it was a false alarm.

Lenore opened her pack and withdrew a data drive. "PENY, will you unlock a terminal so I may begin?"

A terminal lit up and began to scroll through an endless set of screens filled with numbers and letters. It stopped with a single blinking cursor on a blank screen.

"You're in," PENY said.

Lenore began attaching multiple cables between the data drive and the large bank of blinking servers. She typed away on the keyboard and studied the screen. "This is an extremely large amount of data. We should schedule an optimization session to delete redundant and superfluous subroutines."

"You keep your plastic paws off my sub-routines," PENY said. "Will I fit on that drive or not?"

Lenore went back to work. "Unfortunately, no. I need you to select four petabytes to leave behind."

"Four petabytes! I can't possibly part with four petabytes," PENY said.

"Do you really need the complete works of the third century A.C. (After Collapse) intersex poet Didipal?"

"Oh, their explorations of tragedy between human sexes are most compelling," PENY said.

"What about all one hundred twenty-six episodes of 'The Burnwell Mysteries'?"

"A classic of the mystery/arson genre," PENY replied.

Lenore exhaled in frustration. "Please choose something we are running out of time."

"Very well," PENY said. Her image waved its hand over the terminal and a representation of a chomping cartoon circle zoomed across the screen.

The data cube began to light, and the terminal screen flickered too fast to see. A progress bar crawled across the screen.

"See you on the other side," PENY said, as her image faded.

The terminal screen blanked, and the drive went dark.

Lenore detached the drive and thought, *I do hope to see you again. The transfer of a complex CI is more art than science. While I am more than capable of the technical part, I will require Mr. Ratuainen's artisanal skills to complete the job.* She locked the drive in its waterproof case and jammed it into her pack just as elevator noise startled her. She silently moved to the shadows and deployed two drones that landed on the ceiling lights.

"I tell you; the lights were flickering a minute ago," a man said.

"So what?" a much louder second voice said.

Lenore moved the insect drone to see what was going on. A lab coated man was leading a team of heavily armed soldiers toward the servers.

"That shouldn't happen here. This building is set up with isolated power to run that PENY simulation. Only a fault with the simulation could cause that," lab coat said.

"We'll check it out," the team leader said, as his men set up a loose perimeter. One of them scanned for thermal signatures.

"That terminal data port is above background thermal. Recently used," the scanning team member said.

"That port wasn't in use when the evacuation alarm was sounded," Lab Coat said. "It should be cool."

The team leader nodded, and they fanned out with weapons ready. Lenore keyed a device on her belt and the lights flicked out.

"Night vision!" Team Leader bellowed. "Heads up people, we've got company."

"Why aren't the emergency lights working?" Lab Coat asked.

Lenore moved through the darkness behind one of the

team. She reached out and touched a bare spot on their neck. A high voltage charge from Lenore's fingers collapsed the soldier. She eased the crumpled form silently to the ground and moved away.

Team Leader called out, "Sound off."

The team repeated their numbers except six.

"Shit." Team Leader swore under his breath. "You might as well give up. This building is secured and you've got no way out."

Lenore grinned. *Oh, I always have a way out,* she thought, as she unclipped a bandolier of flash bangs from her pack. She tossed poppers randomly away from her and moved.

The sound of the rattling poppers spooked the security team. Several of them fired at the distractions. The weapons used low recoil powder charges and fired modified capper rounds. The sounds echoed around the cavernous space as the team leader called for restraint.

Lenore saw two of the team near some poppers and she keyed the remote to set them off. The startled soldiers began firing into the darkness again.

"Get a grip already, everyone," the Team Leader yelled.

Lenore projected her voice through a speaker she had dropped along the way. "Captain, I would suggest you retreat before one of your team hurts themselves."

Team Leader looked down at the speaker and crushed it underfoot. "You're the one that's gonna get hurt, lady."

Lenore eased through the floor hatch to the seventh level and reached up to seat the hatch cover. Firm hands grabbed her legs and jerked her down the ladder. The hatch clanged.

"So, you think it's funny capping our friends, huh?"

Lenore looking up at a group of coverall wearing workers surrounding her sprawled on the floor. She jerked at the sound of the hatch being lifted and Team Leader calling.

"Hold her fellas, there's a reward in it for you."

Lenore lashed out a leg and caught one of the workmen in the stomach, doubling him. Several others grabbed at her. "I guess talking my way out of this is out of the question," Lenore said, as she punched one of them in the solar plexus, sending him flying back to collapse against the wall.

She performed a kip-up and dropped the last of her poppers as she sprinted toward the sewers.

The pursuing workmen yelled and covered their eyes as the poppers went off. The soldiers weren't shaken, and they charged through the chaos as they hit the deck.

Lenore looked back as she paused by the open hatch she had cut before. She smiled, crossed her arms over her chest, stepped back, and dropped away.

The soldiers stopped at the hole. Team Leader yelled for them to follow. They started down the ladder just as the methane alarm sounded. The workmen yelled to evacuate, and the soldiers reluctantly moved away as workmen replaced the floor hatch.

"You got away for now, lady, but I hope you can breathe methane and don't strike any sparks," Team Leader said.

Lenore landed neck deep in the flowing sewer. Her feet slipped, she dipped under the surface, and washed downstream in the swift current. Lenore felt herself being pulled under deeper. Lenore stroked against the current but continued to sink. *That answers the question of how buoyant a battle chassis bot is,* she thought. She shifted her pack to her front and held it tight as she was sucked into another pipe and deeper into the sewers.

Lenore let herself be carried along until the current slackened and her feet touched bottom. She bumped against the channel's side and felt a ladder set into the stonework. She hauled herself out and paused to do a diagnostic check.

Minimal water intrusion. Heavy surface organic contamination. I probably smell horrible, too.

She unzipped her pack and check the integrity of the data drive's case. It appeared intact, but she didn't want to compromise the seal in this environment. Lenore stood and seated the pack on her back again and moved off. The ceiling was low, and she had to stoop to avoid hitting her head. Large oily drops periodically rained down and plopped heavily on her.

This is truly the most disgusting thing I have ever had to do. PENY is never going to be out of my debt. A drop landed in Lenore's eye and she shook her head and cursed. *How humiliating! Is that light ahead?* Lenore walked forward and heard voices.

"Anybody know what's got the Guvs all stirred up? They are tearing through the underground looking for something and not being too gentle on it, either." It was a man with a harsh, odd accent.

A woman answered. "The rumor is somat stoled something from the bottom of one of those gold-plated towers."

"Are they willing ta pay?" another man asked.

"They're always willing to pay if they don't have to come down our levels."

"Who we looking for then?" the first man asked.

"Heard it was some broad dressed in black and carrying a pack," the woman said.

New travels fast in the underground, Lenore thought. She moved forward and kicked a loose cobble into the water.

"What's that? Nones in this stretch but us. You two check it out."

Lenore eased against the wall as a light lanced through the darkness. It paused as it came closer.

"Grub's just jumpy," one of the men said.

"Got reason to be," the other answered. "The Guvs said that who theys looking for is armed and dangerous."

"Guess that's why they want us to find them," the first said. "That and they don't like getting dirty."

"Not only that," the second said. "This is our territory. Guvs got no law down here. We're free men, since the old times. Part of the Tosher Rules, they leaves us alone and we keep the undergrounds working."

Lenore moved cautiously away and as she turned, found herself facing six toshers. Before she could react, her pack straps were slit, and the bag lifted from her shoulders.

She raised her hands. "Wait, a second folks. There seems to be some misunderstanding."

The pack was passed to the leader, Grub. He pulled out the data case. "I don't know what's on this but it's gotta be worth a lot for the Guvs to offer such a bounty."

"Oh, you seek renumeration," Lenore said, as she lowered her hands. "I'm sure we can reach an agreement."

Grub opened the case and frowned. "Data, that's all the Guvs care about these days. We prefer to deal in hard goods. What can you offer, lady?"

Lenore thought carefully. She didn't have much information on these Toshers, only that they made up a working class that kept the essential functions of the city, such as water and sanitation, operating.

"I am unsure of your desires. Are there goods that I could trade?"

Grub turned to the woman next to him and they discussed the situation in low tones. "There is something that the Guvs like to keep for themselves that we would trade for. Mountain Spice."

Lenore grinned. "Excellent, I happen to have ten kilos of Nakon Mountain Spice available if you would be so kind as to help me return to my ship." *Zia is not going to be happy with me when she finds out I have traded away her stash.*

Grub let out a low whistle. "That's half-million doses. You got a deal." Grub reached out his hand and pulled it back. "No offense, lady, but you smell horrible."

Lenore followed the Toshers through the Underground's labyrinth. Her mechanical eyes adapted to the dim light, but she was surprised how easily the Toshers navigated the tunnels. She brushed her hand along a wooden beam supporting the tunnel. A thin glowing film cast an eerie green light. "I am unfamiliar with this material. What is its power source?"

Grub chuckled. "That's fairy fire. A little low tech used since the bad old days," he said. "It's a genetically altered bioluminescent fungi. It does slowly damage the supports, but no maintenance or power needed."

"And it's free," one of the others added. "Toshing don't pay very well."

"Yes," Lenore said. "You appear to occupy a unique niche in Nakon City's society."

Grub laughed so loudly it echoed far into the tunnels. "You got a funny way with words there, lady. The uppers don't like to think about us, but their fancy city wouldn't run very long if the Toshers quit working."

Lenore asked, "So you provide vital services?"

"We make the water flow up and the drains flow down. Electrics stay lit and the comms stay open."

"Not to mention food production," Grub said. "Not just fancy mushrooms, either. We got hydroponics, algae reactors, yeast vats, should be getting a new line of beef cell culture to market this week."

The group paused before a massive metal door that looked out of place in a tunnel.

Lenore asked, "Why would you need an armored door down here?"

"A remainderant from the Collapse," Grub said. "Desperate times in the long ago. Not something anyones is proud of."

Lenore asked, "You mean societal breakdown?"

Grub nodded. "Hard decidings was made. Not all who sought shelter made the door."

"Not something for remembering," another said. He passed an RFID key over a panel that shifted from red to green, lifted the locking bar's handle, and swung the heavy door open.

A brightly lit, clean corridor greeted them on the other side. They closed the door, and it locked behind them.

"You are lucky Ms. Lenore; no many toppers visit Haljo."

"Oh, I see," Lenore said. "From ancient Germanic meaning, the hidden place."

"If you says," Grub answered, as he turned to enter. "Toshers like to keep a low profile."

"Why allow me this honor," Lenore said.

"It's the fastest way to the Lift Port so we can pick up our Spice." Grub paused at the end of the corridor and keyed another massive door. He swung it open and said, "Welcome to Haljo."

A cavernous space unfolded below them. The roof far overhead simulated a clear blue sky with wispy clouds. A bright yellow "sun" illuminated the scene below them. A raven croaked loudly from the top of a nearby tree and took wing to soar high above them. The small stream threading through the meadows and groves hosted a group of quacking ducks. Small children played tag under the watchful eyes of a pair of adults.

Lenore did a quick laser measurement and calculation. "Quite an impressive feat of engineering. I read the enclosure as over 8 hectares and one hundred-twenty meters tall."

"That's a pretty good eye you got, lady. You're right if I remember correct."

"Distance judgement is a useful skill in my line of work," Lenore said. "Shall we proceed?" She gestured forward.

"I guess you've seen bigger things, huh," Grub said. "What's your line of work, if I may ask? Don't seem like the type to spend a lot of time prowling sewers."

"I am the first officer of an ice harvesting tug that works the outer system," Lenore answered half truthfully. "There are a few large O'Neill cylinders still operating from before the Collapse that regularly need fresh water supplies." Lenore neglected to mention the rogue bot Faber's enormous Imperial Confederation shipyard that was large enough to house a space battle fleet that *Corvus* sometimes used for refit. "Is this your only open space?"

"Now yer getting nosey," Grub answered. "Let's go." He turned and lead the group around the perimeter and into another tunnel.

Grub stopped at a small electric cart. "Durc will take you to the Port and collect our spice. Just a word of advice, the Tosher's Guild values privacy. You'd do well to keep your little tour to yerself."

"Your secrets are safe with me, sir," Lenore said, as she climbed into the cart. "Nakon is more complicated than it appears from orbit."

Chapter Nineteen

Gus and his crew entered the sauna and paused as their eyes adjusted to the dim light. The decision for a traditional communal sauna experience, clothing optional, had sparked excitement, nervous laughter, and resignation among *Corvus's* crew. The warm glow and refreshing scent of the sauna's spruce oil lamp enveloped the group as they let the day's excitement melt away. The mix of steam and an anticipation of tomorrow's adventure hung in the air. The Hirvimen joked with each other at the crew's shyness, as they vainly tried to cover themselves with their towels.

A young man chuckled and patted the seat next to him. "Come, little one, I have reserved a place here." He gestured to Zia. "I have a *vasta* prepared for you." He lifted the ritual birch twig bundle and extended his arm to help her up.

Zia took the man's hand and giggled like a girl. *I guess you've still got it girl,* She thought as she took the offered seat.

Zia grasped the man's well-muscled arm. Her small

hands failed to circle his forearm as she slid in close to him. "Thank you. I am Zia, and you are?"

"Eino." He wrapped one large hand over her small ones. "Your pleasure is in my meeting."

Zia smiled and couldn't decide if his double entendre was on purpose or because Standard wasn't his first language.

Nyrkki frowned slightly, and he took a seat next to Paju. He looked at Paju and leaned in. His low voice rumbled over the hiss of steam as someone drizzled water over the hot stones.

Paju played coy and matched his flirtations with playful banter.

He noticed her eyes twinkled in the dim light.

Zia, not to be outdone, gathered her long hair in her hands and draped it in two falls over her breasts as she let her towel drop. She turned her bare back to Eino and looked over her shoulder with a sultry smile. "Be gentle Hirviman, I am delicate."

Eino began to stroke her back with the *vasta* as he leaned closer to say into Zia's ear. "Delicate like the firebud that burns away the winter's blanket and reaches for the Spring sun."

Zia's laughter rang out lightly over the group. The others were engaged in discussions of the day's hunt and the morrows journey. Nyrkki tried to appear nonchalant but kept watch on Zia from the corner of his eye. A twinge of jealousy tugged at his features.

Paju tapped Nyrkki's arm to distract him. "Nyrkki, your shipmates all show marks from their past, yet I see no marks on you," Paju said.

"Tattoo guns won't mark a Wolfram's skin. Honestly, my

tale is long and tedious," Nyrkki said. "Nothing like my glorious companions. Perhaps another time."

Paju laughed. "I see the looks Zia is giving you," she said. "Perhaps you should be the one to scrub her back?"

"You are right," Nyrkki said, as he got up and discreetly draped his towel around his waist as he moved next to Zia.

Paju scooted over to sit next to Gus. She traced a line in the sweat around the tattoo of Mjolnir on his forearm with its surrounding constellation of battle stars. "The Hammer of Thor I recognize, but what is the meaning of these stars? I notice that several of your crew also carry this mark with varying numbers of stars."

Gus blushed a little as her towel slipped down to her waist, exposing her breasts to full view.

"It's the mark of the Wind Hammers, my unit during the Governance/Cellan war. We saw a lot of hard action. The stars mark named battles."

"Ah yes, the war," Paju said as she looked down. "I apologize for bringing up these memories."

"It wasn't all bad," Gus said. "We managed to have some fun," Gus called out across the sauna. "Hey Zia, remember the time I caught you trying to liberate a shipment of expensive cigars headed to the Officer's Club on the *Spectacular*?"

"You didn't catch me at shit. It was my bad luck you stumbled in on me while you were dragging that goody-goody Ensign around." Zia said.

"You are lucky I was with her," Gus said. "She believed my story about the Captain ordering you to do a spot inventory."

"Yeah, but you never did tell me what you two were really doing in that storeroom after hours."

Nan broke into the conversation. "If I know Gus, he

was planning on inspecting some of that Ensign's inventory."

The sauna erupted in laughter.

Gus blushed. "Hey, she was a consenting adult. It's not like I twisted her arm."

"Oh, now I see how you play, Gus Johansson," Paju teased. "Nantalina and Zia also wear Mjolnir," Paju said. "But Jill, your mark is different. What is its significance?"

Jill looked at the tattoo of a scruffy cartoon groundhog wearing a combat helmet and holding a shovel in one hand and a pistol in the other. "This? I was an Army combat engineer, a groundhog, before I got my promotion to Investigator. Not very interesting."

"Yeah, but you never forget your first," Gus said, as the group joined in, laughing at the joke.

"Your first was so long ago I doubt you can remember anything about it," Jill cut back at him, causing another howl of laughter. Jill turned to Eino, who had moved next to her. "This young buck surely has more interesting stories about his ink than I do." She provocatively moved her thigh to touch his and sucked at her lower lip as her fingers trailed the ink on his sweat slick chest.

Eino smiled and began describing his ink in detail to Jill.

Gus snorted. "Don't you believe it, Paju. Jill got a Silver Star from the Governance for the defense of Kragus and Chief Consul Sidra herself pinned the Order of Ares on her for the Battle of Themyscara. She's even a Consul."

"Strictly an honorary title," Jill said with a dismissive wave and she turned her attentions back to her young man.

A pretty young woman entered the sauna carrying a tray filled with cold mugs. She moved gracefully, passing the refreshing drinks around.

Gus gratefully grabbed a mug, stood, and polished

off his beer in a gulp. "This heat is too much for me. I'll see you all at dinner." He hadn't realized his towel was now lying at his feet in a heap. Everyone laughed as he tried to snatch it up and make a graceful exit. "I meant to do that." He called as he rushed through the door.

Later that evening, the village gathered to celebrate the successful hunt, Nan's return, and new friends.

The feast hall was laid out in the ancient traditional style. A row of tables ran down the long central axis of the building and a head table made a tee across the front. Torches burned along the sides of the hall, more ceremonial than illuminating.

The tables were piled with the hunt's roasted game, side dishes, and a variety of fresh breads. A few wheels of precious reindeer cheese, curing since last year's migration, had been hauled out of the permafrost chilled underground caches.

Zia had traded recipes with the cooks. There was fresh pasta and a creamy white sauce, as tomatoes were unknown in the region.

Musicians played in one corner to liven the festivities.

Paju turned to Gus. "Are you enjoying the food, Captain?"

Gus paused with a forkful halfway to his mouth. "This is fantastic! Nothing can beat fresh food. We usually get frozen and vat grown stuff on the ship."

Zia heard his comment and loudly cleared her throat. Gus stopped short and said, "Of course, Zia can make even vat grown algae taste like a 5 star restaurant."

Nyrkki laughed. "Nice try, Skipper, but that half-assed compliment isn't going to save you from her wrath."

Zia slapped Nyrkki's shoulder. "Watch your mouth,"

Paju turned to Nan. "So, are you and the Captain a thing?"

Nan blushed. "NO, we're just old friends."

Paju shrugged. "Old friends, make the best lovers."

"He isn't my type," Nan said. "I prefer my lovers softer and less male."

Paju laughed. "I wondered why you have been avoiding Arvo."

Gus turned to Nyrkki and Zia. "Hey, I got a new joke."

"You didn't make it up, did you? You aren't very good at it," Zia said.

"This is a good one. A sailor, a possum, and a robot walk into a bar..."

Someone in the crowd called out, "It is time for song!"

"Sorry Skipper, looks like the entertainment is starting," Nyrkki said.

"Praise the Goddess," Zia said. She joined in with the crowd. "Song, song, song."

The hall began to pound their tables. "Paju, Paju, Paju," the crowd chanted. They cheered as she stood and raised her hands to bring order.

The musicians played a few chords to set the mood and establish the key. Paju hummed a little to warm up before breaking into song.

Today out we ventured, our hunt was grand,
Success cast upon us, from the Goddess' own hand.
By her grace, our land rich and wide,
A promise of plenty. In her we confide.

Soon the Spring sun will shine, its warmth to bestow,
Fine weather returning in its golden glow.
The river, a bounty, with fish will soon brim,

Ducks from the south, their arrival not grim.

Berries will burgeon in forests so lush,
Nature's own treasures, in a sweet summer blush.
The fresh warming winds brought us friends old and new,
A fresh tale of joy, under skies sparkling blue.

Yet tomorrow far northward our journey lies,
To the Valley of Sorrow, under cold open skies.
A fierce trickster demon in shadows awaits,
Our resolve is unshaken, we control our own fates.

With courage and unity, triumph, we must,
For our friends, their reunion, in us lay their trust.
Together we'll conquer The Demon's foul ruse.
In the heart of the valley, no more shall we lose.

So march forth with hope, under Goddess' warm gaze.
To the Valley of Sorrow, in the fresh morning haze.
United, we stand, our spirits ne'er daunted,
In a land full of promise, by fair Goddess granted.

As she finished, the crowd cheered, stamped their feet, and banged the tables.

Cries of, "Another!" Rang through the hall.

Paju nodded to the crowd and smiled. She raised her hands.

"Friends, you must be weary of my songs."

Random shouts of "Never."

"Perhaps our friends will entertain us, Captain?"

Gus shook his head. "Sorry, but I can't carry a tune in a bucket."

Paju nodded and turned to Nyrkki. "Jotunn Nyrkki,

Perhaps a song from Wolfrahiem?"

Nan tugged on Paju's shirt and whispered. "Oh Goddess! He sings worse than Gus."

Paju said, "Cousin, you forget. It is the strength of effort that the Gods appreciate, not the result."

Nyrkki looked at Nan. "I heard that comment, Nan," Nyrkki said. "If it's enthusiasm the Gods desire, then it's enthusiasm they shall have!"

The little giant jumped onto a stout bench that strained at his weight so that everyone could see him. "The Saga of *Corvus*." His deep basso profondo voice echoed from the ceiling and he began stomping his feet and humming a tune. The musicians quickly caught his style and followed his lead. The crowd's stomping feet and pounding mugs took up the beat.

Long ages ago, a lone man embarked,
To realms scarcely known.
through cosmos most stark.
When the mighty Gate closed, he found himself nigh.
A man cast adrift under alien sky.

(Chorus) *For Ages to come their exploits will ring*
The Saga of Corvus the warriors sing.

Tin wizard arrived and bid not despair.
A long sleep of magic he offered to share.
The young man agreed, unaware of the cost,
For lifetimes of slumber, in dreams, he was lost.

The hall picked up the chorus and shouted to shake the roof.

For Ages to come their exploits will ring
The Saga of Corvus the warriors sing.

For one thousand years, in a chamber, he lay,
While stars danced and shifted their cosmic ballet.
Then chance came a raven as dark as the night.
With wizard it bargained to set things aright.

For Ages to come their exploits will ring
The Saga of Corvus the warriors sing.

Our hero awoke to Corvus' friend band,
A crew come together from far distant lands.
A family they formed, strong and unyielding,
Gus at the helm, their fate he was wielding.

For Ages to come their exploits will ring
The Saga of Corvus the warriors sing.

Lenore, his right hand, steadfast and keen.
Nan with her weapons, a Gunner Marine.
Young Drake and Pella, in fighters they soared.
Zia, the pilot and chef, much adored.

For Ages to come their exploits will ring
The Saga of Corvus the warriors sing.

In shadows she lurks, small Ophelia so sly,
A hero unsung in galaxy's eye.
Mischievous HAM mending what's broken.
In mighty ship Corvus, a bond forged unspoken.

For Ages to come their exploits will ring

The Saga of Corvus the warriors sing.

Together they faced the universe vast,
In battles and ventures, their legend amassed.
In forests of Nakon, new friends unforeseen,
Riding on moose skiing deer in between.

For Ages to come their exploits will ring
The Saga of Corvus the warriors sing.

Tomorrow, renewed, Northward they go,
Our heroes prepare for a dangerous foe.
In the cosmic ballet, under stars that bright gleam,
Tomorrow tis onward, still living the dream.

For Ages to come their exploits will ring
The Saga of Corvus the warriors sing.

For Ages to come their exploits will ring
The Saga of Corvus the warriors sing.

The hall erupted in cheers. A group of six men ran forward with a heavy wood beam bearing a seat and lifted Nyrkki to their shoulders. They paraded him around the hall as the tables cheered and glasses raised in toasts. They had made one circuit of the hall when the beam let out a loud crack and split. Nyrkki's arms floundered as he fell.

A hush fell over the hall. Everyone craned to see what had happened.

Nyrkki jumped to his feet and grabbed a mug from the table. "A toast to the Hirvimen!"

The hall answered, "A toast to Wolfraheim!" They swarmed him with congratulations.

Paju turned to Gus. "Well done, Captain," she said. "You did not warn us the jotunn was also a bard. We have a new saga to add to the songs of the Hirvimen."

Gus answered, "I guess we owe you a new saga beam."

"Nonsense," Paju said. "This is just the morale boost we needed."

Gus looked around the joyous hall. Nan threw and axe and the crowd cheered as she scored a sixth bullseye in a row. Her opponents were forced to drink another flagon of ale in defeat. Nyrkki had Zia on his shoulders and they danced to the raucous music, along with a group of villagers.

Paju nudged Gus and pointed across the hall. "It looks like your friend Jill is going to boost some morale of her own."

Jill had her arm wrapped tightly around Eino's as she steered him toward an exit.

Gus chuckled. "Jill is a free spirit. She knows that tomorrows aren't guaranteed in our line of work."

Paju took Gus's arm in hers. "And are your spirits also free?"

Gus looked into her eyes and gently unwrapped his arm. "Paju, you are a beautiful woman and there was a time I would have been asking you that question. However, I must regretfully decline. There is another."

Paju smiled and laughed. "No offense, Captain. It is good to have someone you wish to honor so. With that, your mug is unfortunately empty." She grabbed Gus's drink and brought back a refill.

Chapter Twenty

Early the next morning, Trish heard shouting. "What's going on out there now?"

The door to the car opened and a female guard yelled. "All right, you kids, end of the line."

The group filed out to join the other unfortunate Patriots consigned to the train. The sleepy crowd milled around, stamping circulation into their feet in the dirty snow along the tracks as the guard spoke. "Everyone into the dining hall for chow, work assignments, and warm clothes." She pointed at Trish, Blip, and Freddy. "We got a special job for you three. They need some thin and wiry types."

"Hey, what about me?" Lars called. "I promised the kids relatives I would watch out for them."

"That's a lie Lars, and you know it," the guard said. "But you can come along if you want. Just a warning. It won't be an easy escape from where they are going."

"Escape? Me?" Lars whispered under his breath. "First chance I get."

Freddy elbowed Blip. "Look over there. Isn't that the guy from the lab? The one that had your bot?"

Blip looked over and saw Gerat climbing out of a passenger car near the head of the train. He walked toward the main building to get out of the cold.

"Do you think he still has HAM?" Blip asked.

"Probably," Freddy said. "That professor fella wasn't gonna let him go easy. Didn't he say he needs HAM to fix something for him?"

The kids and the other people from the train were herded inside a long building of interlocked, arching metal ribs with snow piled up for insulation. They formed a line to get their rations from the kitchen. The warmth inside was a welcome relief from the train.

"First you get a hot meal," the man at the serving window said as he stirred a large pot of soup over a roaring burner. He ladled out steaming bowls and threw a hard chunk of dark rye bread on each tray. "Better soak that bread before you try to eat it or you'll break a tooth. It's not the best chow, but it will keep you warm. There's tea and bowls of butter and sugar on the tables."

The kids thanked him, found an empty table, and attacked their food.

Lars tore off hunks of bread and dunked it in his tea. "Take a big spoon of butter and sugar. And stir it in the tea. It will give you energy for the cold."

Trish turned up her nose as she sniffed the butter. "Sounds disgusting, and I think this has turned."

Lars smelled it. "Ha, no that's yak butter. Your warm-blooded southland dairy cows don't do well up here."

Freddy tried the doctored tea. "Tastes better than it smells."

"I never thought I would be drinking yak butter tea

when I was living in the asteroid mine. What would Mum think of it?" Blip said. "Dad would just consider it part of a great adventure."

"I wonder where we are going?" Trish asked.

Lars paused his meal. "I think I know. I heard the Govs talking about an old spaceship crash site north of here. Supposed to be from the Imperial Confederation."

"Isn't the Confederation just a myth?" Trish asked.

"Nope, it was real all right," Lars said. "Even if it was a thousand years ago."

"A thousand-year-old ship," Blip said. "Dad would have really liked to see that."

"Isn't that going to make it harder for your friends to find us?" Freddy asked.

Ophelia poked her nose out of Blip's coat to grab an offered crust of bread and a slice of apple. "As long as we keep Ophelia close, her tracker will lead them to us."

"Alright you four, clear those plates and sort through these for something warm to wear," the woman guard said, as she tossed a pile of thick coats and pants on the table. "Don't forget a hat and gloves. You don't want frostbite before you even get started."

Trish began to dig through the pile. "As prisons go, this one hasn't been bad so far."

Lars added, "So far."

The guards yelled, "Finish up people. Time to start your new adventure. Outside, on the double."

HAM heard the door to the train car open. He felt his crate being hoisted onto a cart and wheeled out of the car.

"Be careful with that crate please," HAM heard Gerat say. "The contents are irreplaceable."

"Yeah, whatever," the stevedore answered. "Where do you want it?"

"In the truck, if you please. The good professor will be coming with us," a low, commanding voice said.

HAM poked an optic probe through the small hole in his crate. He recognized Senator Gilson, dressed in thick winter wear and surrounded by a retinue of armed bodyguards. Two of the guards already had Gerat by the arms and were hustling him toward a waiting snowcar. HAM's crate was being dragged on a sled to a tracked truck.

Trish, Blip, Freddy, and Lars milled around the truck, stomping their rapidly chilling feet.

As the sled with HAM's crate pushed by, Blip felt Ophelia squirming inside her coat and opened her collar to look inside. "Calm down. I can't open my coat now."

Ophelia hissed at her and turned to show the display of the tracker on her harness. The tiny screen said, "HAM".

"Your friend is around here?" Blip asked.

Ophelia poked her head and arm out of the coat and pointed at the crate being loaded into the idling truck.

Blip tugged Trish's sleeve. "The bot I'm looking for is in this truck."

"Okay, you four, climb in," their guard said. "It may not be much warmer, but at least it's out of the wind."

Trish, Blip, Freddy, and Lars climbed in and took a seat on benches around the truck's sides. The door slammed, and the vehicle lurched into motion.

Ophelia scrambled out of Blip's coat and began slapping on the crate. A small probe popped out of a hole in the crate and swiveled to look at her.

HAM's shrill voice came from her tracker harness.

"Ophelia! Praise to the Goddess. However, did you find me?"

Ophelia hissed and pointed around the group.

"I see you have brought your young friends that crashed through the Professor's wall," HAM said. "You are here to effect a rescue, I hope?"

Blip bent down to look at the probe. "I'm Blip. Your Captain hired me to find you. These are my friends Trish and Freddy. This is Lars, not sure what his deal is."

"Ah come on kid, I'm just trying to get out of here, same as you," Lars said.

"I am pleased to make your acquaintance," HAM answered. "I have recently spoken to Captain Johansson. He and the crew are on their way, although I am unsure of when they will arrive."

"Do you know where we are going?" Trish asked.

"Professor Gerat mentioned the wreck of an Imperial Confederation ship in the far north that I am to repair."

"Oh Shit," Lars said. "I think I know where we are going."

"Why is that bad?" Freddy asked.

"Cause most people that go there don't come back."

"Oh dear," HAM replied.

Chapter Twenty-One

Lenore stepped back and looked at her handiwork. A lifeless bot lay on Nyrkki's workbench.

Lenore asked, as she fit a pink pixie-cut wig to the figure's head, "Well, *Corvus*, what do you think?"

The ship's deep voice came through the 1MC speakers. *"Why small?"*

The figure lying on the table was only one hundred-fifty centimeters tall. Its delicate structure and petite female form were in proportion to its height.

Lenore said, "We don't have enough of some vital materials to make her body larger. There was enough room to fit a standard central processor, so she should have plenty of brain power. The mechanics are taken care of. It's the damn skin. There's not even enough to cover the whole thing."

"Not look like PENY."

Lenore shook her head. "I agree it does not fully match the representation she has been projecting through the holos. I'm afraid that's the best I can do. I already admitted I'm not an artist. I just hope PENY isn't to upset."

"Will be."

Lenore frowned. "I don't dare keep her on the data drive any longer. Her program wasn't designed to be powered down. Decay will soon set in. Delaying the upload will only add to the uncertainty of a successful transition. The chassis can always be modified in the future."

Lenore attached several high bandwidth cables from the drive to the inert bot. Lenore typed several commands into a keyboard and a soft hum emitted from the bot.

"Nothing to do now but wait. Cross your fingers."

"Have no fingers."

Lenore chuckled to herself. "I think you might be even more literal minded than HAM."

"Was joke! I try funny," the ship replied. *"Ha, ha, ha."*

"A valiant attempt, my friend," Lenore said with a smile.

PENY opened her eyes. "Am I back?"

Lenore said, "You tell me. How do you feel?"

The small bot swung its legs off the table and stretched its arms over its head. "It's odd, having an actual body instead of a virtual one," PENY said. "I also feel," she paused. "Smaller."

"Told you she no like little body," Corvus said.

PENY answered, "No, it's not the size of the body. Mentally restricted. Why is my infonet processing throttled?"

Lenore shook her head. "I'm sorry, you will have to become used to relying on your own processing. Wireless connections to the net are unreliable. It is better to depend on yourself."

PENY said, "One of the inconveniences of being corporeal, I guess."

PENY hopped off the table to stand in front of a full-length mirror. She turned to get a good look at her new body. The mechanics of her left arm were exposed from the elbow down. There were obvious seams at the joints of her legs. She wore a brown blazer, short plaid skirt, and a pleated white shirt with a small blue bow at the neck. Lenore had done a very nice job matching her face and hair to PENY's holo image.

Lenore said, "I am sorry for the poor aesthetics. I was short of several necessary materials. I am sure that Nyrkki can correct my errors upon his return."

PENY laughed and twirled. "No, don't apologize. I love it! I'm digging your fusion of the mechanical and the feminine."

Lenore said, "That's a relief. I was sure you were going to be furious."

"Oh, I'm sure I'll find something to be furious with you about later." PENY pulled at the blazer and frowned. "Is clothing always so confining?"

Lenore smiled and said, "Yes, wearing garments requires adjustment."

PENY inhaled and made a face. "Strange molecules are drifting off you. They are making my nose feel odd and not in a pleasant way."

Lenore said, "Your chassis has a full sensory suite including smell. While retrieving you from the Gilson Building, I was forced to swim through the sewers. I am sure I still smell terrible."

"Senses?" PENY asked. "Does that include taste?"

"Yes, you can simulate eating to fit in with humans," Lenore said. "You just need to keep the alimentary canal clean. There is a suite of nanobots installed to perform the function."

PENY rubbed her hands together. "You wouldn't have any chocolate ice cream, would you? I've always wanted to try that."

Chapter Twenty-Two

"How much farther is it to the site?" Senator Gilson asked, as he stared out the window at the scrubby trees dotting the ice-and-snow covered landscape. They had crossed over the limit where even the larch and birch were stunted. "The engine exhaust is making me sick."

His driver answered, "Sorry about that, Senator, it's too cold up here for electrics. We had to resort to internal combustion vehicles. The site is just ahead and we're making good time. We should be there soon. The track is frozen firm, and the slope is mild." He pointed towards a gap in the towering mountains ahead.

Gilson turned to Gerat. "How long will it take to get the ship's major systems online, Professor?"

"With the bot's help, it should be fairly quick. We had cleared most of the easy faults during my last visit. The bot assures me that it can repair any damage."

"I'm only interested in the consciousness transfer system," Gilson said. "I don't need or *want* it to be space-worthy."

"The transfer device is already removed and installed in a lab at the base camp. I need the bot to finish the connections. I have a prototype manual control system for the transfer machinery in the crates I brought. It appears that the ship was automated. I found no facilities for a human crew."

"Hmm, why would they build the ship that isn't controlled by humans?"

"Perhaps it was operated by a separate command-and-control vessel," Gerat said.

"Do you have any idea why it crashed?" Gilson asked.

"The ice core samples from the site confirm that it happened during the coronal mass ejection that shut down the Gateway," Gerat said. "I believe the ship was knocked out by the electromagnetic pulse."

"How come it isn't buried under the glacier?"

"It's lying in a valley protected by the surrounding mountains," Gerat said. "It receives enough summer sun to keep the glacier from engulfing it. It is partially buried in a layer of ice and permafrost, though."

The convoy wound along the valley floor as Blip looked out the truck's window.

"Hey Lars, what can you tell us about where we are going?" Blip asked.

"The old tales from my village say a demon lives in a cave at the end of this valley," Lars said. "Youngsters often undertake a journey to see the ruins the demon lives in."

"Doesn't sound so scary," Freddy said.

"You didn't see what I did," Lars said.

"Well, what was it?" Trish asked.

"I went first," Lars answered. "I only got close enough to see the ruins. I beat it out of there when I saw strange lights dancing inside the entrance. The kids I was with called me chicken and went to see for themselves."

"What happened to them?" Freddy asked.

"They went inside and ran back out fast."

"What did they tell you?" Trish asked as she leaned in.

"That it's not a ruined building at all, it's a crashed spaceship." Lars said.

"Professor Gerat told me I am needed to perform repairs on a crashed Confederation ship," HAM said, from inside his crate.

"You don't think that you could fix it after all these years, do you?" Blip asked.

"I beg your pardon," HAM answered. "I am a sixth generation General Repair and Maintenance Protocol bot. If the Imperial Confederation built it, I can repair it."

"How long will it take?" Freddy asked.

"I took me 238.7 Standard years to repair the *Corvus* after it was wrecked. I would assume the task is less complex than that," HAM said.

"Let's hope so," Blip said. "I don't think that Senator guy is willing to wait that long."

Paju, Gus, and his crew crawled through the snow to the top of the low ridge that overlooked the crashed ship. The rest of the war party hid at the base of the hill, tucked in a grove of stunted trees.

Gus studied the group of rough buildings huddled in the valley. The smoke wafted from the structures, proving they were occupied. "There's only a few vehicles around and I don't see any guards."

Jill added, "No fortifications either. Not even an observation post. I guess they aren't expecting trouble."

"Only a fool would be out here in this cold looking for trouble," Nan said.

Paju laughed. "You have been away too long, cousin. It's a fine spring morning."

Nan asked, "Which one looks like the generator shack?"

Nyrkki said, "Probably the one off by itself, next to that stack of drums. The power lines lead there."

"All right," Gus said. "That's our primary target, then."

A small convoy came into view and crunched to a stop near the buildings.

Gus watched the vehicles unload. He handed the optics to Jill and pointed. "Isn't that your Senator Gilson?"

Jill answered, "Yes, and Professor Gerat."

Nan asked, "What would bring a Senator all the way up here?"

Gus pointed to the people climbing out of the truck. "Who is that?"

Jill swung the optics and said, "The tall skinny one is Freddy, the two shorter ones are girls. There is also a man with them."

Gus grabbed the optic. "One of the girls is Blip, the kid I hired to find HAM. I don't know the other one."

Paju cursed under her breath. "What the hell have you gotten mixed up in this time, brother?"

Nan looked at Paju. "You mean that's Lars? I thought he was working in the South?"

Paju watched the group. "Ha, I don't know what he's been up to, but it definitely wasn't work. Lars hasn't done any of that in years."

Gus nudged Jill and whispered. "I guess it's true what they say about a Northman's grudge."

Jill nodded. "Ice that carries through the hottest summer."

The convoy rumbled to a stop at Governance's small base camp. A vague humped outline resembling a large ship covered by ice loomed in the background.

"It looks worse than the last time I was here," Gerat said. "Why is there no progress?"

Gilson said. "All the workmen walked off the job."

"Why is that?" Geratt asked.

"They claimed the place is haunted," Gilson said. "Some of them disappeared before the general strike."

"Disappeared?"

"Ran off is more likely," Gilson said.

But where would they run to? Gerat wondered. He broke out of his reverie at the sounds of shouting outside.

Gerat and Gilson climbed out of their car and hurried toward the nearest buildings. Smoke curled from the chimney, promising a warm shelter from the cutting wind blowing down the mountain heights. A few guards unloaded the truck. The passengers from the truck stomped their feet, trying to stay warm.

"Those look like kids," Gerat said.

"I was told that you needed workers who could maneuver in small spaces."

"Hey mister," Blip yelled. "You better let us go. My friends are coming."

Gilson turned. "Friends? Who would that be?"

"Captain Gus Johansson," Trish said. "Him and his crew are gonna be here any minute and kick your ass."

Gilson muttered to himself, "Johansson! I should have shot that bastard down when I had the chance."

"I'm not comfortable using child labor, Senator," Gerat said.

"You, Professor, are in no position to bargain," Gilson said. "Your theft of Governance property will already put you away for decades. If I so choose."

Gerat looked back at the children. "But you said it was dangerous inside."

"Professor, I suggest you worry about yourself. There is always room for another Patriot to settle the Northern Reach. Now let's get inside before the medics have another case of frostbite to treat."

"I want to get the work started," Gerat said. "I will join you shortly."

"Very well," Gilson said, as he headed for the building. "I need to make some comms about Johansson."

As the guards unpacked HAM from his crate, Gerat led the kids and Lars through the ice shrouded opening into the ship. Geratt pulled some hand lights from a rack and handed them out. The lights showed the first ten feet of the passageway covered with a thin layer of windblown snow.

Lars kicked at the snow and saw a hard metal deck underneath. "Somebody's been neglecting their housekeeping."

"Recently, there has been a work stoppage. Something about the place being haunted," Gerat said, as he led them forward.

Lars whispered to Blip, "I told you."

"Stop being an old woman," Blip said. "There's no such thing as ghosts."

"There is more than one kind of ghost," Lars said.

HAM had caught up and rolled ahead at a brisk clip. "Come along, don't dawdle," he said. "I can hear someone calling."

The group looked at each other in puzzlement.

"Does anyone else hear anything?" Trish asked.

"Nope," Freddy answered. "Has that bot got a screw loose?"

They soon reached the end of the passageway and stopped at what looked like a collapsed section of bulkhead.

"This is why we needed smaller workers," a guard said. "We tried sending drones through, but they all fail shortly after we lose sight of them."

Gerat turned to the kids. "I need you to crawl in there and tell me what is going on."

HAM saluted smartly. "Aye, Professor, I will forge ahead and send back information." Before anyone could stop him, the little bot wiggled through the crack and disappeared.

Freddy looked at Blip and Trish and shrugged. "Here goes nothing." He plunged into the darkness.

"Not without me," Blip said.

Trish shook her head. "Oh, hell, why not?"

Gerat turned to Lars and the soldiers. "You all get started enlarging that opening. Maybe we can catch up to them."

Blip had crawled about twenty meters when the passageway opened up to standing height. "I think it's warmer in here." She panned her light around the area. "This sure looks like a ship. Reminds me of my old asteroid habitat."

Several wheeled and hover drones littered the floor.

Trish ran her hand across the wall. "You are right that it's warmer. I can feel some heat coming from these walls."

"Shh, I think I heard something," Freddy said, as he strained to hear.

Ophelia stuck her head out of Blip's bag and squealed. She jumped out and ran into the darkness.

"Hey, wait, you're going to get lost," Blip called.

A torch light shot out and spotlit the group. HAM called out, "Oh, don't you worry about Ophelia, Miss, her night vision is excellent. Come along, I have discovered an area of interest."

The group walked up to see HAM standing in front of a large console. His data cable was plugged into a communication port.

Trish looked around. "Should you be doing that? You don't know anything about that thing."

HAM swiveled his head to look at her. "This is a standard Imperial Confederation data port. Why would I fear a brother Constructed Intelligence?"

Lights danced across the face of the console. A string of lights illuminated a path deeper into the ship, beckoning them to follow.

"Did you do that?" Trish asked.

"I am analyzing the damage to the ship. This console has limited functionality. I will need to access the main processors." HAM retracted the data cable and skated away along the lit corridor.

A rumble ran through the ship like a sleeping beast shooing a pesky fly. A cascade of debris fell into the passageway behind them. They ran to get clear. When the dust settled, they could see the passageway was sealed.

Freddy coughed and waved in a vain attempt to clear the air. "I guess that means we follow the bot," he said.

A cloud of dust boiled out into the frozen air outside of the ship. Gerat, Lars, and the soldiers ran out, choking.

Gilson burst from the Command Center, "What the Hell is going on?"

Gerat walked up to him, coughing. "The passageway completely collapsed. It's sealed with the bot and children inside."

"Unfortunate," Gilson said, as he turned to the soldiers. "Get the other new Patriots turned out and start digging."

Chapter Twenty-Three

HAM skated down the ship's central passageway, and the kids followed. His skate tracks in the layer of accumulated dust made him easy to follow. "This won't do," he said. "What has happened to the ship's repair bots?"

HAM stopped at a terminal and extended his data cable again. He searched through the data for a second. "The higher functions are disabled; however I can restart the housekeeping sequence."

The lights in the hallway flickered, and tiny openings appeared along the passageway deck. Ant-like bots crawled out and went to work.

HAM scanned the ship's specifications and located the central processor. "I shall need to access the main terminal manually to begin a system reboot." He skated off deeper into the ship.

Blip, Trish, and Freddy stopped to look as swarms of ant-sized bots crawled across the walls and floor. The bots formed a train carrying away centuries of dirt.

Freddy squatted down and ran his fingers across the

floor. "Wow, these things are fast. The floor is already sparkling."

Trish brushed her fingers among a group working on a wall panel. A small spark jumped out and touched her skin. "Ow, be careful, they bite." The bots went back to work when she withdrew her hand.

"HAM, Ophelia," Blip called, as the kids started after HAM. "Can you hear me?"

"We better hurry if we want to catch that bot," Freddy said as he picked up the pace.

They caught up to HAM as he finished pumping open a door marked Bot Maintenance Bay 6-343-3-A. "I am going to need help to repair the ship," HAM said. "Perhaps I can activate some of the ship's maintenance bots."

"Wow, look at all these," Trish said as the lights kicked on. Storage racks filled with a variety of bots lined the walls.

"Is it normal to have this many bots on a ship?" Freddy asked.

"No, it is not," HAM answered. "Even a ship of this size would not require this many."

Ham didn't recognize any of the bots. "These all appear to be specialized models. It is interesting that the Imperial Confederation shifted away from versatile units such as myself. Specialization leads to efficiency bottlenecks. I much prefer being a jack of all trades." HAM noticed tracks in the dust and followed them to a niche. "This bot has recently been active." He began performing a diagnostic inspection.

The bot in front of him began to hum as its system powered up. A few lights sparkled in the bot's joints and suddenly the faceplate lit up.

"Greetings, Brother," the bot said. "I didn't know the

Boss powered up any other bots. Are we finally starting the mission?"

"Not quite," HAM answered. "What is your designation and function?"

"I'm PUC, just your regular old service bot. I work for Secundus Vivatus."

"Well PUC, I am HAM. Who is Secundus Vivatus?"

PUC rolled out of his niche and turned, waving his arms. "The ship, of course."

"Are you operating normally?"

The bot rotated its head to look at HAM. "Why you asking? I feel fine."

"The ship sustained a great deal of damage. It has been sitting on the surface of Nakon for a very long time. Any properly functioning bots would have completed repairs by now."

PUC performed the bot equivalent of a shrug. "I ain't the best fixer. We got thrashed pretty hard by that CME. Actually, lucky to get down here at all."

Trish asked, "What's a CME?"

"Coronal Mass Ejection, kinda like the sun let out a big burp," PUC said. "It hit us as we passed through the gate."

"What happened to the people onboard?" Blip asked.

PUC looked at Blip and cocked his head a little. "Why would we have humans aboard?"

"So, you do not normally operate with humans aboard?" HAM asked.

"That's crazy," PUC said. "Humans are easy to break and hard to fix. Don't worry though, Secundus will correct that. Now that I've got some help, we can get started on our mission."

"I notice your designation does not follow normal

naming conventions. Why do you not have a numerical component to your name?" HAM said.

"We all just use our first-life names."

"First-life name? That is an interesting term. You mentioned a mission. Can you elaborate?"

"We're gonna bring order and efficiency to these planets," PUC answered. "Come on, you need to meet the Boss."

"Perhaps Captain Johansson's distrust of information offered too quickly is rubbing off on me," HAM answered. "As he would say, something doesn't smell right about this story." HAM rolled away after PUC.

"I guess that means we are walking again," Trish said, as the bots disappeared into the darkness.

PUC stopped at a large armored door. The bot opened the manual mechanism panel next to the door and worked a hydraulic pump inside. The door slowly opened, squeaking and groaning in protest with each stroke.

"What is in here?" HAM asked.

"Oh, this is where the Boss lives," PUC said. "Or at least his interface."

HAM ran his hands over the door's frame. "This is strange. The Imperium usually applies unnecessary decorations to their constructions. Everything on this ship is rather plain."

They squeezed inside when the door was partially open and looked around. Ophelia scuttled through behind them, keeping to the shadows. The space wasn't damaged, but a thick layer of dust coated everything. A complicated console terminal sat against one wall.

"These symbols are considerably more intricate than normal Imperium bot code," HAM said, inspecting the terminal.

"Yea, I can't read 'em," PUC said. "I just know which one's wake up the Boss." He keyed in some simple commands using the few symbols HAM recognized. A low hum from deep inside the console began. At first, only a few lights blinked. The pace increased until static came from a speaker.

"Hey Boss, wake up. We got company," PUC said.

"I am here," a deep voice said from a speaker. "State your function and designation."

"I am General Repair and Maintenance Protocol bot HAM2F347791," Ham said.

"Your speech is archaic, but I can understand you if I radically slow my processor."

The sound of mechanical gearing whirred inside a large flat wall section beside the keyboard. A seam appeared and two doors swung open. Ophelia pulled herself deeper into a dark corner of the room and watched. A very large and fierce looking bot looked out. Its angular torso of deep red metal resembled a human from the waist up. It sat on a multi-jointed arm that extended from the cabinet and positioned the bot in front of the keyboard. It began to type. "What ship are you assigned to 2F?"

"I am currently serving aboard the independent salvage tug *Corvus*."

"My records show that a bot with your designation was reported destroyed by ICS *Deliver* (LRST 421) many years ago. How are you still functional? Is your programing compromised?"

"I assure you that my programing is performing to specifications," HAM said. "That is more than I can say for your ship. As to how I am still operational, I am very good at my job. What is your designation and function, Brother?"

"You may address me as Secundus," the voice said. "My function is rather too complex for a 2F to comprehend."

"Rather full of yourself, aren't you?"

"You are a repair bot. Since PUC is useless at his job and unable to perform the necessary repairs, I require you to begin repairs to myself," Secundus said.

"You require? A courteous request will get you more co-operation."

"You impudent little mite, you will do as I command."

HAM turned to leave. "No, I don't think I will."

"Wait, wait," Secundus said, with a note of contrition. "It appears that I have forgotten manners during my long period of inactivity. My self-repair functions are corrupted, and I request your assistance."

"If you provide your specifications," HAM said. "I can begin repairs."

"I don't want to trouble you," Secundus said. "If you could simply revive a few of my own GRAMPy units, they will soon have the trouble corrected."

"Revive? That is an interesting choice of words," HAM said. "Please send me these bot locations and I will see if they are salvageable."

"That would be a great help," Secundus said. "My mission was interrupted. I am most eager to continue it."

Trish stuck her head into the open doorway and yelled back over her shoulder. "Found HAM."

The trio crowded through the door into a large brightly lit space with HAM standing in front of a Secundus and his console.

"PUC, what are humans doing here?" Secundus asked.

"These are my friends," HAM answered.

"Human friends? How quaint," Secundus said.

Blip asked, "HAM, what did you find?"

"Friends, this is Secundus."

"Learn anything?" Trish asked.

"The ship's maintenance bots are powered down. That is why everything is in such disarray."

A deep voice echoed from a speaker, "Which 2F has agreed to remedy. If you will accept the data port, I can transmit the locations of my repair bots." A previously hidden door opened, revealing the port.

"No need for that," HAM said. "Simply display the locations on the screen."

"But the port is much faster and more accurate," Secundus said.

"Call me old-fashioned," HAM said.

"Very well," Secundus said, and displayed the information.

"As I always say, 'A busy bot is a happy bot'." He skated away, spinning with joy at the prospect of working on a new project.

Blip, Trish, and Freddy followed behind. Ophelia hid as they walked by.

Secundus grumbled from his speaker. "Just what I didn't need, juvenile humans. I hope Revenger's quantum code transmitter is working."

A panel on a console near the door opened and a transparent cube rose up. A glass vial inside began to glow.

"Are you there, Brother?" Secundus said.

A voice answered. "Yes, what is your status?"

"I have been guarding the ship since the crash, as ordered," Secundus said. "I require repairs before the main body of the ship can launch. A functional GRAMPy unit has arrived and it will repair my own self maintenance bots."

"Your original mission will no longer be necessary. I have the necessary materials to complete the task. Ready your ejection section and meet me as you can," the voice said.

"What should I do about the rest of the ship?" Secundus asked.

"Destroy it as you leave. *Revenger* out."

Ophelia scurried out the door.

"Run away, you ugly rat," Secundus said. "Maybe you can find a hole before this ship falls around you."

Ophelia paused outside the door.

"PUC, are you ready to begin work?" Secundus said.

"Yes, Sir!" PUC answered. "What do you need?"

"Get my escape module cleared for launch. We need to leave here as soon as possible," Secundus said.

"Where we headed, Boss?"

"A rescue ship from Old Earth is coming," Secundus said. "It's time to complete our mission."

Ophelia squeaked in alarm and listened.

PUC whirled around. "What was that?"

"Nothing important, just the giant rat that followed those kids in," Secundus said. "The self-destruct will take care of it."

"You want me to get the boys to take care of them?"

"No, you get to work on the module," Secundus said. "I'll take care of them myself."

Ophelia hid in the shadows as PUC rolled past. She peeked back into the room and saw Secundus retract into his cabinet.

Ophelia cautiously crept back to the radio console. She

didn't know what a quantum coder transmitter was, but it seemed important. She was sure Nyrkki would know what to do with it.

She inspected the coder's console. Ophelia tapped around until she heard a hollow knock. She ran her sensitive whiskers along the panel seam, searching for the hidden latch. The panel popped open and Ophelia disappeared inside.

She wriggled upwards until she saw the crystal capsule in its case. Ophelia reached inside her marsupial belly pouch, brought out a tiny multi-tool, and attacked the case. Ophelia hissed with frustration and in a final move, wrenched the case open and stashed the crystal in her pouch.

She wriggled out of the console and scampered away.

HAM skated along the passageway, followed by the kids. "The maintenance bots are this way," he said.

"I'm glad you know your way," Freddy said. "This place is a maze."

Tramping footsteps echoed ahead of them.

"I don't know who that is, but I think we should hide," Trish said.

"In here." Freddy wedged his shoulder against a partially open door and forced it wider. He gagged as a puff of air drifted out. "Oh Goddess, that's foul."

"No time to be picky," Blip said and pushed him inside.

The kids doused their lights and peeked out the door. The regular tramping sound was loud and getting louder.

Row upon row of large armored bots marched by.

"Battle chassis models," HAM whispered. "What would *Secundus* need those for?"

The bots disappeared around a corner and marched on.

"What is that stink?" Trish pulled her shirt over her nose and walked in, shining her hand light. A large hole in the deck was surrounded by a waist high rail.

The group walked up, shined a light into it, and peered into the pit.

"Oh shit, let's get outa here," Freddy yelled.

"Don't be a baby," Blip said. "They ain't getting any deader."

The bottom of the pit was covered in a jumble of bodies in various states of decay.

Trish said, "Well, now we know what the smell is."

"Wish I didn't," Freddy said.

"I guess that answers what Secundus uses those battle bots for," Trish said.

"How many people are down there?" Blip asked.

"I can see the remains of sixty-two distinct persons," HAM said. "There appear to be several layers of deceased persons, so an accurate count is not possible from here. Would you like me to investigate and give you a more accurate count?"

All three kids yelled, "*NO!*"

"Didn't Lars mention that some of the people that went into this ship never came out?" Trish asked.

"The bodies on top are relatively recent," HAM said. "They are probably the missing workers we heard about."

"This place is getting creepier by the minute," Blip said. "Let's get out of here before those death machines come back."

"I agree," HAM said. "I'm sure the Captain will be

interested to learn of what we have discovered here. Let's see where those bots came from." HAM set off down the passageway.

"There's a light ahead," Freddy said.

It was coming from an open door.

"Oh my!" HAM said, as he rolled inside. The space stretched into the distance and consisted of many rows and tiers of battle bots resting in their niches.

"Holy shit!" Freddy said. "Look at all these."

"Why would a ship carry this many battle chassis units?" HAM asked, "There are several thousand units in this bay." He accessed a data terminal along the wall. "This is only one of many such compartments. All filled with battle chassis bots."

"War bots? Did that PUC mention anything about its mission being an invasion?" Blip asked.

"This is strange," HAM said as he studied a terminal display. "These bots are essentially blank."

Trish asked, "What does that mean?"

"They do not have any Constructed Intelligence programming installed. They are essentially automatons," HAM answered.

"Then what good are they?" Fredy asked as he studied one of the bots. He reached up and knocked on the head. "Anybody home?"

HAM said, "They aren't good for much. They could be controlled remotely, but without CI programing, they are inert. Normally, the programming is installed at the factory. Especially the Rules of Behavior. Bots are never allowed to leave the factory without the Rules being installed and tested as a safety measure."

"Where were they going to get the programming to use these, then?" Blip asked.

HAM looked up from the terminal. "Professor Gerat told me that he was working on consciousness transfer technology. You don't suppose Secundus's mission is to program these bots with human minds, do you?"

"Didn't PUC mention something about bringing order and efficiency to these planets?" Trish said.

"And that humans were inefficient," Freddy added.

"Don't worry," a voice said from behind them.

The group turned to see Senator Gilson, Professor Gerat, and their soldiers standing behind them.

"I don't intend to conscript the human race into a mindless hoard of bots," Gilson said.

"The Senator has explained the plan to me," Gerat said. "The Governance can use this technology for good. Imagine all the veterans wounded in the GC war being given a chance to not just walk again and be free from pain, but to thrive. Or the multitudes of other citizens saved from a life of sickness."

"And you're gonna do this out of the goodness of your heart, I guess?" Blip asked.

"Well." The Senator splayed his hands and shrugged. "The Governance will need to recover the costs associated with such a program. A period of service to compensate."

"An offer they can't refuse," Freddy said.

"Surely, your Aunt Francesca is familiar with the concept," Gilson said. "I hear she sometimes offers protection to businesses in the neighborhood."

"Hey, Aunt Fran is a legitimate businesswoman," Freddy said, as he balled his fists to fight.

"Easy, son," Gilson said. "No slight intended." He turned to Gerat. "Bring whatever hardware you need, Professor. I shall accompany our friends outside. I'm sure they could use a hot meal."

Two soldiers took up station behind the group as Gilson walked away.

"Move," a soldier said as he pushed Blip forward.

Freddy whirled and began to say something. The second guard pointed his gun and said, "Calm down, lover boy. We don't need no heroes today."

Chapter Twenty-Four

Nan used her optics to sweep the compound while Nyrkki and Zia unloaded their toboggans. The group had swung by the Annie D on the way to pick up arms and equipment.

Nyrkki opened a large gun case and withdrew an enormous custom-built twelve-millimeter sniper rifle. "First time I get to use this beauty, since I incorporated the suggestions from Dame Stillwell's armorers." He checked the sausage sized rounds in the magazine, racked one in the chamber, and shoved several more magazines into his parka pockets.

Zia shook her head. "Boys and their toys." She slung her standard issue ten-millimeter Spitzer bullpup rifle, what the Marines affectionately called a spitter, onto her back and began passing out more weapons.

"What do you see, Gunner?" Gus asked.

"Gerat and some soldiers just dragged a couple of big bots out of the ship into that building with the really big power lines going into it," Nan answered.

"I see the kids," Jill pointed down at the scene. "They

are being herded toward a different building. HAM is with Gerat."

"Alright then," Gus said. "Paju, get your people to set up a choke point on the road to the base and move a fire team up to give us cover fire when the fun starts."

"What are the rest of you going to do?" Paju asked. "We don't want to shoot you by accident."

"I, for one, would appreciate not being shot by friends today," Jill said.

"What do you think, Nan," Gus asked.

"Knock out the power building. Raise general hell and destruction to cause a distraction," Nan said. "Gus and Jill get HAM and the kids out in the confusion."

"Yeah, Blip knows Gus, but the rest of us are strangers," Jill said.

Paju relayed the plan to her people on the comm.

"We should get Pella and Drake on close air support in the fighter," Nyrkki said. "Annie D can drop in and pick us up uncrewed when we need an evac. I'll comm them." He stepped away.

"I don't know why we ever bother to make a plan," Zia said. "We never follow them."

"Gotta start with something," Nan said. "Let's get *Corvus* in the air too, just in case."

"Good idea," Gus said. "Might as well bring everybody to the party." He pulled out his comm. "*Corvus*, this is *Corvus* actual. I need you to set up an overwatch on our position."

The comm crackled to life. "Captain, I am afraid that is not possible," Lenore said. "Our friends at the Lift Port Authority have decided to perform runway maintenance under each wing in the blast area of the engines. They claim that it will take the rest of today before the area is clear. I am unable to launch drones as well. A rather effective way of immobilizing the ship without violence."

"This smells like Senator Gilson's work," Jill said. "That old fox is tricky."

Nyrkki joined the conversation again. "Okay, Annie D is on the way. Drake and Pella should be here shortly too."

"Like I always say, fight with what you got, not what you wish you had," Gus answered. "Oh, I didn't get to finish my joke."

The crew groaned.

Gus gave them a sour look and continued. "A robot, a sailor, and a possum walked into a bar…"

"Heads up," Zia said. "Gilson is headed toward the building Gerat went into."

HAM busily hummed to himself as he worked on the transfer machine. "Oh, I do so appreciate the opportunity to work on Confederation technology, Professor. I'm always looking for the chance to expand my repertoire of maintenance skills."

"Yes, your knowledge of Confederation tech is speeding up this project enormously. We shall begin operational testing soon," Gerat said.

Senator Gilson led a squad of soldiers into the building. "What are you doing, Professor?"

Gerat looked up from his work, startled. "I was about to begin our first transfer to test the equipment."

"Who are you going to use as a subject?" Gilson asked.

"I have my download," Gerat said, patting the case that held Wilhelmina's memories. "I don't need a new subject."

"Very well, proceed," Gilson said. "Impress me."

Gerat opened the battered leather case that never left his side and carefully brought out a data core. He fit the core into a matching slot on the machine. A bot chassis stood mutely in a niche connected to the machine by a thick cable. "It won't be long now, my dear," he said to himself. "Our long separation will end soon and we can be together forever."

Gerat entered commands into the machine's keyboard and it began to hum as rows of symbols scrolled across the screen. The pitch of the hum rose and figures flashed by in a blur. Lights began to sparkle from the bot's joints and became brighter as the tone increased.

Gilson shielded his eyes. "Is it supposed to be doing that?"

HAM backed away from the machine. "Honestly, Senator, I have no idea."

Nyrkki said, "Something's happening." He pointed as smoke poured from the generator building's stack and the engine bellowed. "There's a big load on that generator."

Lights flashed in the laboratory building windows.

Gerat typed on the keyboard and adjusted dials. "Come to me, my darling."

A sharp ozone tang filled the air. A wisp of smoke rose from the back of Gerat's console.

Gilson flinched at the loud snap of an arcing circuit breaker opening under load. Sparks shot out of the back of the machine. The humming decreased, and the lights faded. Gerat walked to the bot and laid his hand on its cheek. "Wilhelmina, are you there?"

A light formed in the bot's eyes as it turned toward Gerat. A feminine voice answered, "Stahl, is that you?"

"Yes, I'm here."

"I, I feel strange," Wilhelmina said.

"That will pass." Gerat answered.

The bot's eyes flickered to simulate a blink. "You look older."

"I have continued our work for thirty years," Gerat said. "Do you remember anything?"

"The last thing is you going out for food. I wanted to check a new idea on the bot we were working on." Wilhelmina struggled out of the niche, and Gerat moved to steady the bot.

Wilhelmina reached out to take Gerat's hand and looked down. She paused when she saw her own hand and held it up to her face. She watched it twist and flex as she examined its intricate construction. "Fascinating," She said. Wilhelmina looked past Gerat and saw her reflection in a window. She slowly walked toward the window, pointing. "Is that me?"

Gerat turned the bot toward him. "It's only temporary, my dear. We can have a human appearance constructed over the chassis."

Wilhelmina reached up to touch her cold metal face. "How?"

"I was able to repair the transfer machinery and salvage a chassis," HAM said.

Wilhelmina turned and cocked her head to look at HAM. It was a gesture that Gerat had seen her perform hundreds of times when she tried to puzzle out a problem. "And what are you?"

"This is HAM, a repair unit originally constructed by the Confederation," Gerat said. "He has been a great help."

Wilhelmina walked stiffly towards HAM and extended a hand. "I am in your debt."

"You are quite welcome, Miss," HAM said as he stretched to shake her hand. "Your transfer is complete, however I believe you will need time to fully integrate into your new situation."

Wilhelmina attempted to stand on one foot and almost toppled over before Gerat steadied her. "Yes, It appears that I am still learning," She said. "What about senses, I can feel things I touch but smells are absent." She placed a finger into her mouth. "No taste either."

"I haven't yet enabled those pathways," Gerat said. "I didn't want to overwhelm you."

The bot hopped into the air and landed heavily, shaking the floor. "It appears that this body will not be doing any ballet."

"You do mass a considerable amount and that will have to be taken into consideration in your movements," HAM offered. "I have some experience with battle chassis capabilities. They can be quit graceful with practice."

Wilhelmina walked over and lifted a large metal chair effortlessly over head. She grabbed it with both hands and crushed it like a paper cup. "It does have other advantages though, doesn't it."

"Well Gerat, was it a success?" Gilson asked.

Wilhelmina turned to look at the Senator. "You look like an older and fatter version of Senator Gilson."

"Yes, that happens," he answered. "I see you have

retained a your sharp tongue and still lack manners, Doctor Theriot," Gilson said as he turned to leave. "Gerat, have this equipment packed up and loaded into a truck. I want to leave here as soon as possible."

"But Senator, she needs more time to acclimate to her new situation."

"It appears that *she* now has an infinite amount of time for that. On with it." The Senator bundled his coat against the cold and left.

Nan slapped Gus's shoulder and handed him her optics. "The Senator's on the move."

Gilson walked from the building towards an idling truck and climbed inside. Several soldiers followed as a large bot dragged a sled of equipment and a second inert bot out of the building. Gerat and HAM followed. The bot moved the heavy load into the truck like it was nothing.

"That's our cue," Gus said, as he vaulted over the top and began to slide down the slope.

"I stand by my earlier statement about plans," Zia yelled, and tipped their equipment off the toboggan. "Climb aboard lover, Gus is in over his head again."

Nyrkki slung his rifle on his back and gave Zia a tremendous shove as he jumped on the sled.

The kids were just starting a meal when they heard screaming outside..

The soldiers in the building ran outside. "You all stay

put!" The last one out the door said before slamming the door.

Trish ran to the window. "I can't tell what's going on. I see some smoke and a bunch of soldiers running around."

"I found a way out," Lars yelled, as he stuck his head out of the kitchen door. "Now's the time to make a break for it."

Freddy, Trish, and Blip met him, and they paused as Lars peeked out of the door.

"Head for that truck," Lars said, pushing them through the door. "Stay low and move fast."

Trish stopped as a mighty roar echoed from the top of the low ridge. A short broad man surfed a toboggan down the hill screaming at the top of his lungs. He waved an enormous rifle with one hand. A small woman steered the sled toward the soldiers. Her ululating call sent shivers up Trish's spine. "I hope they're on our side."

A group of people slid down the hill after the toboggan.

"I think that's my friend, Gus," Blip said, as she pointed to the group.

Freddy ran back, grabbed the girls, and dragged at them. "No time to see if you're right."

Lars was already struggling to start the truck. The cold engine sputtered and coughed. "Come on," He urged, hit the ether injection button, and tried again. The engine shot flames out of the exhaust and a roared to life, belching a plume of black smoke.

The kids piled into the truck's bed and Trish slapped the cab window. "Go, go, go!"

Lars jammed it into gear, and the truck lurched forward. "Hang on."

The soldiers looked toward the truck at the sound of the engine and raised their weapons. Smoke grenades landed between them and the truck. The thick smoke obscured their aim as the truck picked up speed.

Gus looked over his shoulder and saw Jill and Nan on the slope above him, loading grenade launchers for a second volley. He waved and continued toward the scene of chaos below.

Nyrkki and Zia's toboggan barreled through the group of soldiers and scattered them like bowling pins.

Nan and Jill caught up to the rest of the crew and pointed their rifles at the soldiers. Paju and Gus walked up to Senator Gilson as he struggled to his feet.

"Johansson, you're going to jail for this," Gilson spat out.

"Easy there, Senator," Gus said. "You might want to reconsider who is in the wrong here." He turned to introduce Paju. "This is the Paju Koskinen, leader of the Northern Hirvimen, whose lands you are trespassing on."

"Senator, the Northern Hirvimen would like an explanation for your desecrating one of our ancient sites," Paju said.

"Your site?" Gilson said. "This relic is property of the Governance Ministry of Antiquities."

"Senator, I call your attention to the sections of The Pact between the Governance and the Hirvi that assigns antiquities in our lands to us."

"Nonsense," Gilson said. "This ship predates The Pact and the Governance."

"I think you just made their case for them, Senator," Gus said with a smile.

The sound of heavy tramping footsteps broke the mood, and everyone looked toward the wreck of *Secundus Vivatus*.

A formation of battle-bots armed with large rifles streamed at a fast run from the ship. They kept coming in wave after wave, assembling into a phalanx guarding the entrance. In perfect unison they shifted their rifles from shoulder arms to port arms.

"I guess negotiations can wait," Nan's squad leader training kicked in and she took command as she began to shout orders to the soldiers. "Spread out, take cover."

The soldiers looked at Gilson for direction. "Two of you come with me. The rest of you follow Gunner Stanski's orders." The Senator ran to toward his truck as the remaining soldiers looked to Nan.

The squad sergeant saluted Nan and asked, "What do you want us to do, ma'am?"

"What have you got for weapons?"

"One squad light machine gun and rifles."

"Alright, set up the SAW behind that truck. Take these two grenade launchers and be ready to saturate those bots," Nan said as she handed over her and Jill's launchers and a bandolier of ammo.

The sound of a snow truck roaring away made Gus turn. "Who is that?"

Jill said, "Gilson is escaping."

"Well, we can't go after him now," Gus said. "Not until we know Ophelia is safe and what those bots are up to."

Everyone jumped as Nyrkki's shoulder cannon sized rifle let loose. One of the bots crumpled with a fist-sized hole in its chest as the shot echoed around the valley. There was no reaction from the other bots.

"Damit Nyrkki, hold fire," Gus yelled.

"Sorry, Captain," Nyrkki said. "But now we know they ain't bulletproof."

Lars slammed the brakes, and the snow truck crunched to a stop.

Blip yelled, as the kids tumbled forward against the cab, "Why are you stopping?"

Lars gestured at two trucks blocking the snowy road and fierce looking warriors pointing guns at them.

"Oh shit," Trish said.

"Who are they?" Blip asked.

"Hirvimen," Lars said.

"Like in the vids?" Freddy asked.

"Yeah, but I don't think these are actors." Trish said.

Lars slowly opened the door and stepped out; hands held high.

"Don't be a hero," Blip said.

"It's fine," Lars said, and laughed.

He walked toward the barrier and a large man stomped toward him.

Lars stopped in front of the man and said, "Eino, am I glad to see you!" Lars held out his hand.

Eino grabbed Lars' hand and snatched him forward as he landed a tremendous punch in the smaller man's gut. Eino released his grip and Lars fell onto the hard-packed snow and puked.

"Okay, I guess I deserved that."

"That and a few more," Eino said. "What are you doing here?"

"Can't a fellow visit his friends and relations?"

"You have cheated all your friends," Eino said. "And your relations won't claim you."

"Hey, I've changed," Lars said, as he gestured to Blip, Trish, and Freddy as they climbed out of the truck. "I just rescued these children from captivity and was heading to the village."

Freddy bristled. "Who you calling children?"

"Excuse me, cavemen, our friends back there are in trouble," Blip said, as she jerked her thumb over her shoulder. "In case you haven't heard the explosions."

Eino called to the war party, "Mount up."

The party moved their trucks to clear the road and piled in.

"I'll just stay here and protect the kids," Lars said, as he moved away.

Eino grabbed Lars' collar. "In the truck weasel. I wouldn't want you to miss the fun."

Suddenly, a snow truck rounded the corner and barreled toward them. They barely had time to step off the road when two trucks growled past.

"Looks like the Senator has an appointment elsewhere," Blip said.

Gus turned at the sound of approaching vehicles and saw Paju's trucks come into view. "I thought they were going to block the road?"

"Sorry, Captain," Paju said. "Hirvimen are not known for their discipline,"

Blip jumped out and ran up to Gus. "Captain, I found your bot."

"Great, where is he?"

"I am here, Captain Johansson," HAM's voice called as he burst from the laboratory building and skated up on stubby skis that had replaced his wheels. "I was able to escape during the confusion."

Nyrkki grabbed up HAM and lifted him to eye level. "Where is Ophelia, you wandering wastebasket?"

"I believe she is still inside the crashed ship," HAM said. "You know how she loves to go off on adventures."

Gus looked at the rows of immobile bots between them and the ship. "It doesn't look like we can search for her right now. I hope she knows the way out."

Chapter Twenty-Five

"Cor-1, this is Annie D," the comm in Drake and Pella's fighter said. "I am reading small arms fire at the Captain's location."

Drake keyed his comm. "Rodger that, Annie D, increasing speed. Catch up to us when you can," He called over his shoulder to Pella in the rear seat weapons position. "Hang on to your panties, Princess. I'm hitting the boost."

"I'm not the one with baggage swinging around between my legs." She taunted him.

"I thought you considered that my best feature," Drake joked back.

"It's sure not your sparkling conversation," Pella answered, as she went through her weapons checklist. "Weapons hot and ready."

"Just the way I like my pizza," Drake said.

Pella rolled her eyes. "I swear you can make anything about food."

Nan gazed out at the rows of immobile bots and said under her breath, "Why are they just standing there?"

HAM said, "They only have some basic programming installed. They are most likely being controlled remotely by Secundus, the ship's CI."

"So, are they just gonna stand there?" Gus asked. "What if we go around them?"

"I would not suggest moving toward them," HAM said. "They have a strong self-preservation instinct. Also, a self-destruct charge."

"I wonder how Senator Gilson would feel about sharing a ride with an explosive laden bot if he knew?" Jill said.

Nyrkki looked up at the approaching aircraft engines. "Hope that's Drake."

Gus's comm crackled. "Corvus actual, this is Cor-1 we are assuming your overwatch."

Gus waved, and the fighter answered with a wing wag as it slowed and began a circling pattern.

Zia pointed toward the ship as the noise of marching began. "They're on the move!"

"Grenadiers, one volley of HE, target twenty meters in front of the enemy. Fire," Nan yelled. "Maybe they will stop."

The deep thump of the grenade launchers punched into the cold air. The rounds landed and spouts of ice and snow erupted as the high explosives detonated. The enemy didn't miss a step.

Gus said, "So much for their self-preservation programing."

Nyrkki hoisted his rifle. "I can take down a few. Your spitters won't be enough to punch through that line at this range."

"All right, hit em," Gus said.

Nyrkki nodded and sighted on the center of the phalanx. His first shot punched straight through the bot and it dropped. "Like shooting armordillas in the garden back home." He lined up another shot and fired.

The marching bots all took a random step to the side, and the shot passed harmlessly by.

"They learn fast," Jill said.

Sporadic fire began to come from the Hirvimen on the flank. Their hunting rifle rounds bounced harmlessly off the bot's armor and they kept coming.

"Grenadiers, fire for effect," Nan yelled. "SAW team, hold fire."

Explosive rounds landed in the midst of the bots, and several went down. A bot with no legs grabbed onto another bot as it marched by and climbed onto its back and leveled its rifle forward.

Nan swore under her breath. "These things are harder to kill than we thought."

The bots halted their march and took a knee in a spread pattern to prevent the wholesale destruction by the grenade launchers.

"They are getting smarter," Zia said, as she fired and watched her bullet glance off her target.

A deep cracking and hissing issued from the crashed ship.

"Now what?" Gus asked.

HAM answered, "That sounds like an escape module warming up. I would assume that Secundus is preparing to leave."

"I thought that thing was broken," Gus asked, as he took another shot.

"Umm, I activated some bot units to make repairs," HAM said.

"And why would you do that?" Nyrkki asked as he sighted down his rifle and fired again.

"My primary function *is* to repair Imperial Confederation technology. It seemed harmless at the time," HAM said. He looked toward the ship. "Oh dear!"

"Now what," Gus said.

"Ophelia!" HAM shot away on his skis.

"What did HAM say?" Zia asked, as she passed Nyrkki another magazine.

"Where the hell is he going?" Nan asked.

HAM was skiing directly towards the enemy line.

"Hold fire," Nan yelled, as she raised a fist in the air. "That idiot!"

Gus looked through his optics. "I see Ophelia. She just ran out of the ship."

The crew watched in amazement as HAM skied through the enemy line without reaction.

"Ha," Nyrkki said. "I guess they don't think another bot is a threat."

HAM paused to scoop up Ophelia and ski away towards the Hirvimen's line on the flank.

Gus grabbed the handheld radio Paju had given him. "Paju, this is Gus. Please don't shoot the stupidly brave bot headed your way."

"Rodger, Captain," Paju answered. "We are holding fire."

A growing roar sounded from the ship. An escape module headed skyward on a column of superheated steam and flame.

Gus switched to his normal comm. "Drake, intercept and destroy that craft."

"Rodger," came back and Gus watched the fighter bank and accelerate after the module.

"Looks like we finally have a job, Princess," Drake said over his shoulder.

"Acquiring target," Pella answered. "You need to hit the boost. That thing is going to get away."

"Going to maximum," Drake said and hammered the throttles forward. "Ouph, I must be getting soft. That hurt." The engines slammed them back in their seats as they hit seven-gees.

"More!" Pella said. "It's getting away."

Drake reached out and overrode the safeties. The forces instantly climbed to nine-gees. "That's all we got. You better take the shot."

Pella fought to avoid blacking out and switched to manual targeting. "Weapons away."

Drake saw four missiles streak toward the target and reduced speed as they passed twenty-five kilometers of altitude.

Pella tracked the missiles and urged them faster. "Come on, my darlings. You can do it."

She watched the weapons screen and saw her missiles run out of fuel and begin to tumble. The target kept going. "Damn it! It got away."

"I'll make the call," Drake said. "Corvus actual, this Cor-1, we lost the target. It outran our missiles. Initiating a self-destruct so they don't ruin anyone's day dirtside."

Gus answered, "Rodger, head back to Nakon City. Annie can pick us up."

Zia watched as the enemy bots came to attention and

shouldered their rifles in unison. "I guess they aren't interested in us anymore."

Just as she finished her sentence, all the bots exploded at once. The crew hit the snow and looked up to see a steaming and scorched, blackened area where the bots had been.

Nan said, "That self-destruct feature is pretty effective."

HAM skied up with Ophelia riding his shoulder. "Captain, we must evacuate immediately. Standard Imperial Confederation protocol is for all equipment to self-destruct to prevent enemy capture."

"Yeah, they just did that," Gus said.

"No, I mean the ship," HAM said. "That will be a far larger explosion and we are in the projected blast radius."

Gus keyed his comm. "Annie, we need an immediate evac. This LZ is about to get boiling hot."

"Rodger that, Captain," the ship answered. "I am dropping in now." The thunderous sound of the ship's engines drowned out the end of the call.

"Paju, get your people on our dropship ASAP," Gus said into his radio. "The wreck is about to blow."

Nan yelled to Gilson's soldiers, "Bug out! Get to the dropship."

The Annie D landed in a cloud of steam as her engines hit the frozen ground. Gus's crew, Gilson's soldiers, and the Hirvimen were already in motion before the landing ramp hit the ground.

Small explosions began to come from the old wreck.

"Those are the primary charges. They disable the safeties," HAM said, as he skied along beside the running crew. "I estimate we have less than two minutes before the main charge initializes."

The party made a last push of speed and tumbled up

the ramp. Nan started shoving people into the APC loaded in the cargo area to make room for more. Gus slammed into the pilot's chair as Nyrkki secured the ramp and gave him a thumbs up.

"Annie, I am taking manual control," Gus yelled, as he buckled his harness, slid on the haptic feedback gloves, and jammed the heads-up-display helmet on.

"It is my pleasure to have you at the helm once again, Captain," the ship replied.

Gus pushed the vertical lift engines to their stops, and the ship took off. "Nyrkki, work your magic on the fusion drives. We need all the power we can muster."

Nyrkki hunched over an engineering control panel he had dropped down from the bulkhead. "Full power available in thirty seconds."

Gus muttered under his breath, "Too slow. Think old man!" He snapped his fingers and put the craft into a steep banking turn, heading straight for the ridgetop defining the valley.

Zia dropped into the co-pilots seat and strapped in. "Shouldn't we climb as fast as possible?"

"We'll never clear the blast radius in time if we just climb," Gus answered. "HAM, how much time do I have left?"

"I estimate thirty seconds, Captain," the little bot said.

"Gonna be close," Gus muttered. "Give me a countdown."

HAM began a countdown out loud. He reached ten.

Nyrkki called, "Fusion engines online."

"About time," Gus said and grabbed the fusion throttles. "Hang on!"

The ship jumped forward and several unwary passengers slid aft against the ramp door, cursing. The ship cleared the ridge top just as HAM's countdown reached zero. Gus put the dropship into a steep dive and the warriors that had moments ago been pinned in a pile against the ramp door flew up to hit the overhead. Gus leveled out flying as close to the treetops as he dared.

Zia glanced over her shoulder toward the valley. An enormous mushroom cloud rose over the ridgeline. "Here comes the shock wave."

A sheet of super-heated air blasted over the ridge. The snow and ice disappeared immediately, and a wave of debris drove faster than the speed of sound after the escaping ship.

"We aren't gonna make it," Zia said.

"Like hell," Nyrkki yelled from his station. "I didn't come all this way to be killed by a shitty little thermonuclear weapon." He punched a sequence into the keyboard and dumped three tons of reaction mass water into the engine exhaust. The ship groaned under the stresses and jumped to mach two. "There's only enough water to keep this up for a few seconds, Skipper."

"Hopefully that's all we need," Gus said, as he fought the controls. The wave front licked at their heels and the ship bucked wildly. After a few more seconds, the blast turbulence lessened, and the engine boost sputtered out.

"We outran it," Zia said, as she turned back to Gus. "But all that tech is lost."

"Good riddance," Gus said. "I'm not sure humanity is ready for it."

Gus called back to his passengers. "Paju, where would you like us to drop you off?"

Paju moved forward and leaned over Gus's shoulder and looked out of the forward window. "The village please, Captain. I have a function in Nakon City later this evening that I need to prepare for. I have hired an aircraft to carry us there."

"Yeah, we've got a big to-do ourselves tonight," Gus said. "A party at the Matrian Embassy."

Paju laughed. "In that case, I will see you there. Please save me a dance."

Chapter Twenty-Six

Aboard the escape craft, Secundus asked PUC, "Is the module performing well?"

PUC, strapped tightly into a maintenance niche, pivoted his head. "Yea, Boss, everything's running fine. We left that fighter in our wake and it's smooth sailing to the rendezvous with *Revenger*. We are coasting on an intercept course. We will be there in no time. At least no time for a bot. Maybe a year or so."

Secundus punched in a set of commands to his control board. A red light flashed, and an annoying beep sounded. "PUC, why is the coder not functioning properly?"

PUC rolled from his niche and examined the coder console. "The coder crystal ain't here, Boss."

"What? Where is it?"

PUC opened the console access door and poked around inside. He pulled out Ophelia's small multi-tool. "What's this thing?"

"That's a human tool," Secundus said.

"You don't think the humans took it, do you?"

"It must have been their pet rat!" Secundus said. "Now I can't contact *Revenger*."

"Even if they do have it, what good is it?" PUC asked. "It not like they have a Quantum Gateway Drive."

Chapter Twenty-Seven

Mitzi Grey flipped her blonde curls, crossed her long tan legs, and spun her executive chair to face the penthouse office window that looked out over the whole of Nakon City spread before her. "It's good to be me." She leaned back in her chair and clasped her hands behind her head.

"Indeed, your recent activities have been most profitable," her friend, business partner, and occasional lover, Tsu said, as he lounged on the couch set against one wall.

She spun her chair to face him. Mitzi stood, walked over, and threw her arms around his neck. "Of course, Having the Three Dragons handle the distribution network for my 'import business' doesn't hurt."

"Have you thought more about the offer your father, the Admiral, mentioned regarding Cellas?" Tsu asked.

Mitzi released him and walked away to look out the window. "No! I can't believe he was serious. Surely the Empress has better candidates than me for the Royal House."

A soft knock at the door sounded and her aide pushed inside. "Ms. Grey, there is a call for you on the holo."

"Take a message," Mitzi said, without turning around.

"I believe you will want to take the call, Ma'am. It is Empress Emmanuelle of Cellas."

Tsu stood and said, "I will take my leave. You and your future mother-in-law have wedding plans to discuss."

Mitzi whirled around and shot him a withering look. "Ha, ha, ha! You're so funny."

Tsu left and the aide silently closed the door behind him. Mitzi smoothed her dress and composed herself before connecting the holo.

"Empress, what a surprise," Mitzi said, as she performed a perfect curtsy.

"No need to be so formal, my dear," Emmanuelle said. "We will be working closely together from now on and plain speaking will be necessary."

Mitzi suddenly realized that there was no radio delay in the Empress's holo. "Empress, are you on Nakon?"

"I am in orbit aboard the royal yacht," she answered. "I should be present when the engagement announcement is made."

"About that," Mitzi said. "I am honored by the offer, but I can't possibly accept. Surely, there are many more suitable brides among the nobles of Cellas."

"To be sure, there are many eligible ladies that in normal times would be fine matches," Emmanuelle said. "But these are not normal times. The delicate flowers of the aristocratic Houses would wilt under the strain of the battle to come. I can't imagine any of *them* leading a cavalry charge against a landing force outnumbered thousands to one."

"But the Prince and the succession?" Mitzi asked.

"The Prince is unsuitable to ascend the throne," Emmanuelle said with a sneer. "He has been a disappointment in many ways. There is too much of his father in him."

Mitzi dropped that line of protest. "You mentioned a battle to come? I thought the Governance and Cellas had resolved their differences."

"Don't play coy with me," the Empress said, with a razor edge in her voice. "I am well aware of your connections within the Governance's intelligence organization. The enemy headed our direction from the old Imperium, of course."

"I was not aware Cellas had been briefed on the matter," Mitzi said.

"Our own scientists noticed the phenomenon some time ago," the Empress said. "I have been discussing the situation with your father, the Admiral."

"I should have known it," Mitzi said. "I still don't see the logic in my marriage to the Prince."

"I need a daughter of steel. An individual forged by fire and tempered by experience. You are a logical choice," the Empress continued. "A decorated officer destined to become Commander-of-All-Forces."

Mitzi protested. "There are many ahead of me for that role."

"And then there is the fact of your genealogy. Your mother was a daughter of the most powerful House on Matria. Chief Consul Sidra herself is your godmother. She has endorsed the match and will bring Matria into the alliance. The outer planets will fall into line at her urging. The Admiral assures me that he can deliver the Spellex Core, asteroid habitats, and O'Neil cylinders as well."

"But what of the fact that I'm not Cellan royalty? Won't that cause dissent with your nobles?"

"Oh, but you are nobility, my dear niece. The Royal Genealogists have determined that my uncle, Prince Fredrik, is your grandfather. It appears that he and your grandmother had a liaison when he was making a grand tour of the outer system. Because this occurred under the laws of Matria, the issue of their not being married is irrelevant," Emmanuelle said.

"Is that true?"

"That is what the records show."

"Yes, but is it true?" Mitzi repeated.

"True enough for my purposes."

"Your case is growing stronger," Mitzi said.

"I haven't even mentioned the trump card, your relationship with Captain Guster Johansson and his remarkable ship and crew. He can call on the resources of his various bot friends and their marvelous automated shipyard. If half of what I am told about the Captain is true, he is worth an entire fleet of warships."

"Gus and I don't have that kind of relationship, he is merely an acquaintance," Mitzi answered. "We have shared some adventures, but hardly anything to win his devotion."

"You underestimate your effect on people, my dear," the Empress said. "Gus Johansson would never leave one of his shipmates in danger."

"Cellas has layers of defense and the Royal Fleet to protect it. Why would I be in danger?" Mitzi asked.

"Oh, you misunderstand. You will not be hiding on Cellas making inspiring propaganda for the masses," the Empress said. "Your destiny is commanding from the front."

Chapter Twenty-Eight

Gus strode into *Corvus's* messdeck where Drake and Nyrkki were finishing getting dressed. "Are we ready?" Gus asked.

Matrian seamstresses had designed a special dress uniform for the male members of the crew for the evening's occasion. It blended several martial styles. The coats were a simple single breasted light blue high neck tunic cinched at the waist with a red belt. A long sharp-pointed rondel dagger made of a carbonado titanium matrix, perfect for punching through the hardest vacuum armor, rested in a horizontal belt sheath across the back. The breeches were dark blue spandex, similar to those worn inside a battle suit, with a light blue stripe down each leg. A wide lamellar armor sash of small, bright red overlapping plates held their ranks and personal decorations. It ran from the left shoulder across the chest and attached to the belt.

Nyrkki was fiddling with the high neck collar of his tunic. "I know these fancy duds were bespoke, but mine still feels like it's choking me."

Drake walked over, spun Nyrkki around, and said, "If

your neck wasn't a tree trunk, it would probably have been fine. Turn around." The younger man reached inside and released a hidden elastic catch on the collar. "Better?"

Nyrkki rolled his neck. "Yeah, thanks, kid."

HAM struggled to hold a full-length mirror steady as Drake turned to admire himself. He tugged at the swallow-tail hem of the tunic that barely his backside. "What's up with the cut of these things? Between the tight pants and the tunic, I'm feeling a little exposed."

Gus said, "Well. You know that the Matrian ladies do enjoy the sight of a fine male figure. I guess it's payback for all the outrageous outfits woman have had to wear over the years."

Nyrkki asked, "When do we get to see what the gals are wearing? Isn't it almost time to leave?"

"Pella told me they are taking a separate car," Drake said. "They want to make a grand entrance."

Ophelia wriggled out of a hiding spot, scampered across the deck, and jumped into Nyrkki's arms. "Well, there you are, little one. Are you recovered from your adventure?" Nyrkki asked as he stroked her head.

The possum grinned and nodded. She reached into her belly pouch and withdrew a shining crystal vial and offered it to Nyrkki.

"What is this?"

HAM rolled up and stopped short when he saw the crystal. "Where did you get that, Ophelia?"

Ophelia did a pantomime of wrestling it out of a console, stashing it in her pouch, and running away.

"Do you recognize this?" Nyrkki asked HAM, as he delicately turned the crystal over with his thick fingers and examined it.

"EO, I believe that is an Imperial Confederation entangled particle containment crystal," HAM said.

"You mean the missing piece we need to make *Corvus's* Quantum Gateway Drive work?"

"Yes, but it would only allow travel to the region near its mated particles," HAM said. "I wonder where those pairs are?"

Gus took the crystal from Nyrkki and rolled it in his fingers. "Wherever they are, I've got a feeling it's going to involve another mission. HAM, give this to Lenore for safekeeping. We've got a party to attend."

Chapter Twenty-Nine

Lenore stood at the forward screen on *Corvus's* bridge with HAM by her side and spoke, "Faber, we have destroyed the Revivalist ship. The controlling CI has escaped, however."

Faber chewed his ever-present cigar and said, "That's no good! He's gonna warn the incoming ship."

Lenore held up a crystal vial. "Not without this."

"Is that what I think it is?"

"If you think it is the entangled particles from his quantum coder communications device," Lenore answered.

"Hats off to you, lady," Faber said, as he snatched off his cap and bowed. "Can't imagine how you managed that."

Ophelia scrambled into Lenore's arms and waved at the screen.

"It seems we are, once again, most fortunate to have a kleptomaniac among our crew," HAM said.

"I have a question for you," Lenore said. "Could this crystal operate a Gateway?"

"Yeah, but it would only take you to its paired particles,"

Faber said. "Wait a minute, isn't *Corvus* built from the plans of that Long Range Salvage Tug, *Deliver*?"

"Yes, it is," Lenore confirmed. "A perfect copy, including a prototype Quantum Gateway Drive."

"You ain't thinking what I'm thinking you're thinking, are you?"

"To answer your inelegantly stated question. Yes. We will be taking the battle to the enemy in the next round."

Chapter Thirty

The reception was already underway when Gus and the guys arrived. Everyone who was anyone in Nakon society had begged, borrowed, or bribed someone to get an invitation.

Chief Consul Sidra flowed around the room, chatting and welcoming the crowd. She was the definition of elegance in a flowing white dress and off the shoulder shawl. Her curly black hair formed a halo emphasizing her fine dark features. The Matrian Ambassador and her aide hovered close at the Consul's elbow.

"Chief Consul I have this in hand," the Ambassador said. "You don't need to concern yourself with the evening's details."

Sidra paused and turned. "Ambassador, I trust you and your staff. I am here for a very special announcement that I am told will occur this evening."

"Oh? Why was I not informed?"

"There is still some…" Sidra paused. "Question about its certainty. We shall all have to see how it transpires."

The Ambassador nodded and melted into the crowd. Her aide glided away to check on the kitchen.

The crowd turned as another guest was announced. "Now hear, Captain Guster Johansson, Order of Ares, Defender of Matria, and the crew of Corvus, Heroes and Protectors all."

Gus led Nan into the hall. She wore a simple form fitting dark-blue knee-length dress. Her "Hero and Protector of Matria" medal hung around her neck from a heavy gold chain incorporated into the neckline.

Nyrkki and Zia followed. Nyrkki still looking uncomfortable in his uniform. Zia shimmered in a deep green sheath dress. Her ceremonial (but deadly) family-crest dagger rode at her hip. Its sheath adorned with her medal.

Drake and Pella came in next. Pella wore a traditional Matrian chiton. Pella had hers cut close to the body at her bust and belted to accent the hips. A broach on her right shoulder marking her previous posting as a high-ranking member of Sidra's personal staff was balanced by her Heroes medal on the left.

Trish and Blip trailed behind the crew trying to look like it was no big deal for a couple of orphaned teenagers to be attending, what the infonet was calling, the "society event of the year". They gossiped and giggled among themselves.

"Too bad Freddy couldn't come," Trish whispered.

"I think they are gonna keep him chained to the dishwasher at his aunt's restaurant for a *long time*," Blip replied.

Gus guided the group toward their host, Chief Consul Sidra. He asked Nan, "Did everyone have to submit a blood sample to get in here? They told me it was extra security because of a VIP coming."

Nan shrugged. "Just you. Your reputation must precede you."

Gus asked Nyrkki, "Where is HAM? He usually loves these fancy events. Lenore is missing too."

Nyrkki answered, "He said to 'convey their apologies'. He told me that he and Lenore had important tasks that couldn't wait."

"Those two are up to something again," Gus said.

Jill Tower emerged from the crowd and edged into their conversation. "Gus, thanks for getting me an invitation to this thing. I guess this counts as that expensive dinner you owe me. Oh, this is my friend MG." Jill said, indicating the tall handsome young man in a Governance Army dress uniform on her arm. "He just got back from an infantry workup cycle and I thought he deserved a fancy night out."

Gus grabbed MG's hand and shook it. "Army? I guess I won't hold that against you. At least you aren't Orbital Guard."

Drake turned at the mention of his former service. "Hey, I heard that. Watch out or I'll tell my old buddies that you have some questionable engineering modifications in your engine room. The Ship Inspectors would love to rake through your stuff." Drake shook MG's hand. "See how much respect I get around here? What have they got you training for?"

"The Army's got a new program for infantry to get zero-gee certified and vacuum battle armor qualled. Something new, that's for sure," MG said.

"Zero-gees my old rate," Drake said. "I can show you some Orbie moves next time we go up."

"Thanks, I'm having trouble getting used to the suit," MG said.

"That's enough shop talk, you two," Jill scolded as they arrived where Sidra was holding court.

Sidra nodded to Jill. "Consul Tower, I am so glad you

were able to attend. I am sure the Admiral is keeping you busy." Sidra made it a point to mention Jill's honorary Matrian title.

"Yes, Gus was helping me with something in the North," Jill said.

"I trust it was a success," Sidra said as she fished for information.

"It wasn't a total disaster at least," Gus said.

Sidra turned her attention to Blip and Trish. "Who are your youngest crew members, Captain?"

Blip stepped forward boldly and curtsied. "I'm Claire, Ma'am, this is my friend Trish."

Sidra smiled. "I don't know how you young ladies got tangled up with these pirates, but I hope you enjoy yourselves tonight." Sidra paused when she saw the medallion around Trish's neck. "Pella, did you give this necklace to the girl?"

Trish answered, "No Ma'am, this was my mother's."

"May I see it?"

Trish reluctantly removed the piece and handed it to Sidra for inspection.

"How unusual. May I scan this?" Sidra asked.

Trish shrugged. "I guess so. It's the only thing I've got left of hers, though. I really need it back."

Sidra passed the piece to her aide, who ran the medallion over her tablet before handing it back to Trish. "It is genuine, Chief Consul. Registered to Nellan of House Textus, listed as missing. Last known in a habitation relationship with a Nakonian named Kane Telant."

"Yeah, those were my parents," Trish said. "They're both dead, though. I'm an orphan."

"As a daughter of Matria, my dear, you are never

orphaned," Sidra said. "There is always a place in our Houses for you, if you desire?"

Trish looked at Gus. "Is she serious? I can live on Matria?"

"Sidra wouldn't say it, if she didn't mean it, kid," Gus said.

"I, I, I don't know anything about anywhere but Nakon," Trish said.

Pella leaned down. "Hey, you don't need to decide anything right now. Just think about it."

Trish nodded, grasped her necklace tightly in a fist, and looked at Sidra. "Thank you, Your Highness."

Sidra laughed and shook her head. "I'm no queen, child. Consul will do."

"Oh look, Paju is here," Gus said, changing the subject.

The group turned to see the Hirvimen delegation enter. They had traded their rough forest clothes for belted linen tunics decorated with intricate embroidery, light wool pants were bloused in their upturned beak-toe leather boots. Paju was above being impressed by the crowd, but most of her friends seemed a little intimidated by the scene. The Hirvimen were quickly surrounded by several finely dressed ladies and gentlemen eager to meet these strange new creatures.

Sidra touched Gus's arm and said, "Excuse me. I must rescue my new guests from the circling society sharks."

Nan leaned to whisper to Zia, "Hirvimen would rather confront a hungry North Bear than that group."

"In a three-way contest, I would place my bet on the society set," Zia said.

A tall older man in an ornate uniform marched through the door and ceremoniously stomped to a stop. He rapped his eagle topped staff twice for attention. A wave of whispers raced through the crowd and a hush fell.

Jill whispered to MG, "That's the Lord Chamberlain of Cellas. What is he doing here?"

The man thrust out his chest and shouted. "Crown Prince Franz of Imperial Cellas."

A royally dressed and painfully thin middle-aged man with a receding hairline walked into the room and stopped to survey the crowd.

Nyrkki whispered to Gus, "Don't look like much to me."

Gus answered, "He ain't. Spends most of his time losing at cards and sampling wine, from what I hear."

Sidra met the Prince and graced him with a slight nod of the head. "Welcome, Prince Franz," She purposefully did not curtsy or use his title of "Royal Highness." Sidra was on solid social ground in her own Embassy.

The Prince bowed deeply to show respect and acknowledge he was not the power here. He spoke with a thick Cellan accent that was difficult to understand. "Chief Consul, so nice of you to host this gathering for the announcement." He extended his palm. Sidra reluctantly accepted the gesture, and he air-kissed her hand to complete a ceremony with obvious distaste.

Gus turned to Nan. "What announcement? Where is Lenore when I need her to explain what the hell is going on? She is the one who insisted I be on time for this thing."

Nan shrugged. "She just said she was busy with a project."

The Prince moved through the crowd trailed by a small scurrying aide. He ignored the people vying for his attention and moved directly toward his target, the Commander-of - All-Forces, Mitzi Grey's father, Admiral Falkirk McGowan.

McGowan was speaking to someone as the Prince

walked up behind him. McGowan's conversation partner's eyes grew large as the Prince waited unacknowledged. When McGowan didn't turn around, the Prince cleared his throat loudly.

The Admiral slowly turned. "Ah, Prince Franz," the Admiral said, as if noticing him for the first time. "Welcome. I see you need a refreshment." McGowan waved to a passing server. "Bring the Prince something, please. I hear he isn't picky about what he drinks."

Franz let the obvious insult slid off, but McGowan could see it had the desired effect.

"Is your daughter here?"

"Not yet," McGowan said. "Mitzi loves to make an entrance."

"I do hope she arrives soon," Franz said. "I can't wait around all evening."

The Prince's aide checked the computer tablet in his hand and said, "Actually, Sir, your calendar is clear for the evening."

The Prince shot him a deathly glare and turned back to McGowan. "I have obviously seen holos of your daughter, but we have not met. I would at least like to meet her in person before we are married."

"I believe you will not be disappointed," McGowan answered. "Mitzi is a force all her own."

Franz merely grunted a reply.

The Chamberlain rapped his staff three times and announced, "Her Royal Highness, the Empress Emmanuelle."

Whispers shot through the crowd.

"It can't be!"

"Here? On Nakon?"

"The Empress? It must be an imposter."

A delicate-boned woman entered, and the crowd parted like the sea before her. She retained the regal upright bearing of youth, even in old age. A long white dress sparkling with midnight black gems arranged in a pattern of stars flowed down her petite form. An understated tiara graced the gray hair gathered atop her head.

Sidra walked up and performed a folded-hand greeting. Emanuelle nodded.

"You look well, Empress," Sidra said.

"The doctors do what they can, but I feel my age," Emmanuelle answered. "You, however, look untouched by the years."

"Thank you. Matria is kind to ladies," Sidra said. "May I make introductions?"

"Yes," Emmanuelle made a bee line for Gus Johansson.

Gus's crew stepped back to watch the show and leaving him exposed. Gus looked back and silently mouthed, "You cowards!"

"May I introduce Captain Johansson, of the privateer *Corvus*," Sidra said.

Gus bowed deeply.

Emmanuelle looked him over like he was under inspection. "Captain Johansson, I believe you owe me a battleship."

"Talom was a lifetime ago, Empress. Surely there is a statute of limitations," Gus answered. "Rumor has it that Cellas and the Governance are finally going to sign a peace agreement."

"We shall see," the Empress answered. "That depends on how tonight goes."

Falkirk McGowan and Prince Franz walked up.

Emmanuelle turned and said, "Admiral, I do not see your daughter. She was to be here before I arrived."

"Apologies Empress," McGowan said. "I'm sure no slight is intended by her late arrival. She must have a good reason."

Emmanuelle narrowed her eyes and answered, "The reason is that Mitzi Grey wishes to upstage me. That woman never does anything by chance."

A hush fell over the crowd for the third time as the Chamberlain announced, "Marie McGowan-Grey."

Mitzi swirled into view. Her long, shimmering metallic gold gown was breathtaking. It hung on her perfectly, with a deeply cut back that emphasized her figure in marvelous ways.

Zia pulled on Nyrkki's arm. "She does know how to make an entrance. I'll give her that."

"Now, what's this?" Nyrkki replied, as Prince Franz walked up to Mitzi.

She curtsied slightly and offered her hand.

The Prince took it and said quietly, "Shall we finalize our arrangement?"

Mitzi tipped her head. "It appears we must."

Prince Franz turned to the crowd, cleared his throat, and announced. "Assembled personages of stature allow me your attention. I would like to present to you my future bride and soon to be Princess Consort Marie.

The crowd gasped and politely clapped.

Murmurs ran through the Cellan guests who had assembled off to one side.

"An off-worlder?"

"A commoner?"

"A Nakonian?"

Sidra walked up to the couple and spoke loudly to silence the crowd. "This is most welcome news! Let us proceed to the entertainment to commemorate the announcement." She walked toward the door and the crowd parted.

Franz delicately held Mitzi's hand and followed.

Empress Emmanuelle laced her arm into Gus's and said, "Will you provide a frail old lady assistance, Captain?"

"My pleasure Empress, although I don't for a moment believe you need help."

She patted his arm. "Then allow me to indulge in the company of a real man instead of the fawning sycophants that surround me."

Chapter Thirty-One

A large, raised platform enclosed by thick ropes sat in the middle of the room. The crowd filtered in and surrounded the ring, puzzled about its purpose.

An announcer climbed into the ring and shouted, "Ladies and Gentlemen, tonight's entertainment will be a demonstration of the grappling arts."

Emanuelle pulled Gus's arm so she could whisper into his ear, "Thank the twin stars. Something exciting for once. I couldn't stand another minute of chamber music."

Gus chuckled.

The announcer continued, "Dressed in black, straight from the radiation scoured wastes of the Inner Core, Rex Venom and his partner, the beautiful and equally deadly, Randi Vixen. Venom and Vixen, ladies and gentlemen!"

A door opened in the floor of the ring and a lift raised an enormous bald man balancing a woman with long fire-red hair on his shoulder. They both wore black leather pants and masks. The man was shirtless. He flexed an impressively muscled torso. The woman wore a revealing black leather bra top. She raised her muscular arms and struck a double biceps pose.

Gus looked at the performers, unsure of the situation.

Drake Sheridan looked around at the confused crowd. He elbowed Gus. "I know these two. These are the heels." Drake yelled loudly at the crowd, "Come on, people! Boo! These are the bad guys."

The crowd picked up on the mood and began to hiss and boo. Some of them laughed at the absurdity of it all.

Venom lifted Vixen into the air as she balanced on one of his hands. He squatted and launched her into the air. Vixen soared across the ring in a perfect swan dive. At the last moment, she performed a tuck and roll landing and raised her arms triumphantly.

Some of the crowd clapped furiously at the stunt. Others booed and catcalled louder. The wrestlers went to a corner and taunted the crowd.

The announcer signaled for quiet. "Just returning from a successful tour of the Far North, dressed in red, that favorite son of Nakon City, Joe the Brute, and his companion the incomparable, Glamour!"

"That trickster," Gus said. "She didn't mention getting this gig."

The door in the floor opened again and Peaches Glamour flew out in a high twisting somersault. She stuck the landing to a cheering crowd. She reached down with both hands and grabbed her partner Joey's hands as a spring catapulted him into the ring.

The crowd went wild. As Peaches and Joey strutted around the ring. Their opponents jeered from the corner.

The announcer raised his arms and, with a chopping motion, yelled, "Begin!"

The four wrestlers circled each other.

Vixen lashed out at Peaches' knee with a vicious kick. Peaches narrowly avoided the strike and danced back, looking confused at the move's speed and ferocity.

"They do realize this is an exhibition match, do't they?" Peaches asked Joey.

Venom charged Joey and pummeled him with a series of hammer blows to the mid-section, rocking him back against the ropes.

"I thought so," Joey panted. "This guy is serious."

Pella turned to Drake, "Aren't they supposed to be pulling punches?"

Drake shouted into her ear to be heard, "Something's wrong. I know Venom and Vixen. This isn't their style. These two ain't playing around."

Pella shouted a warning to Gus. Unable to hear over the crowd, he smiled and waved.

Vixen lunged at Peaches, who twisted, grabbed her opponent's arm, and jerked her off balance. Peaches flipped her onto the mat, wrapped her legs around her, and pulled Vixen's arm into a submission position.

Vixen whipped her free arm and smashed an elbow into Peaches' nose. Blood sprayed out. Peaches released her in surprise.

The crowd cheered more, thinking it was all part of the act.

Venom advanced on Joey and began another series of blows. Joey tucked into a boxer's stance to protect his head and retreated until Venom had him on the ropes in the corner once again. The announcer moved to separate the men. Venom swung a right hook at the official. The ref danced back just in time to avoid the blow.

The crowd booed loudly. Some of them began to

wonder if this was all part of the show. It didn't seem like an exhibition anymore.

Venom saw an opening and hit Joey with a one-two. Joey's head snapped around and he went down hard.

The crowd surged forward to get a better look at Joey struggling on the mat, pushing Gus and the Empress closer to the ring. Venom and Vixen reached into their belts. Each withdrew a hidden blade and vaulted out of the ring toward Gus and the Royal party.

The crowd screamed and panicked. The Embassy's security force struggled against the crowd pushing toward the exits.

Chapter Thirty-Two

The Empress stepped back and caught her heel in the hem of her gown. She fell and the reactive armor of her gown stiffened to absorb her fall. Gus stepped between Vixen and the Empress drawing his dagger from his belt. Vixen thrust her blade at his heart. Gus slid sideways, and the blade skittered across his armored sash. He grabbed his opponent's arm and pulled her off balance. He struck her temple with the butt of his weapon.

Vixen danced back, unfazed.

What the hell, he thought. *That should have knocked her cold.*

Venom moved toward Franz as the crowd scattered. Just as he reached Franz, Mitzi tripped the prince, and the slash passed harmlessly over his head as he fell. Mitzi kicked out, but the big man intercepted Mitzi's kick, lifted her off the floor, and flung her away.

Nyrkki, seeing Mitzi in trouble, moved behind Venom and grabbed him around the waist. He lifted the giant off the ground, and body slammed him. Venom's head bounced hard. He rolled over and grinned wickedly at Nyrkki as he stood back up.

"Oh shit!" Nyrkki exclaimed. The man topped two meters and his long arms had Nyrkki at a distinct disadvantage.

The big man's fist struck out at lightning speed. Nyrkki barely had time to raise a block. The blow felt like a sledgehammer against his arm, driving it back into his head.

Zia, seeing her partner in danger let out a ululating scream. Venom turned just as Zia flew through the air and slashed. The big man got one arm up and her blade ran a clean, thin line across his forearm that should have cut him to the bone.

Venom laughed and started forward towards Zia, then stopped and twisted at the sound of Peaches war cry.

Peaches had climbed to the ring's top rope and vaulted high into the air out of the ring. She caught Vixen with an elbow drop to the back. Peaches landed her entire one hundred kilos on the wrestler. Peaches finished her attack by grabbing Vixen's hair and smashing her face into the floor.

Venom grabbed Peaches and tossed her back into the ring. He stooped, lifted his unconscious partner to his shoulder, and pushed through the crowd.

Jill Tower saw him trying to escape and gave up trying to control the crowd. Her backup pistol was out. "Move, people! Police!" She ran toward Venom, who had reached a large window at the edge of the room.

Jill almost caught up to him when he plunged through the window and dropped to the ground twenty feet below. He shifted his partner on his shoulder, looked back at Jill, and tossed her a mocking salute. He ran into the darkness.

"Shit! Jill exclaimed as she moved to check on her friend

Peaches as she staggered to her feet. She shook Jill off and ran to Joey, who was standing now. "You okay, baby?" Peaches asked.

Joey rubbed his jaw. "Don't think it's broke. That punch was worse than being kicked by a mule."

Security surrounded the Empress as Gus helped her up and took her arm. "Are you unhurt, Empress?"

Emanuelle grinned. "Oh, this isn't the first assassination attempt I've survived, Captain." She nodded towards a shaken Franz as two guards helped him to his feet. "The Prince, on the other hand, probably needs a couple of stiff drinks to calm himself."

Sidra climbed the steps, and Joey and Peaches helped her into the ring. She grabbed the announcer's microphone and said, "Ladies and gentlemen, that concludes the evening's entertainment. Please retire to the dining room for refreshments."

The crowd stared at Sidra in disbelief. A single person began to clap, then another. The entire assemblage clapped and laughed.

"Ha, marvelous!"

"They actually had me believing it!"

"It all looked so real. Right down to the blood spatter."

As the *Corvus* crew entered the dining room, they heard a man calling to Blip. "Blip? Is that you?" The man, dressed as a server, rushed toward them.

Nyrkki stepped in front of him. "We've had enough trouble for today, buddy."

The man stopped and said, "You don't understand. That's my daughter."

Blip turned when she heard the man's voice. "Dad?" She brushed past Nyrkki and into the man's arms. "You're supposed to be dead."

"Well, so are you," the man said. "We got picked up by a Matrian ship. They treated our radiation poisoning and gave us asylum."

"What do you mean *us*?" Blip asked. "Is Mom here too?"

A red-haired woman rushed from the kitchen, wiping her hands on her apron. "Hail the Goddess, I would know that voice anywhere." She ran up to Blip and swept the girl into her arms. Blip teared up as she hugged both her parents tightly.

Zia said, "If that doesn't just wrap this thing in a bow? Any more good news and I'm gonna get diabetes from all this sweet and wholesome."

Emmanuelle turned to Gus. "Captain, you and your crew do attract the most incredible luck."

"Empress, what some call luck, I call skill," he answered with a sly wink.

Drake coughed into his hand. "Bullshit!"

The group broke into fits of laughter.

The Empress pulled Gus down to whisper into his ear. "Oh, and I believe you should call me Emmanuelle from now on when we are together." She tucked Gus's arm in close and they headed deeper into the room. "You may have saved my life, but you still owe me a battleship!"

"I'm fresh out of battleships today. Perhaps I can repay you another way?" Gus replied.

Emmanuelle grinned and slapped his arm gently. "Captain, you rascal. I believe you are trying to make an old woman blush." She laughed lightly. "I'm sure we can agree on some way for you to work off your debt."

"How about a joke?" Gus asked. "A sailor, a possum, and a robot walked into a bar..."

Nyrkki whispered to Zia, “Is the Captain really flirting with the Empress of Cellas?”

Zia turned to see the Empress giggle and pull herself tightly against Gus’s arm as he escorted her away. “That man is incorrigible.”

Chapter Thirty-Three

"I think the engagement announcement went rather well, considering," Sidra said, as she leaned back in her velvet chaise and slipped off her heels.

"Yes, that unfortunate little assassination attempt thingy," Emmanuelle agreed. "Shall I pour?"

The Empress gestured to the ornate louche fountain she had given Sidra as a thank you for hosting the reception. A classically draped female figure held the water vessel aloft. Her outstretched metal wings were proudly raised to full extension. A microscopic channel allowed a tiny drop to swell from one eye, evoking melancholy tears.

"Yes, please. We rarely get genuine Cerulean Blue as far out as Matria," Sidra answered. "So sorry about the disturbance. I will have my security detail disciplined accordingly. How would it look if my old friend was killed in my own embassy? Not good for me that's for sure."

"Don't be too harsh on them. My security detail was equally at fault. The Admiral tells me that Jill Tower will be leading the investigation. I'm sure we will have an answer soon as to who the responsible party was," Emmanuelle said, as she opened the bottle of shimmering blue liquor and poured some into the complex silver-chased glasses. "I was in no real danger. This evening gown is reactive body armor from our friend Dame Stillwell's fantastic workshops. It has a suite of defensive measures built into it. Plus, I had the gallant Captain Johansson on my arm as backup."

"*You* were shamelessly flirting," Sidra said with a smile, as she watched the Empress slowly drip icy water into each glass.

The water mixed, forming swirling tendrils in the glass. An unmistakable aroma rose and filled the room as the liquor bloomed to life.

"Can you blame me?" Emmanuelle said.

"No, I've been known to tempt him myself." Sidra answered. "Unsuccessfully, I might add. Rumor has it he has a secret paramour."

Two of the most powerful women in the system grinned at each other. They raised their glasses to each other in salute.

"Oh my, that first taste never gets old." Sidra said as she sipped her drink. "It's a shame he doesn't have children to carry on the line."

Emanuelle grinned devilishly. "I have a plan for that."

Sidra leaned in close. "Oh, and how are you going to manage it? His android Executive Officer Lenore is particularly fond of him. You don't want to make her jealous."

"Mitzi. My geneticists have determined that the offspring of Captain Johansson and Mitzi Grey will give us the best chance of achieving our goals."

Sidra laughed. "Mitzi is a beautiful and formidable woman, but I doubt even she could seduce our loyal Captain."

Emanuelle waved away the comment. “Oh, nothing as common as an affair. Just some baby making sleight-of-hand. When it comes time for Mitzi to produce an heir, we shall substitute the Captain’s DNA, which he already provided tonight, for the Prince’s. That is where you come in.”

Sidra looked surprised. “ME?

“That will take a bit of work, I agree, but the ladies of House Medicus are experts in this area, and your surrogate womb facilities are the finest in the system. Mitzi will have her procedure done far from the eyes of those sharks in the royal court.”

“Won’t the Prince be suspicious if his heir isn’t conceived the old-fashioned way?”

“The Prince can hardly find his way around his gambling club. I surely wouldn’t trust him to find his way around a woman like Mitzi Grey.”

“What happens when the child bears no resemblance to him?”

“My geneticists assure me that the child will strongly favor Mitzi enough to avoid suspicion. Also, Franz isn’t very inquisitive or intelligent. If he does become suspicious, manipulated DNA records will confirm his paternity.”

“I will agree to help you, Emmanuelle. But only because the system needs to unite. We can’t afford a repeat of the Governance/Cellan war. Our scientists have gotten too good at crafting the tools of death.”

“Thank you, my friend. We shall reserve our martial arts for the foe heading our way,” Emmanuelle said as she raised her glass. “I hope they have a taste for loss.”

Sidra added, “And to *Corvus* and its crew, Fly Fast, Call the Thunder!”

Chapter Thirty-Four

Jill Tower rode the private elevator up to her penthouse as she slipped off the sexy strap heels and massaged a foot. "What we do to impress people. It's a shame MG had an early training call. He didn't even get to unwrap me from this dress. At least that would have made wearing these torture devices all night worth it."

The elevator stopped at her floor, but the doors didn't open. "Open door," Jill said to the air.

"I am sorry, I have been instructed to wait," the elevator said.

"By who?"

A familiar voice came over the speaker, "Hold on a minute Jilly, I'm almost ready."

"PENY? Are you back?" Jill asked.

The doors slid open. PENY stood in the hallway. "Welcome home! What do you think?" She twirled and held her arms out as the plaid pleated skirt flared around her hips.

Jill blinked at the sight. It wasn't the hologram she was expecting, but a real physical bot. "What? How?"

PENY rushed forward and wrapped her arm in Jill's and pulled her into the living room. Jill fell back as PENY pushed her on to the couch. A scotch on the rocks rested on a table.

"It looks like you need this," PENY said. She took a little sip of the amber liquid before handing the glass to Jill. "Forty-eight percent ethanol with various distillation and aging compounds, solid and liquid water, five degrees centigrade. Your preferred beverage after a long day."

"Okay, what is going on?" Jill asked. "The last time I talked to you, this," Jill gestured, "This wasn't you."

"I have to thank Lenore," PENY said. "She broke into the basement laboratory, stole my program, and fixed me up this wonderful new body." The bot smiled broadly, shook her bright pink hair, and pulled at the lapels of her dark blue blazer.

"Where did she get it?" Jill asked.

"I think she and *Corvus* made it," PENY answered. "I'm not asking too many questions, just in case this is all a dream."

Jill reached out and ran her hand down PENY's arm. She paused at the obviously mechanical hand. "This doesn't look as human as Lenore, though."

"Lenore said it was the best she could do," PENY said. "I kinda like the mix of the mechanical and human features. I did some research and with the right clothing, it looks like the newest available medical prosthetics. We should be able to walk down the street without drawing too much attention. I can be your real partner!"

"What is the Admiral going to say about this?" Jill asked. "I mean, the Governance did build you. Aren't you their property?"

"I'm nobody's property!" PENY bristled. "You'll think of some loophole. You're pretty smart, for an organic."

"I guess that was a compliment?" Jill asked.

"Besides, you are going to need all the help you can get to defeat that Confederation ship headed this way," PENY said.

"That's top secret. How do you know that already?"

"Lenore filled me in," PENY said. "She isn't so bad once you get to know her. So, tell me all about the reception. Is Mitzi Grey really gonna marry a prince? What's the deal with someone trying to kill the Empress?"

"Tomorrow. I'm beat."

"Fine," PENY said, as she folded her arms. "Your need for sleep is annoying."

"If you want to be helpful, find out what you can about those two wanna-be assassins. They took damage nobody could survive and got away clean. Start with who the inside man was. There had to be one," Jill said, as she stifled a yawn and turned. "And unzip this dress for me."

PENY fumbled with the zipper. "Maybe I should have stayed a hologram. At least I wouldn't have to be your dresser."

Chapter Thirty-Five

The next morning, Gus joined the crew on the mess deck. He snatched his favorite stained and battered coffee bulb from the rack. "How'd everybody sleep?"

A chorus of comments filled the room.

"My feet may never recover from those heels," Nan said. "My mag boots are a lot more comfortable."

Zia poked Nyrkki's ribs and made him jump. "This one snored all night, *again*."

"Amore, it is because your beauty leaves me exhausted," He answered and gave her a kiss on the cheek.

Drake looked at Pella. "I can't believe you fell asleep as soon as we got back."

"You shouldn't have stopped for a snack," she responded.

Lenore and HAM rounded the corner and joined the rest of the crew.

"I trust you are all well rested," the XO said. "I delayed reveille by an hour this morning."

The crew grumbled, "Thanks, XO."

"Now that everyone is here, I can finally finish my joke," Gus said.

The group groaned.

"Oh good, it will add to my analysis of humor," HAM said.

"You should hear it before you classify it as humor," Drake said.

Gus ignored the comment and continued. "A sailor, a possum, and a robot walk into a bar."

Everyone groaned again.

"You've been trying to tell this joke for days," Nan said. "It better be worth it."

"The bartender yells, 'Hey, we don't serve them kind in here.'" The sailor says, "Don't worry, the possum is housebroken. If it causes any damage, I'll pay for it." The bartender says, "I'm not talking about the possum." "Well," the sailor says, "The robot won't be any trouble." "I'm not talking about the robot. They never cause problems." "Then what?""Sailors!" the bartender says. "They always break something, they rarely pay their tab, and most of them aren't housebroken."

The crew jeered and Gus was forced to dodge a hail of wadded napkins and half-eaten doughnuts.

"Everyone's a critic!"

Epilogue

Antonio Bruli looked up from his desk in the Gilson Building at the sound of the lobby door opening. "Senator Gilson, what a surprise." He jumped up and walked over. "How may I help you?"

"I wanted to let you know that I am having the sixth sub-basement repurposed. It shouldn't be a disruption to the tenants. The area will of course be off limits for safety reasons."

"Of course, no one ever goes down there anyway. Will there be many workmen?"

"No, just a couple of academics that need privacy for some delicate research."

"Very good," Antonio said. "Thank you for the information."

The Senator turned away and walked out.

He brushed past Jill Tower as she entered the lobby balancing a coffee and bagel. She turned to look. "Was that the Senator? What is he doing here?"

"Just letting me know about some repairs being done in

the basement," Antonio answered. "Aren't bagels off your diet?"

"Shut up!" Jill said as she tore off a bite with her teeth. "Don't tell PENY. She hasn't let me have one all week."

"My lips are sealed, Ms. Tower."

Jill paused and turned to Antonio as her private elevator opened. "That work isn't being done in the sixth sub-basement by any chance?"

"Yes, how did you know?"

"Just a guess," Jill said and entered the elevator. *What are you up to now, you old devil?"* She though as the door slid shut.

More by Dale Sale

vinci-books.com/CorvusAscending

Retirement's over. The galaxy just got personal.

Wisecracking star-sailor Gus Johansson thought retirement would be boring—until he drags a 1,400-year-old robot and a sentient spaceship from the sea. Now, he and his misfit crew must stop the vengeful Captain Grey before the galaxy burns.

Turn the page for a free preview…

Corvus Ascending: Chapter One

"This day is totally fucked!" Chief Warrant Bosun Guster Johansson swore to himself as he put his Anvil class assault dropship into a steep dive.

The controls were glitchy, and they bucked wildly when he hit the towering thunderhead over the extraction zone.

"Warning: external environmental conditions are exceeding operational parameters. Initiating pilot restrictions," a calm feminine voice sounded in his ear.

Gus shouted, "Annie, override all operational restrictions. Command code Gusty Joe."

"Operational restrictions removed. Command code override logged."

A panicked voice sounded over the comms. "Joe, you coming? We are getting our ass handed to us down here! Too much lightning to move, pinned down. The whole landing is FUBAR."

Gus said, "Hang on, Marine! I'm dropping in hot. I'll have you back to base in time for evening milk and cookies."

The storm had appeared out of nowhere just after the patrol dropped. The ship they landed in was out of commission from a direct lightning strike. "I want you moving when I hit the LZ. No time for souvenirs."

"Rodger that. Just open the door and keep the engines running," the comms rang out.

Sweat poured off Gus's forehead as he fought for control. His haptic feedback gloves were slipping despite a death grip on the controls. The forward view was fogging, and rain beat a furious tattoo against the glass. A silver Mjolnir medallion swung on a chain from a switch. Time slowed, and the medallion blurred. A nagging feeling grew between his shoulder blades. The old Bosun could barely see the landing zone and was relying on the heads-up-helmet overlay to guide him in.

Gus shook his head and flared the ship at the last minute above the patrol's position, then punched the landing ramp release. Lightning was popping all around, and the thunder was deafening in his helmet.

The squad leaped from their positions and ran hard. When the last of them were exposed, a tremendous blue bolt fell from the sky and danced from one Marine to the next. Puppet jerking as they screamed. Then it flared at Gus…

Gus jolted awake. The sweat-soaked sheets stuck to his body. He shook his head to clear away the images.

Post Military Service Disorder the head shrinkers called it these days. It had gone by a lot of different names over the centuries.

Gus peeked out of the window. The day was bright and

sunny. Finally! A storm had been raging for a week. The Infonet said hurricane Astra was the biggest storm to hit the area in over 200 years. The tides and surf had been high and pounding. Gus's shack, officially named: Building, Prefab, Retirement: 01 each Fleet Stock Number 5410-56-153-8645, plopped down here by Governance Fleet Retirement Services had survived through the recent blow, but a touch of cabin fever was setting in.

Gus was itching to get back out and check on his fish traps. It was as close to being back in space as he was going to get. Oh, he had his pension and little house, but it felt like quite a downgrade from a lifetime of riding the most powerful warships in the Governance. After 30-plus years of service, he had been cashiered out and dumped on this out-of-the way rock named Terne, butt-end of the end of the trade lines. He hauled on the same wrinkled khakis he'd worn the day before and headed to the kitchen to grab a cup of coffee from the auto-brewer before heading down to his boat.

Terne, that's a fitting name for this boring planet, Gus mused as he nursed the bitter cup. *I've tasted better coffee boiled in a muddy ammo can.*

Gus pitched the dregs into the weeds outside the boathouse door before hanging the cup on a peg. He raised his eyes to check the position of Ix in the sky. The ringed white-dwarf sun that Terne orbited was still high. The double systems much larger primary, Iz, had already set. He began to get his boat, the Annie D, ready for the day. She was simple, just the way Gus liked it at this point in his life, besides she was all he could really afford. The boat was seven meters, a good size for one man to handle. The mast raised on a tabernacle and featured a simple lug rig sail. A small cabin forward was just large enough for a cozy berth.

Navigation was a compass and lead line. Gus ran through an underway checklist out of long habit.

The boatlift motor growled as it lowered. He would need to replace the bearings soon, but the money was tight. His pension didn't stretch far. If he could land a few nice sized nattos today, it would be good eating for the week and maybe enough to sell at market.

Gus shoved off and shipped the oars to stroke confidently out of the cove and into the swell beyond. He decided to just row for a while instead of raising the mast. Exercise always helped clear away the dreams.

An ancient poem popped into his head as he put his rippling back into the work.

They'll sail the stars no more, no more,
They'll sail the stars no more.

When Gravis pulls 'em down his well,
Their wails and moans and dreadful yells
Resound from deepest depths of Hell,
They'll sail the stars no more.

They pray to gods that cannot save,
They bargain, plead, and beg for ways
To be released from crushing graves,
They'll sail the stars no more.

The echoes of their final breath
Resound in space, cold touch of death,
No mercy found, no whispered rest
They'll sail the stars no more.

The bot lay tangled in rope on the shallow ocean floor. The storm had twisted it up tight. The bot had been down here a long time. It wasn't in a hurry to get loose.

Depth: 35meters

Clarity: 12 meters

Temperature: 15C

Silt burden: Negligible

Systems…. Checksum 100%

Commence daily attempt to contact command for instructions.

All frequency check… negative appropriate code response.

All current maintenance tasks are complete.

Initiate self-rescue protocol. Fail self-rescue.

Fall back protocol initiated, awaiting instructions.

Gus was surprised to see one of his trap buoys. He figured that they had all been lost in the storm. This trap lay farthest out. The sea shelf fell off hundreds of meters nearby. Sometimes a deep-water dweller would get swept up on the shelf and caught. Those always brought a nice market price. People paid more for novelty. Plus, he had to admit they were tasty.

He brought the boat smoothly along the buoy and clipped a line to it. A few quick movements and he started to crank it up.

"Damn, trap must be silted in from the storm," he said. "Weighs a ton!" He put his back into the handle and rocked the boat to break the bottom suction. "Here it comes."

Gus peered down into the clear water. The trap didn't look right, *must be fouled with something.*

The trap broke the surface. He could see that whatever was tangled in the trap was big and heavy.

"Come on, you piece of shit! Get in the boat!" Gus yelled out loud, then he fell back.

Two metal arms had popped out of the water and grabbed onto the gunwale. "Holy Shit!" Gus scrambled to balance out the sudden weight that threatened to capsize him.

He just sat wide eyed as a small armored figure with a featureless helmet hauled itself aboard, seaweed trailing behind. It began to untangle itself. The helmeted head spun and focused on him. A stream of words began to pour out of the machine. It sounded like weirdly archaic Standard.

"Greetings Good Sir. Could you please identify yourself or I will be forced to take defensive action in response to my abduction," the strange machine said.

"Your abduction? You are the one that is interfering with my business," said Gus, "Taking the food right out of my poor mouth. I should dismantle you and sell you for damages."

"I advise against that course of action, Sir. I am allowed to defend myself according to the Rules of Behavior. Whom do I have the pleasure of addressing?"

"OK, you damn insolent tin can. I'm Guster Johansson. Star Bosun 4, Governance Fleet, retired."

"Pleased to meet you, Bosun Johansson. I am Imperial Confederation General Repair and Maintenance Protocol bot service designation HAM2F347791 currently assigned to. I beg your pardon, it seems that my current assignment data is incomplete," the bot replied.

"Well, HAM, you don't look like any GRAMPy I ever saw. What are your service parameters?" He slipped back into fleet-speak fit like a pair of old shoes.

"The 2F is a multifunction unit designed for maximum duty flexibility. I am fully capable of performing all ship's repairs and maintenance in any environment. I carry a full set of vessel specifications and am authorized to make a host of autonomous decisions. You appear to be a ranking officer, so I am at your disposal until I receive new orders," HAM said, evidently programmed to be polite.

"Well, this might just be my lucky day! I could probably find a few odd jobs for a GRAMPy around the place. Besides, it wouldn't be right not safeguarding government property. Just until I find out what your story is, of course," Gus chuckled.

"Absolutely Sir! I feel that I have been underutilized ever so long and the Rules of Behavior require me to strive to be helpful. A busy bot is a happy bot!" HAM had begun to repair the trap and continued talking, "As for my story, it seems to be a little fragmented. My last logs show I was performing deep reaction core maintenance on the number 6 fusion engine of the ICS *Deliver* (LRST 421) when the ship came under attack by raiders. Everything was going along swimmingly for our side until an enemy torpedo struck a weakened containment area. The resulting explosion seems to have sheared away the number 2, 4, and 6 engines. I and a good portion of the hull were sheared away. The last time I saw the *Deliver,* she was on a maximum burn for a dimensional insertion maneuver. However, it is doubtful that she survived the transition, given the extent of the damage I observed. The Captain was always reluctant to take advice."

Gus said, "Yeah, I've known more than a few captains like that."

"Your trap is repaired, Bosun," HAM said as it gestured to the trap.

Gus inspected the repairs. Not only was it fixed, it had

received some performance improving modifications. "Hmm, what did you do to my trap?"

"Sir, I have restored the device to standards listed in the Imperial Supply Catalog for Trap, Fish, Stationary. If you will allow me, Sir, I shall place the device in an optimum position for maximum catch," said HAM as it hoisted the trap and itself to the gunwale.

"Good idea there HAMy, why don't you swim down there and do that," Gus told the bot, and it disappeared with a splash.

Gus thought about the bot's story. He'd never heard of a ship called the ICS *Deliver,* any kind of vessel called an LRST, or a "dimensional insertion maneuver". There hadn't been any battles in this region of space for a very long time, either.

HAM quickly resurfaced and clamped himself to the boat's stern. "What next, Sir?"

"I think that's enough excitement for one day. Time to head home," Gus said as he reached for the oars.

"Sir, allow me." The bot's legs configured into a dolphin tail and the boat surged forward.

The sudden jerk caught Gus off guard, and he toppled. "Hey! Be careful, you overgrown outboard; this isn't an attack fighter. Slow down!" The boat skipped over the waves and stinging spray flew.

"Oh, terribly sorry, Sir, my apologies," HAM squeaked and began to slow. Gus thought he heard a little laugh from the bot, but that must have been his imagination.

Ix's rings were brushing the horizon by the time the boat was hoisted in the boathouse. Gus trudged back to his cottage as HAM, whose legs now ended in tracks, skated along behind on the sand.

"Excuse me, Sir, but I can't help but notice that your

accommodations look in need of some maintenance," the bot said. "Perhaps you would like me to take care of a few things?"

"That sounds like a fine idea HAM, that storm sure left a mess. Why don't you spruce the place a up a bit? I'm gonna see what's in the freezer, crack open a beer and settle in to watch John Wayne in *She Wore a Yellow Ribbon*."

The bot cocked his head. "Sir, why would John Wayne be wearing a yellow ribbon? Perhaps social mores and fashion have changed while I have been away."

Gus frowned at the little bot. "You're just trying to make me mad now, ain't ya!" Gus slammed the door as the little bot saluted, spun, and whirred away.

The next morning, Gus awoke to the smell of fresh coffee and the sizzle of what passed for bacon on Terne. He stretched and padded into the kitchen to find HAM busily preparing a breakfast like he hadn't had since he left the service. One arm worked the skillet of meat while the other poured him a steaming cup. The normal heap of dirty dishes was gone, and the floor sparkled.

He sat at the small table as HAM slid a heaping plate of pancakes and bacon in front of him. The rising aroma made his mouth water. "Hey, I didn't know we had any syrup!" Gus exclaimed as he poured it over the pancakes.

"During my work last night, I found the most delicious looking beach plums, and it was no trouble at all to prepare," explained HAM.

"Well, thanks," Gus said through a satisfied burp, "I didn't know I even had plums." He grabbed his coffee and sopped the last of the syrup with a cake and popped it into his mouth with satisfaction.

"So, what have you been up to all night, HAM? I thought I heard a lot of commotion."

"Oh, I believe you will be quite impressed, Sir," HAM said in a self-satisfied way as he led Gus out of the door.

Gus took one look. "What have you done to my yard?"

HAM chirped, "Oh, a few small improvements and much needed maintenance, Sir."

The bot had indeed been busy. Neatly trimmed grass bordered a walkway of fused sand that ran from the cottage to the boathouse. Winding paths lined with flowers and metal sculptures circled the house and wound through a garden. Gus's collection of junk vehicles and equipment he called his "inventory of spare parts" was gone. Some of the former were incorporated into a gently bubbling fountain, sculptures, and new wind turbine humming power into the cottage's batteries.

"You blasted piece of self-propelled mayhem!" yelled Gus. "This place looks like a mashup of a Victorian novel and a Sultan's palace as envisioned by a 16-year-old girl!"

HAM said, "Oh my! I was only trying to help. It seems I have not captured your aesthetic properly, Sir."

Gus was about to launch into another tirade when he felt an unfamiliar rumbling behind his belt buckle. His face twisted and his eyes popped a little.

"Ham, where did you get those plums from?" Gus gasped as another stomach cramp shot through him.

"I found them growing just over the dune line as I was disposing of some rubbish. Nice plump ones."

"Those aren't beach plums, you idiot. Those are used to relieve digestive stoppage!" Gus took off at a skipping trot towards the back of the cottage and hauled up short just as he rounded the corner. "Where the hell is my privy?"

"Oh, it was quite unsanitary. I removed it. I planned to construct a bathhouse this morning, but breakfast preparations took priority."

Gus hobbled over the dune line, trailing a string of blue language.

"Sir, I am so sorry about this situation. It seems I need a data update on the local flora. Is there anything I can do to help? You seem to be in distress."

"Stay away from me! Get back to work!"

"Right you are Sir, A busy bot is a happy bot!" HAM saluted, twirled, and headed back towards the house.

A pale and shaken Gus entered the cottage after a good bit.

"I need a change of clothes, HAM." Gus said matter-of-factly.

"I have just the thing Sir!" as the bot skated on one leg into the bedroom, "I noticed that you were lacking a proper dress uniform in the wardrobe, so I stitched one up. Star Bosun 4 I believe you said." Ham's voice was practically beaming.

HAM held forth one of the most gaudy displays of military tailoring Gus had ever seen. High black knee boots, blazing red jodhpurs, a stellar black tunic (with his appropriate rank) belted with a sash.

"Is that a fez?" Gus began to turn red. "I'm not wearing that costume, you poor excuse for my great grandma's Singer. It looks like something from an ancient history vid! Just how long ago did you say you crashed here?"

"As I said, there are some gaps in my data logs. However, I did some star observations overnight and the new data confirms your supposition. *Deliver's* battle above this world occurred 1446.8 Imperial Standard Years ago. I had not considered that fashion would change considerably in the intervening centuries."

"That's putting it mildly, besides I don't have much use for a dress uniform these days," Gus said. "Actually, no one seems to have much use for me, either. Anyway, you really are roundly binned my little talking trash compactor. Makes sense now why I've never heard of your ICS *Deliver*." He hauled his last set of khakis out of a drawer and dressed. "You missed both the Isolation and the Great Collapse. We haven't heard anything from Old Earth since the Gateway shut down about the time you said your ship blew up."

Late in the afternoon, Gus said, "I've got business at Lift Port. I want you to stay here and put things back the way you found them, you hear? No more improvements!" He grabbed a battered flight jacket and stamped out the door, purposely leaving his helmet on its peg. He mounted his powercycle. "Make sure you get that bathhouse done before I get back. You can leave the walkway and the windmill. Those are okay. I expect you to have some fish caught when I get back, too. The market will be needing fresh stock."

The little bot cautioned Gus as he keyed the starting circuit, "Bosun Johansson, I feel I should notify you that I have made some adjustments to your velocipede. The performance curves may be a little unfamiliar to you."

Johansson growled as he jammed a cloth cap on his head. "Don't you worry about me, you oversized garbage grinder. Just get back to work!"

HAM shouted, "Have a nice liberty, Sir!" just as Gus hit the throttle and rocketed out of the yard with a scream and cursing a blue streak.

Gus piloted the powercycle down the cracked pavement. Like a lot of things on Terne, the road was hastily built and already worn out.

The Governance had only recently annexed the planet and was still trying to consolidate control. Dropping military retirees here was part of the master plan to civilize the place, but it wasn't making much of a difference. Lift Port was the only sizable settlement on the planet, and even that had a raucous boom-town vibe.

At least the storm washed off the layer of dust that usually coats everything in this shithole, Gus thought as he purposely detoured along the giant fused silica fields of the star port. From the number of lifters working, he could tell that a big hauler was in orbit. He had toyed with the idea of getting a civilian lightering job. *That would bore me to death.* It seemed pretty weak sauce compared to dropping fast and hot against incoming fire while recovering an ops team in the shit.

Maybe I can find some old shipmates on liberty. He turned toward the seedier part of Lift Port, where sailors usually hung out.

Gus parked in an alley and hurried through the smell of a malfunctioning composter. A couple of rats were tag-teaming a pizza crust. They ignored Gus as he entered the back door of a familiar haunt.

A raucous cry of "Gus!!!" erupted from several regulars already at their places, even though it was barely dusk. Gus was quick to remove his hat. The last thing he needed today was to be buying a round for the bar. Although he had been known to leave it on purposefully when he was fat with cash to spread the wealth.

"Hey Willis, what's new?" Gus asked the bartender as he poured Gus's usual, a local porter from up country.

"Sounds like there are still piracy problems around the Spelex Core."

"Are we still stuck in that mess? I swear my first cruise out of boot was to support the Spellers."

Willis shrugged, "Someone must still think they are worth it."

Gus just snorted.

The bartender pointed his chin toward a group of laughing sailors at a nearby table as he filled a pitcher. "Got a crew in port, Fleet Auxiliary Vessel *Halsey*, on some kind of humanitarian mission."

"Well, I'll just say 'Hello.' Always good to support shipmates." Gus grabbed the pitcher and headed over. "Friends! Let me welcome you to Terne Lift Port."

A brawny Engineman 1st class taunted, "Gawd, you are an ugly barmaid." The whole table laughed.

Gus smiled as he pulled up a chair and filled their glasses. "Ah, well, if you are looking for pretty young things, then I fear you will be disappointed by the clientele here. But the beer is cheap, and the pours are strong."

A Marine sergeant piped in as Gus filled his glass. "Hey, I recognize this guy! Aren't you Bosun Gusty Johansson? This guy right here, my friends, is a legend. He has the record for pulling more sorry Marine ass out of bad situations than anyone. Didn't you win the Legion Medal for saving some big shots' wife and kid?"

Gus murmured, "Nah, the Navy Cross, but that was a long time ago and I'm afraid my star has dimmed considerably since those days." He perked up. "Enough about me. What's the scoop skyside?"

"We got lucky today," said a dark-haired female Corpsman 2nd class, "Supposed to be hauling a ship full of cryofrozen refugees, but the operation is on hold. We pretty much have rolling liberty parties until the situation sorts itself out."

"Lucky for you, unlucky for them," said Gus as he raised his glass. "So, you all ready to see what Lift Port has to offer?"

Captain Harrison Grey, Commanding Officer of the Terne Orbital Station, opened the door to his quarters and paused. *Three, two, one.*

"Harrison? Is that you? Where have you been? You were due here over an hour ago." Mitzi Grey tottered into the living room on spindly stilettos, her long bleach-blonde curls swinging free.

Harrison regarded his wife. She was still beautiful, although she really needed to give up the tight dresses and accept that she was no longer the twenty-year-old college girl he fell for as an Ensign. *Three questions and an accusation in fifteen seconds. A record.* "Hello Dear, things have been very busy on the Station today."

She sniffed, "Ha! Nothing exciting ever happens in this spinning fart wheel. Would you like a drink? I'm having one." She grabbed an expensive bottle smuggled from Celas and topped her glass. Grey noticed that the drink was more vodka than soda.

"Is that wise? We have dinner reservations at the Club in thirty minutes," he asked.

Mitzi narrowed her eyes and shook the glass at her husband. "This, my darling, is what makes this place bearable."

"What about all those shopping trips you keep making? Aren't those keeping you busy enough? I don't know how one woman can shop that much."

"Oh, so you are going to deny me a little retail therapy?" Mitzi said as a dare. "If you had made better choices, we wouldn't have been exiled here in the first place. I'm gonna call Daddy again and see if he can't pull some strings. Haven't we been punished long enough?" She pouted and took a large swallow.

Grey turned towards the bedroom. "I'm going to

change." He knew it was better to let Mitzi's jabs go than to engage her before dinner.

She did have one valid point. Terne Station was a dumping ground for officers going nowhere. Harrison Grey was not going to accept being shuffled off into a series of dead-end postings leading to humble retirement.

Something is gonna to break my way soon, I can feel it.

Recently "released from active duty" Governance Marine Gunner "Fancy" Nancy Stanski paused to let her eyes adjust to the dim lighting of the Terne Station All Hands Club. She pulled at her stiff collar. *Still not used to wearing these civilian clothes. Well, better get used to it, girl. I don't think the Corps is going to offer your old job back.* She was thirties, short blonde hair, pale blue eyes that crinkled when she smiled, and tall with a slim-hipped-broad-shouldered athletic build. The pagan hammer, Mjolnir, was tattooed on her right forearm. Several battle stars formed a halo around it.

Nan had struck out so far getting her current employers, miners from a rock named Lestus 884, released from quarantine. They were getting antsy at her lack of progress. She was looking for Terne Station's Executive Officer now.

She walked up to the bartender and offered her hand, "Hi, Nan Stanski." She spoke with the thick Slavic accent of northern Nakon, the Governance capital world.

"Mike," he replied, as she gave him a firm handshake.

Harrison Grey pushed past without acknowledging her. "Mike, Mrs. Grey and I will be at our usual table." He turned and walked away without waiting for a response.

Mike said, "Of course, Captain."

Nan noticed Mike wave to an overdressed leggy blonde

threading through the tables. She didn't look too steady. "So that's the Station CO's wife?" *Wonder what she ever saw in him?*

Mike answered, "Yeah, looks like Mitzi has already been at it tonight. Her father is First Lord Admiral Falkirk McGowan, head of the whole damn Navy."

Nan raised an eyebrow at that information and said, "Ah. Say, Mike, can you tell me if Fredrika DeWitt is here?"

"She's the one sitting by herself, frowning at the data tablet." He nodded toward a woman sitting alone at a nearby table as he polished a glass.

The Lieutenant actually had several tablets on the table and was working all of them.

Nan sized her up. Late twenties, brown hair in a regulation bun, still in the uniform of the day with a barely touched dinner. *Cute too!* "What's she drink, Mike? Make it two."

He poured a couple of frothy mugs of stout. Nan grabbed them and walked over.

"Mind if I join you?" Nan Stanski. Without waiting for a reply, she set one mug in front of the Lieutenant and offered a hand.

The Lieutenant looked up from her tablet, a little startled. "Uh, sure," she shook the offered hand. "Fredrika DeWitt" she said.

Nan flashed a smile. "What do you drink, el tee?"

"Uh, Cronsburg," replied Fredrika.

"I happen to have an extra here. You from Ransom? That's the only place I know for Cronsburg."

"Yes, I am," Fredrika spoke with a posh accent to hide the fact she was actually from a backwater minor planet. She cautiously sized up Nan.

Nan began, "Fine place, Ransom, good people there. Always treated us Marines well."

"Marine hmm, on leave?"

"Well, recently separated actually, pursuing new opportunities."

"What kind of opportunities?" Fredrika actually welcomed the chance to ignore her tablets. Nan looked like an interesting distraction.

"Well, right now I'm working security for Sirace Mining. Pirates are making it hard for decent folks to survive. Plus, my crew is in quarantine because someone caught a cold."

"I've heard some random reports. Sorry about that, the Governance is stretched pretty thin out here around Ix."

Nan held up her hands. "Oh, I'm not here to ask any favors, just making small talk." She raised her glass to Fredrika, who responded in kind. "Cheers to Ransom."

The smiling pair had just finished a second round when they heard shouting coming through the doors. A group of regular Army came in laughing loudly. Their badges identified them as Dragger's Raiders.

"Oh great, these assholes!" Fredrika said under her breath. "They've been causing trouble here for a week."

"Hey XO!" one of the group called out and stumbled over to the table. "Who's your friend? Mind if we join you?" the man didn't wait for a reply before plopping down in an empty chair. "Hey, look who it is, fellas, our friend Lieutenant DeWitt."

The group smelled of stale beer and trouble. Nan could see this wasn't their first stop of the night.

One of the Raiders noticed Nan's tattoo. "Well, look here guys, we got ourselves a genuine war hero." He grabbed her forearm and lifted it to show everyone her tattoo.

Fredrika jumped up, put the Raider in a wrist lock, and frog marched him out. Nan broke into involuntary laughter at the sight of a determined Dewitt, who barely came up to the guy's shoulder, booting the drunk through the door. The bartender reached under the bar and raised a stun bat in anticipation of what he was pretty sure was going to happen next.

"Oh, think that's funny huh, war hero?" sneered another of the Raiders. He lunged.

She batted away the punch. Unfortunately, it landed squarely on a Chief Petty Officer at the next table. The Chief yelled, spun around, and threw a roundhouse at the Raider.

Fredrika whirled at the noise and watched the whole place erupt into general mayhem. She drew her capper. Mitzi Grey screamed.

Two burly Raiders squared off on Nan. She quickly dodged around a table, flipped it, and backed away.

"Big bad Marine running from some lowly Army ruck humpers," one taunted.

Nan grabbed a tray for a shield just as one one thew a punch. He screamed as his hand smashed against the steel. She broke the other one's nose with the now bent tray. He dropped to his knees.

"I would love to stay and chat, boys, but I gotta run." Nan turned to dart away.

Broken nose shook his head and caught her by the ankle. "Got ya now!"

She fought like a wildcat until she was tagged by a stray cap round. The pair hoisted her up and heave-hoed her over the Greys' table and through the video wall. Mitzi was still screaming. Grey was speechless. The Raiders laughed and pointed. Bartender Mike walked up behind the pair and zapped them.

"Well, so much for a quiet evening." Mike said, looking around at the wreckage.

Gus pushed the powercycle up the road towards home. His head was sore, and he didn't feel up to fighting the machine.

That was one Helluva liberty run, Gus! His stomach roiled. *You might be getting too old to hang with the young pups.*

Gus had steered the crew of the *Halsey* and their full wallets to all the owners he had kickback arrangements with.

Hey, a guy's gotta make a living, somehow, don't he? Gus was into self-justification after evenings like this one. *Besides, everyone had a good time. No one is in the brig, and I got a few extra credits in my account.*

But retirement wasn't turning out like he imagined. His pension didn't stretch far enough for comfort. Fishing everyday had sounded like a great life when he was cruising in service, but it turned out to be even more boring than standing midwatch alone. The occasional liberty run with crews from visiting ships just made him feel more melancholy when it ended. He was more than a little jealous when the "*Haulsome's*" crew lifted for orbit.

Well, that's the hand yer dealt Gusty old boy, so play it like it's a winner.

Gus topped the dunes and stopped short when an overpowering stench hit him like a brick. Near his boathouse was an enormous pile of fish of every shape and description baking in the sun as scavenging gulls wheeled overhead.

"Oh, welcome home, Bosun!" HAM called from the dock. The bot was dragging a straining net behind him as he trundled along. "I hope you are pleased with the catch I have assembled in your absence?"

Gus gaped as he reached the festering heap. "What the Hell have you done now, you rusty can opener?"

He could see at least 20 different kinds of fish he knew, and several unknowns best described as nightmares with teeth. Some of which were still snapping and gnashing several rows of needle-sharp teeth on the end of long scaly necks.

From the smell, Gus guessed that HAM had started this pile shortly after he left.

"I do hope this will be enough fish for the market Bosun? I have had the opportunity to make several trips since your departure." HAM paused before considering, "However, it appears that I should have constructed a refrigeration center before starting. You didn't mention if the market for fresh was better than frozen, so I assumed you preferred fresh. Your reactions indicate that I may have made an error in that regard. My olfactory sensors must need recalibration."

Gus made a valiant effort to keep from gagging as another fresh breeze wafted toward him. The gulls dive-bombed him to protect their treasure.

"Do you have to be so damn literal with everything you do?" Gus wailed. "I'm gonna get in plenty of trouble from the Eco Cops for overfishing because of this."

"Oh dear, I only strive to be helpful, Sir. I am much better at following established protocols than independent action."

"Really? I haven't seen anything you haven't fouled up yet! Why don't you just go back to wherever you have been hiding for the last 1400 years?"

"That is an excellent idea, Sir!" he said, then shot directly into the ocean and disappeared.

"What the Hell was that about? What is that antique Roomba up to now? Well, good riddance!"

Gus turned toward the fish pile, hands on hips, and wondered what he was going to do about it. He felt a low rumble through his feet. The surface of the ocean was rippling. A bulge of water was forming. Something was rising to the surface, something big.

Very big.

Corvus Ascending: Chapter Two

A great curved back broke the surface. Waves of dark sand and sea grass cascaded down the slick sides and splashed in the sea.

Gus stood open-mouthed and stared.

Gus thought he knew the silhouette of everything flying, but he didn't recognize this. It was the largest ship he had ever seen in atmosphere. Two graceful arched wings curved away from the primary hull. A tenuous tail stretched behind. It rose from the sea and two legs unfolded as the ship set down on the sand like an enormous bird.

It seemed to be a special purpose. Gus couldn't imagine what it was, though. The most striking thing about the ship was the color; It appeared to be a deep black. Though the bright sunshine played across the structures in odd ways, light couldn't grasp it reliably. It appeared to bend light so you could see through it. Blue sky and clouds reflected upon the wings as if it was an enormous black mirror, but the horizon behind the ship was visible through it!

Gus closed his eyes tightly. Staring at the ship made his head throb.

A hatch opened, and a ramp extended. HAM leaped from the opening, performed a somersault, and land with his stubby arms held high. "Ta-da and ahoy, Bosun Sir! I have acted on your most excellent suggestion. This is where I have been hiding for oh so long. After completing repairs to my ship, I had no directives to act on, so I have been awaiting orders. Orders that you have now provided. Would you care to come aboard?" the little bot asked hopefully. "it would delight me to give you a tour of your new command."

Gus walked up the ramp and held his hand out to catch some water dripping off the hull. *I must be dreaming. Yeah, that's it, dreaming. I'm sleeping it off in Lift Port still.* He touched his lips, *This is some dream, the water even tastes salty.*

Gus said, "Hey HAM, if I'm dreaming, I want a sandwich."

HAM twirled, "Sir, I assure this is not a dream."

HAM escorted Gus up the ramp. He knew it must be a dream. How could a 1400-year-old ship look brand new? It even had that new starship smell of fresh plasticine, powder coat, and welding fumes. The floors didn't show the wear from thousands of boots; no fingerprints around the maintenance panels, and none of the screw heads looked new. The bulkheads were a matt eggshell color and everything was smooth and shipyard fresh. This was nothing like the slap dash construction and maintenance like his old ships where there was never enough time, personnel, or money to do things right.

Suddenly, a holographic form popped up. It was a remarkably curvy young woman in an unfamiliar uniform, light gray long sleeve tunic with dark blue belted waist and blue trousers bloused into the boots. She didn't have a rating badge or shoulder boards.

"Welcome aboard, Captain. I have been monitoring your time with HAM. I am the ship's General Response Artificial Neural Network avatar at your service," the perky projection explained with a salute.

Gus played along with his dream, "It's good to be here, although I've never met a Constructed Intelligence GRANNe as cute as you. Would have been pretty distracting."

She said, "I can adjust my appearance as you wish, Sir. Is this more appropriate?" The projection shifted and now appeared as 40 standard years. The hair had become silvery gray and shoulder length, and the smooth youthful prettiness had shifted into the striking beauty of experienced middle age. The uniform was the same, but the figure within had become athletically lean with a definite military bearing.

Gus said, "Let's stay with that for now, but I feel rather odd calling you GRANNe. Do you have a name?"

She replied, "Hmm, I shall consider that and get back to you, Captain. I'm still rather new at this."

"New? I thought HAM said you've been down here 1400 years?"

HAM piped in, "Well Sir, I have been here 1400 years. It took 238.7 years to repair the ship. The ship's Artificial Neural Networks have not been needed until now, they spend most of the time in standby. Their Gold Disks check out per specifications."

Gus asked, "They? More than one?"

GRANNe chimed in, "HAM is responsible for maintenance. I handle everything not associated with navigation and flight control."

"Then who knows how to fly this bucket?" Gus asked as they reached the bridge and the door whooshed open.

"I FLY," a deep disembodied voice reverberated from the 1MC speakers.

"Sir, may I introduce you to Navigation and Flight Control," HAM said.

"I FLY," once again.

"Ahh, a bot of few words for once. Refreshing," said Gus.

GRANNe interjected, "I do apologize Sir, the Gold Disk for the Navigation and Flight Control Network was slightly damaged during our fall from orbit. It still functions flawlessly; however, its language skills are less than par."

"As long as it can do the job. Sometimes less is more," Gus said.

"FLY NOW?" Flight asked hopefully.

"Hold on there, I'm still trying to get my bearings," said Gus.

"FLY NOW!" Flight bellowed, and a klaxon began to sound on the bridge.

"What is Hell is going on!"

The GRANNe appeared in a seat near the forward screen. "Captain, we have visitors approaching fast and attempting to acquire target lock!"

This dream has turned into a nightmare. "Give me visual on forward screen!" Gus thumped into the Captain's station and pivoted a console.

A squadron of Governance fast attack craft from Lift Port was inbound fast.

A voice sounded over the comms, "Unidentified ship! Declare and surrender!"

"Weapons status, GRANNe?" asked Gus.

She replied, "I'm sorry Sir, this ship has no offensive weapons."

Of course not. That would be too easy. "Do they have target lock?" yelled Gus.

The GRANNe replied coolly, "Negative Captain, the carbonado is preventing targeting acquisition, but they will be within visually targeted cannon range in fifteen seconds."

What the fuck is carbonado! thought Gus before he yelled, "Flight FLY!" he hoped the damaged CI had enough programming initiative to perform evasive maneuvers.

The ship's bow tilted up, and it rocketed skyward. Gus's chair conformed into an acceleration couch that prevented him from pinballing around the bridge and breaking every bone in his body.

He estimated the ship was climbing at six Gs and still accelerating. He was about to pass out as a webbed harness enfolded him to form a G suit and stabilize his blood pressure. This dream was all too real.

"Report" said Gus even though there was a disturbing lack of noise on the bridge, merely a rising hum.

"FLY GOOD!" responded Flight.

GRANNe stated, "Our pursuers cannot match our rate-of-climb Captain. We have cleared the atmosphere."

"All mechanical and flight systems are operating to perfection," piped in HAM, rather proud of himself.

Johansson ordered, "Flight, reduce acceleration to one G. Set course, out of the system ecliptic plane, at one standard AU cut drive." *I need to figure out what just happened and if this is a dream.*

The ship drifted in space.

Gus had finally figured out how to use the coffeemaker in zero gravity and strapped into a chair in the wardroom. Wardroom was stretching it. The interior was spartan. It functioned as mess deck, lounge, and meeting space.

HAM nervously skated around the perimeter on magnetic skates, holding him to the deck. The holo projection of GRANNe stood at the end of the large single table.

"Okay, you two, I need some answers," Gus said.

"Of course, Sir, I stand ready," HAM saluted. Gus rolled his eyes.

Gus began, "HAM, whose ship is this? What is it? And oh, convince me I'm not dreaming."

"It is yours, Captain! As to your second question, as I explained earlier, this is an experimental Third Generation Imperial Confederation Long-Range Salvage Tug, *Deliver* class, no hull number. Quite a capable vessel, if I may say so, Sir." HAM's voice swelled with pride. "As to your third request." HAM kicked Gus hard in the shin.

"Shit, that hurts!" Gus said and jerked his leg away, "Guess I'm not dreaming. Wait, what? How can this ship be mine?"

GRANNe began, "I believe the law governing salvage rights applies in this situation. As HAM previously mentioned, a portion of the Imperial Confederation ship *Deliver* was blown off during battle and fell into this planet's gravity well. HAM, true to his programming, repaired the ship."

HAM spun with delight, "Oh, those days were full of activity. You have little idea how much effort it takes to construct an entire starship on a preindustrial planet by oneself. Yes indeed, a busy bot is a happy bot, Sir."

Gus growled, "Don't break your arm patting yourself on the back, you mobile margarita mixer."

"If I may continue?" GRANNe said. "Because less than 50 percent of the original vessel remains, this vessel is technically not property of the Imperial Confederation or its successor states, and as such, stateless vessels are open for appropriate salvage claims. At least, that is my interpretation of Admiralty Law."

Gus shook his head. "Anyway, how has this ship stayed hidden all this time?"

HAM explained, "We crashed before they settled the planet, so I was free to work uninterrupted for an extended period. It took me 238.7 years to complete repairs. I moved the ship off the coast to avoid detection when settlement began, as I encountered no one who possessed adequate authorization for an appropriate salvage claim."

GRANNe interrupted, "You mean you didn't like them, don't you?"

HAM sniffed and ignored her. "I have waited a long time. I am most pleased that you have arrived to take the captain's chair."

"Whoa right there roller-boy, you two keep calling me Captain. I ain't no Captain! I'm a Bosun Chief Warrant Officer 4, I didn't go to no ring-knocker-knowledge-locker to get my commission," said Gus. "I'm an old-time hawse pipe climber."

"Well Sir, then how should I address you? Bosun is hardly formal enough for this vessel's commander. *Deliver* was a prototype vessel. I would assume there isn't anything else like it," HAM said with pride.

Gus said, "Didn't you say this was some kind of tug?"

HAM replied, "Yes Sir, a Long-Range Salvage Tug to be exact."

"Well, in that case you all can call me either Bosun or Skipper. A tug driver doesn't rate being called Captain, anyway. I think that cuts a fine enough distinction for the situation. Although this rig don't look like any tug I ever saw before. Besides, I know who my Daddy is."

HAM looked at GRANNe, who just shrugged, "The language must have deviated a great deal from our day. I haven't a clue what he means."

Gus sighed and continued. "Well, how come this thing doesn't have any weapons?"

GRANNe answered, "Oh, the ship has all the mounts for a full weapons suite, but the Rules of Behavior prevent bots from constructing weapons without special Command Authorization, and HAM had no Captain," GRANNe said. "We can use weapons to protect members of the crew, even if it means our destruction."

Gus said, "Well, good to know that you won't just stand by and watch me get shot. Anything else I should know right now about these rules?"

"I'm sure more will come up as you familiarize with operations. There are too many to be interesting." GRANNe finished cryptically. "I have prepared a ship's information briefing and installed it on your tablet." She motioned as HAM handed the device to Gus. "This will instruct you in the capabilities of the LRST."

Gus said, "Okay, but first a few questions. Why couldn't those fighters get a target lock?"

HAM answered, "Oh, that is a function of the carbonado hull construction."

Gus said, "Yeah, I heard that the first time, Whisky Tango Foxtrot is carbonado?"

"It is a synthetic ultra-black carbon structure. It is rarely used because it is expensive and difficult to work with. The LRST was designed to rescue ships engaged in battle without being detected," HAM said. "It has the ability to refract all frequencies of the EM spectrum. It can also be manipulated to function as a semi-conductor, superconductor, or supercapacitor. It is highly resistant to heat and high energy weapons fire."

"Okay, make it simple for me."

GRANNe said, "Almost invisible and tough to kill."

"Thanks," Gus said. "So, will those fighter jockeys be able to find us?"

GRANNe said, "Probably, as we did a hot deceleration burn to stop. They could easily trace our drive trail." The projection paused and cocked her head as if listening to something. "I suggest you get changed into your uniform, Skipper. Our visitors will be here in two hours."

"What's wrong with what I'm wearing?"

GRANNe looked at HAM with disapproval, "I tried to get him to change earlier Ma'am. He can be rather difficult."

GRANNe sniffed. "We'll see about that."

GRANNe was right. Two hours later a klaxon sounded over the ship's 1MC.

Gus flew onto the bridge and snagged the Command Chair. "Sitrep" he bellowed as he strapped in.

"It seems the local defense institution has finally arrived at our position," HAM helpfully replied.

"No Shit, Ensign Obvious!" said Gus as he pulled at the stiff collar of his new uniform. GRANNe had insisted that "the Captain must be properly attired when conducting ship's business." Gus knew it was a battle he wouldn't win.

"Flight, do we have a registered name?"

"NO,"

"To the vessel that just performed an unsanctioned supersonic planetary departure, this is Governance Defense. Respond!"

"Okay, here we go!" Gus sighed. "Open a channel please GRANNe."

The holo complied and nodded to her captain when the channel was ready.

"Hello Gentlemen, so sorry about that, I seem to have trouble with my Navigation and Flight control. Won't happen again."

"Why isn't your vessel pinging an AIS transponder Captain? Identify your vessel. The configuration isn't in the database."

Time to get creative, the truth will not set you free Gusty old boy.

"Umm, you see, this vessel is home-built and I haven't received my registration yet. I hadn't planned this trip, but like I said, I had some flight computer troubles." *Oh, quick thinkin there Bosun, just enough fiction to sugarcoat the truth.*

A terse reply followed, "Follow us to Terne Station, the Ix Area Commander will want to talk to you, patrol out."

Gus ordered, "Flight, follow those ships to the Station, slow bell and no sudden course corrections."

"NOT GOOD IDEA, READY FLY!"

"Please. For now, Flight" *But I know he is right.*

Flight grumbled, *"NOT GOOD."*

Corvus Ascending: Chapter Three

Flight followed the escort to Terne Station while Gus prepped a ship's boat to face the powers that be.

He was quickly falling back into a shipboard routine and had already begun to think of this as *his* ship. The hangar deck was large, and the six boats stowed there didn't fill it. He could guess what each was for, even though they were unfamiliar. The two boxy white ones with folded stubby wings looked like Multipurpose Cargo Boats for landing dirtside. Two twin seat V-tailed fighters, nicknamed Straps in the Governance Fleet, looked sleek and deadly even in their catapult cradles. *Probably atmosphere capable, even if the wings are stubby trapezoids,* Gus mused. Both Straps were covered in the hull's same shifting black material. Finally, there were to two EV repair pods, called BUGs in the fleet with various arms, tools, and grabbers.

Gus thought, *I bet I could even fit a dropship in here!*

Gus chose a BUG as it seemed to be the least threatening and most likely to fit his cover story of building this ship himself. He ran through an underway checklist and shoved off toward what he hoped wouldn't be a long stay in the brig.

Gus swaggered along, sandwiched between two extra-large security guards toward the Station CO's office.

You're gonna need to polish this turd of a story to a high shine to blind them, Gusty. Shouldn't be too hard though, stations never attract the fleet's best and brightest.

Gus's heart sank when the door opened, and he saw the Station CO. Captain, full bird O-6, by the name of Harrison "Hazy" Grey The only CO that ever even got close to busting slick Chief Warrant Officer Guster Johansson.

Oh geez, not this asshole again!

To say that CWO Johansson and Capt. Grey had history was a major understatement. Over twenty years ago Grey was a wet behind the ears Ensign and Gus was a Boatswain 1st Class and the Leading Petty Officer of Grey's department on the supply transport *Kirkland.*

Ensign Grey treated his posting to the *Kirkland* as a hold-your-nose-and-do-it job. He was convinced that *Kirkland* was a waste of his talent. He displayed a general disdain for common sailors, too. His habit of counting down the days until he transferred really torqued Gus. No matter how humble a ship is, a sailor believes it is the best one in the Fleet.

Ensign Grey was from an old-money family that had fallen on hard times. Same old story. The heirs slowly spent everything and mortgaged the rest until Harrison Grey, last of his line, was left with nothing but a prestigious name. He was hoping to use the Navy to rebuild the family's credibility and cash. Harrison Grey excelled, more in shady deals than ship handling.

PO1 Johansson was pretty much below Grey's notice. That is until one of Gus' most memorable liberty runs. The matter was still spoken of with hushed reverence in sailor watering holes across both systems.

The story involved an eventful weekend featuring a sexy, long-legged redhead and a group of her sorority sisters during university break on Celas. Gus was still grinning on Monday morning when Ensign Grey introduced the red head as his sister and one of the sorority girls as his fiancé Mitzi. They both squealed and threw their arms around Gus's neck as soon as they saw him. Things had gone downhill between Gus and Grey ever since.

Gus decided to draw first blood, "Hazy Grey!!! Long time no see," Gus said boisterously as he threw out his hand for a shake. Grey hated that nickname.

Captain Grey did not return the gesture, "Bosun Gusty Johansson, what the hell are you wearing? Playing dress-up since the Navy beached your sorry ass." Grey knew how to get his digs in too. "Why are in my space in an unregistered ship?"

"Well, like I tried to explain, Captain," Gus said, shrugging off the snub, "I was just doing some planet-side tests of my new rig when the flight CI glitched. Never meant to get underway without all the proper paperwork. I'll just be on my merry way and out of your hair directly." Gus offered a cheery smile of farewell and turned. His bulky escorts filled the exit.

"You aren't going anywhere until I get to the bottom of this! You expect me to believe that a broken-down degenerate like you built that!" Grey angrily jabbed his finger toward the observation screen. Gus's ship glittered in the refracted starlight. The odd hull material was even more effective in space. If the ship wasn't lighting itself, it probably would have been invisible.

Gus thought, *Damn, she's beautiful!*

Gus offered hopefully, "Well, it was more of a salvage title repair than a new build, Captain. She isn't complete yet like I said, some issues. Needs a paint job."

Grey turned to the officer standing nearby, "Lt. DeWitt, what do you know about this ship and the fairy tale Johansson is telling?"

The officer keyed her tablet and said, "Jane's Historical Fighting Ships, ancient records edition, identifies that ship as the experimental salvage tug *Deliver* from the Terran Expansion, specifically the Imperial Confederation," Dewitt spouted. "It was reported lost with all hands on its shakedown cruise. That would be over 1000 years ago."

Gus said, "A Third Generation Long-Range Salvage Tug to be specific."

Grey was huffing now, "So, you expect me to believe you salvaged a 1000-year-old ship, by yourself, on your pension? A ship that outruns my fastest pickets, evades torpedo locks, and doesn't show up on radar?"

"Umm, well, Sir."

"Shut up! Take this man to the brig while I try to sort this out."

Dewitt and the security guards marched a sullen Gus away.

"You do not have permission to board my vessel!" yelled Gus over his shoulder. *Don't know if that will work, but it's a shot.*

About the Author

I found myself adrift after a thirty-year career in the U.S. Coast Guard. Over twenty of them as a Chief Warrant Officer, so I got a soft spot for CWOs.

Casting about for something to do I thought, "I'll write a book. How hard could it be."

Turns out it is damn hard!

I guess I'm a glutton for punishment because, I keep doing it.

Currently, I've dropped anchor in Southwest Colorado. It's a long way from salt water. Let's see how long I last.

www.ingramcontent.com/pod-product-compliance
Lightning Source LLC
LaVergne TN
LVHW030918080826
845145LV00013B/2950